SELBY PUBLIC LIBRARY
1331 FIRST STREET
SARASOTA, FL 34236

# Praise for The Myth Adventure Series

"Asprin's major achievement as a writer—brisk pacing, wit, and a keen satirical eye. Breezy, pun-filled fantasy in the vein of Piers Anthony's *Xanth* series"—ALA *Booklist*

"A hilarious bit of froth and frolic. Asprin has a fine time with the story. So will the reader."—*Library Journal*

"Witty, humorous, a pleasant antidote to ponderous fantasy."—*Amazing*

"The novels by Asprin are loads of fun, extremely enjoyable humorous fantasy. We really like it."—*The Comic Buyers Guide*

"...an excellent, lighthearted fantasy series..."—*Epic Illustrated*

"An inspired series of magic and hilarity. It's a happy meeting of L. Sprague de Camp and the *Hitchhiker's Guide* trilogy."—*Burlington County Times*

"Humorous adventure fantasy at its rowdiest."—*Science Fiction Chronicle*

"Recommended."—*Fantasy Review*

"All the *Myth* books are hysterically funny."—*Analog*

"This is a fun read and series enthusiasts should enjoy it."—*Kliatt*

"Stuffed with Rowdy fun."—*Philadelphia Inquirer*

"Give yourself the pleasure of working through this series. But not all at once; you'll wear out your funny bone."—*Washington D. C. Times*

"If a reader is searching for sheer reading enjoyment, they need look no further than Robert Asprin."—*SF Digest*

"The Myth Adventure books are modern day classics. Again and again, Robert Asprin proves with effortless skill that he is one of the funniest writers alive today."—Nick Pollotta

# Myth Alliances

by

## Robert Asprin

and

## Jody Lynn Nye

SELBY PUBLIC LIBRARY
1331 FIRST STREET
SARASOTA, FL 34236

Meisha Merlin Publishing, Inc.
Atlanta, GA

This is a work of fiction. All the characters and events portrayed in this book are fictitious. Any resemblance to real people or events is purely coincidental.

All rights reserved by the publisher. This book may not be reproduced, in whole or in part, without the written permission of the publisher, except for the purpose of reviews.

Myth Alliances Copyright © 2003 by Robert Lynn Asprin and Jody Lynn Nye

PLEASE HELP FIGHT INTERNET PIRACY. Scanning and uploading this novel to the internet without the author's permission is not an act of flattery. It is an act of *theft*. It is not only disrespectful to the author; it violates the author's copyright and takes money from the author's pocket by disseminating copies for which no royalties are paid.

## MYTH ALLIANCES

Published by Meisha Merlin Publishing, Inc.
PO Box 7
Decatur, GA  30031

3 1969 02142 2406

Editing by Stephen Pagel
Interior layout by Lynn Swetz
Copyediting & proofreading by Teddi Stransky
Cover art and interior illustrations by Michael Komarck
Cover design by Kevin Murphy

ISBN:   Hard Cover    1-59222-008-8
        Soft Cover    1-59222-009-6

http//www.MeishaMerlin.com

First MM Publishing edition: September 2003

Printed in the United States of America
0  9  8  7  6  5  4  3  2  1

# Myth Alliances

by

Robert Asprin

and

Jody Lynn Nye

# Introduction

You have in your hand something both familiar and also new. In a way this is a bit frightening. The best selling Myth Adventures series has had a unique place in SF literature. And a surprising number of the readers of this series are amazingly knowledgeable about every detail and nuance. This is a new novel in the Myth Adventures series. That is the familiar. What is new is the second name on the cover. This book is a collaboration between Robert Lynn Asprin, who created the series and wrote the earlier novels, and Jody Lynn Nye, the author of over two dozen other books.. It is a further adventure, or series of calamities, featuring Skeeve and many of the same characters you have enjoyed in the first dozen books. This adventure takes place just after the end of volume 12, *Something Myth Inc.*

A few years ago Jody and Bob created another novel set in contemporary New Orleans, License Invoked. They have also done several short stories, which have been collected in the *Myth-Told Tales* (a Meisha Merlin book). Incidentally those stories actually set the scene for this book, though aren't needed to read it. So why Jody Lynn Nye? Simply put, Jody had already demonstrated the ability to fit comfortably in other author's worlds with other collaborations, most notably four novels written with Anne McCaffrey. She has herself written several humorous novels. It didn't hurt that Jody and Bob have known each other for almost two decades as well. So when the decision was made to add collaborations to the series, Jody Lynn Nye was first choice.

Note I said "add collaborations". This is not to say there won't be more solo novels from Robert Lynn Asprin as well. There will be.

So what is happening beyond this new Myth Adventure that has both writers so busy, especially Robert Asprin? Both contributors are also working on other books. Robert Asprin has already delivered to Penguin Putnam the first of two really action filled fantasy novels in a series titled "Wartorn" and as of writing this is getting close to the deadline for the second adventure. He is also in the process of expanding a second mystery novel in a series not yet placed. Jody has herself just completed a new novel in her Taylor's Ark SF medical series, titled The Lady and the Tiger. From that list of projects you might be beginning to get the idea on why a collaboration became a good idea. It's called deadlines... and finding the time to do it all. Both the readers and the publishers were asking for another novel. You see above how busy Bob is, and it is also hard, often slow work to write humor, and the gentle situational humor in the Myth Adventures series is one of the most difficult. This is not to mention the effort it takes to keep things fresh after having already writing a dozen books in this series over what is now just short of twenty years. The second writers adds a new perspective, a fresh look, shared laughter...and a second pair of hand typing away when time is limited and we cruel publishers demand at least one new Myth Adventures book a year.

You will find many of Bob's trademark writing styles in Myth Alliance such as  the quotes starting the chapters and Bob's penchant for rarely using the word "said" (Had you noticed?). Since this is a collaboration you may find some differences in the way the familiar characters and dialogue are presented. That is inevitable in any collaboration, if subtle. When you speak with either of Bob or Jody about this book, the parts you really like should be assumed to have been written by whichever author you are talking to. Those you don't like were most obviously should be assumed to have been written by the absent one. (Hmm, now that is a real advantage to collaborating.) Though most likely each will credit the other with the good ideas.

So here you have it. A collaboration that once more brings you the adventures of Skeeve the Magnificent and his companions. This time they are taking on one of the most frightening forces that can be found in all of the Dimensions in a book that will be both comfortably familiar and a little something new as well.

Enjoy.

The Editor

# Chapter 1

*"Not much of an inn, if you ask me."*
H. Johnson

I stared at the candle in the brass holder in the middle of the cluttered table. *Light the candle,* I thought, concentrating hard. *Light it!*

Anyone who might have looked in the window would have seen a young, blond man from Klah, if they knew Klah, gazing hard at an unlit candle. Anyone from a few dozen dimensions might have identified that young man as The Great Skeeve, Magician to Kings and King of Magicians. None of them would have guessed that in spite of my reputation, which was that of a wonderworker, diplomat and organizer, as far as magik went, I was still a pretty rank...apprentice.

Apprentice. I sat upright on my bench to rub my back, and gazed at nothing in particular. The term caused all kinds of emotions to well up in me and distract me from my self-assigned task. The first: regret. I just walked away from my entire life to date: money, a position as Court Magician I could have held on to infinitely just on my reputation, a business that was thriving even beyond my ability to cover all the opportunities that came my way, but the thing I most regretted leaving was friends. The best and most important friend I had left behind was the chief reason I had gone. Aahz, denizen of the dimension Perv, had been my mentor, guide, partner, teacher and, yes, friend, since the untimely death of my master, the magician Garkin, who'd just finished this very lesson when he'd been killed by an assassin.

The second was fear. I hadn't mastered the candle trick then, and though I could do it now with ease I hadn't progressed much farther than that in my studies. I'd come back to Klahd to start over again with the basics and work my way up.

How long would it take? I had no idea. What if, after all this time, I turned out to have no real magik talent? How would I deal with that? What if I couldn't learn to be the wizard everyone but my partners thought I was?

The third was loneliness, but I suppose that was good, in a way. I left behind friends who'd been my support through thick and thin, who'd given me the confidence to take over situations that I, as an apprentice magician (and would-be thief) never dreamed I'd be controlling, let alone involved in. It was time to strip away that protection and find out who I was. I also needed the solitude to study magik. I couldn't do it in front of a crowd. I needed to be able to fail, and learn from those mistakes without anyone correcting them for me. I needed to know my limitations, hard as that was. I also needed to learn how to deserve the friends I had. There had been times I could look back on now with the shame they deserved when I had been an unimaginable jerk to the people nearest and dearest to me. Being on my own for a while would be good for me.

I wasn't entirely alone in my self-imposed exile. Here, in the inn that we had sort of inherited from a madman named Isstvan and which I now more or less owned, lived myself and three friends. Gleep was my young green dragon. Buttercup, a war unicorn I'd acquired from a retired soldier named Quigley, was Gleep's best friend. Bunny, a drop-dead gorgeous woman, was the niece of my former sort-of-employer (there are a lot of sort-ofs in my life), Don Bruce, Fairy Godfather of the Mob. Bunny, for all her baby-doll looks, had a great brain. She'd been M.Y.T.H. Inc.'s bookkeeper and accountant, and had come with me to be my assistant and connection with the rest of the dimensions.

I turned my attention back to the candle. The spell had become too easy for me. I'd stopped feeling the connection between will and power, the connection I'd fought to attain to master the energies that abounded in earth and sky.

The bell rang. I heard light footsteps on the stone floor, a pause, then more footsteps coming towards me.

"Can you handle this, Skeeve?" Bunny said, poking her head into my room. "It's much more up your alley than mine."

I rose from the table and the unlit candle, and hurried toward the door. A glance through the peephole revealed a couple of eager-faced Klahds with luggage. The inn had been abandoned for years, but I'd cleaned it up enough to make it habitable. Unfortunately, a rumor had gotten around that the hostelry was operating again, not what I had in mind. Normally Bunny would politely send them on their way, but I understood why she wanted me to do it. The eager-faced couple on the doorstep were the kind of tourists who didn't take a subtle hint.

The one magikal talent I had mastered without a doubt was illusion. Immediately I filled the hall with illusory spider webs and broken beams hanging crookedly over the gallery. I cast a disguise spell over myself to make me into an aged hunchback with matted hair crawling with vermin. I blotted Bunny out completely behind the image of a sarcophagus with skeletal hands crossed on the chest under a skull-like face. Then I opened the door.

"Ye-ees?" I croaked.

"Hello!" the man beamed. "Do you have a room for the night?" As he glanced over my humped shoulder at the ruin of the room his face changed. "I mean...er...do you know of a nearby hotel where we could spend the night?"

"Come in, come in," I urged them, beckoning with a gnarled hand. The man backed away. Gleep chose that moment to stick his head around the door. I changed his scaled visage from dragon to large and mangy dog. There was no need to alter his breath, which was bad enough to send maggots packing. The man and woman stepped back another pace.

"We'll just be going," the woman said weakly. The two of them, apologizing hastily, sprang back onto their cart. The man whipped up their horse, who lurched into a trot. I waited until they were out of sight, and had a good laugh.

"Thanks, Gleep," I praised my dragon, patting him on the head. His tongue lolled. I let the disguise drop, restoring his large, round eyes to their normal baby blue. The tongue snapped up and slimed me across the face. I gagged. He romped away a few paces, then thundered back to me, making the floor wobble under his weight. He looked hopeful.

"Skeeve...play?"

"Not now. I'll play with you later," I promised. "I've got to keep working. Why don't you find Buttercup?"

"Gleep!" He thundered off, his passage shaking dust down from the rafters.

I turned away from the door. Bunny emerged from the shadows. The beautiful woman with luxurious red hair had a figure that made it hard for men to remember to look up at her face...which, by the way, was well worth the effort. She resembled a wood nymph appearing suddenly from a copse of trees. I let the illusion fade away, to be replaced by the ordinary walls and furniture.

"Thanks," she sighed. "I just knew when I saw those tourists pulling up they weren't going to take no for an answer from *me*."

"No problem," I assured her. If we'd been back in the Bazaar at Deva there was not a soul who'd give trouble to the niece of Don Bruce, the Fairy Godfather, or to a member of M.Y.T.H. Inc, for that matter, but Klahds, denizens of my own dimension, were notoriously unable to appreciate subtleties. It took a good scare to send them off.

I was a Klahd, too, but I knew I'd changed in the years I'd associated with my friends, especially Aahz. Looking back, I finally understood what the Pervect meant when he said, "You can't go home again." In the past I'd been puzzled by that, since all I had to do to go home was unlock the door of the tent in the Bazaar, and there I was. *This* was the home I couldn't come back to. I knew I didn't belong here any longer, but this was the appropriate place to do what I'd come here to do.

"Lunch in ten minutes," Bunny said, heading back toward the kitchen. I snapped back to reality long enough to lift my head and sniff the air. Bunny's cooking was much better than mine. It was an unexpected bonus when I'd asked her to come back to Klah to be my secretary. I had had visions of endless meals of squirrel-rat stew, something I could prepare with my limited culinary skills. Now I still hunted for most of our meat and cut herbs from the wild tangle of weeds that surrounded the inn, but she prepared those simple ingredients with a gourmet's hand. She had numerous unheralded talents, and was always surprising me with the things she knew or was studying. I had a sneaking feeling that she'd be a much better magician than I, though she seemed to have as little interest in the Arts Magikal as she did in going into her own Family's business.

I sighed, glancing back into my study. The candle still sat on the table unlit. Drawing the lines of force that ran through the earth deep under the inn into my body, I formed a hot spark in my mind and sent it to the wick. The candle blazed brightly into life. *Too easy,* I thought sadly, as I turned toward the kitchen. The lesson no longer taught me anything. I'd have to look elsewhere for inspiration.

"Massha sent a new collar for Gleep," Bunny bubbled, as she dipped a ladle into the simmering pot of soup. "It was a present from her friend, Princess Gloriannamarjolie. It's there on the table." She pointed with the non-dripping side of the spoon. I unwrapped the package. The collar, made of a thick hide I hoped was fireproof, had been dyed a soft baby blue that would match Gleep's eyes. It was studded with cabochon jewels, also light blue, each bigger than the last joint of my thumb. Automatically a part of my brain calculated the value of the gems. If fortune did not go my way, each of them could feed us all for a year. Disgusted at myself, I shook my head, to chase away the thought. I had plenty of money, countless times more than I deserved for the work for which I'd earned it.

Bunny must have noticed that I was in a dark mood. Never a prattler under other circumstances, she began to talk cheerfully about other subjects at random.

"My uncle has a new tailor who's trying to sell him a whole wardrobe. You've never seen so much purple fabric anywhere. I don't think ruffles are him, if you know what I mean..."

The bell rang softly. I rose to my feet. Bunny looked dubious. "You don't suppose they've come back, do you?"

"I hope not," I agreed. I wasn't in the mood for any more interruptions.

Before I reached the hall, the bell had sounded again twice more, but with only a mild jangle, as if the person had pulled the string gingerly. It had to be those tourists again, I thought, my ire rising. I didn't even bother to put on a disguise as I flung wide the door.

"We're not open!" I shouted. The man on the doorstep jumped back, flinging his hands up to protect his face. "Go away!"

He gawked at me, then vanished. I blinked. I hadn't used any magik to dispel him. I thought. Puzzled, I closed the door and turned around.

He was standing there looking at me. "Please," he begged. "I need to speak to you."

"No, you don't," I stated. "The inn is closed."

I noted that he had hazel eyes with horizontal slitted pupils, giving him the look of a herd sheep. He tilted his round head, which was topped by a mass of pale curls, adding to the ovine semblance. "But you are Skeeve the Magnificent, aren't you?"

"Yes! I mean, no!" The surprise of being recognized momentarily unsettled me. "I'm not magnificent. I mean, I'm on sabbatical."

"But, we need your help."

"Not mine," I contradicted, firmly, walking toward him. He cowered until he was standing in a corner with me looming over him. "Go away. Scram."

The sheep-man reached into his tunic. I readied a defensive spell, but I didn't need it. He disappeared. Relieved, I started toward my study.

He appeared in front of me again, hands out, beseeching. "Please, Master Skeeve, you must listen to me..."

My hands went up automatically, spreading out a web of protection. The sheep-man rose in mid-air, his body twisting as the strands of power surrounded him. It was a spell Aahz had taught me to tangle up intruders. He looked so miserable and helpless I felt terrible for tying him up in it. I hurried to undo the enchantment, all the while listening to him babble.

"...They'd kill me if they knew I was here, but we can't take it much longer...I heard you were the only one who could, well, convince them that what they're doing is a bad idea...I mean, I think it's a bad idea, but other people might think I'm wrong...I mean, I'm willing to concede that I *may* be wrong..."

By the time his feet touched the ground I was interested in spite of myself. "Who would kill you?" I asked, curiously.

The sheep-man sputtered, as if embarrassed by his own choice of words. "Did I say that? Well, I mean they'd be unhappy with me. Really unhappy with me. Not that it would be unjustified, my questioning their judgement like this, but..."

Bunny swept in and took the man by the arm. "Why don't you just come and sit down and tell us all about it. Maybe Skeeve can recommend someone to help you with your problem if you talk it out with us. How do you like that idea?"

The sheep-man was almost bleatingly grateful. He turned his large eyes toward her. "Oh, I'd love to! But only if it's all right with you. I mean, I am so sorry to intrude on your privacy. I'd never dream of it normally..."

Once Bunny had settled him in the inglenook with a hot cup of tea, our visitor was somewhat more composed. I sat in the big armchair between him and Bunny in case he seemed inclined to become hysterical again. He remained calm, if a little incoherent, as he outlined his mission.

"My name is Wensley. I represent the government of Pareley in the dimension of Wuh," he began. "Well, it *was* the government before...but I'm getting ahead of myself. My people have never been very worldly. It's terrible to have to admit it, and I don't want to speak ill of others, but I think, well, I *think* I think that it comes from our never having needed anything much from outsiders before. Our land is fertile, our animals and crops plentiful, our climate more than clement."

"It sounds like a paradise," Bunny put in.

Wensley laughed bitterly. "And well you might put it that way, dear lady. It was a pair of dice and a few other devices of the Deveels that landed us in the situation that led to our present plight—but I'm being far too direct." He looked abashed.

"Not at all," I assured him. "Lots of beings have lost money to the Deveels. Does your problem have something to do with gambling?"

"Not exactly," our visitor waffled, with an uncomfortable wriggle. "If our leaders had in truth been *gambling*, but I think that perhaps in retrospect the games might have been a tiny bit tilted away from strictly fair?"

"If they were Deveel-run, there's no way they would have been fair at all," Bunny stated firmly, "not to anyone from outside their own dimension. Deveels are in business strictly to earn money—all of it, if they can."

"Well," Wensley hesitated, relieved that someone else had put it more strongly than he seemed inclined to, "it might have been a little like that. Our representatives were persuaded to put our treasury surplus into a game of chance or two. It seemed like a good idea at the time. It was a can't-miss proposition. If we made a large wager, the returns were to be astronomical. They put the idea up as a referendum to the population..."

"Pareley isn't a kingdom?" I asked.

"Why, no," Wensley replied, surprised. "Well, it was. That didn't seem at all fair as a system of government. When the old king abdicated, his son announced that he didn't feel wise enough to tell his people what to do, so he wanted everyone to have a voice in deciding how to run the country. That way none of the wisest ideas would be lost, you see."

"And no one would have to take the blame for bad decisions?" Bunny concluded wryly.

"I suppose so," Wensley conceded. "Everyone seemed quite happy about it at first. Then it became rather cumbersome, collecting everyone's opinions on every single matter of state. It was only logical that those of us in a large geographical district should pool our opinions and have them presented by one person, although for anyone living close to the border between two zones it was difficult to decide which group one ought to give one's opinions to, and some ended up putting in their suggestions twice..."

"Why did they send you?" I interrupted. Even a small sample of this brand of logic was enough to cross my eyes.

Wensley looked modest. "You see, I'm considered—by some—to be more decisive than most. But I don't know if that's true. It might be. I don't really know."

"Go on," I prodded him.

"Er, yes. Well. Naturally, in retrospect it would have been worthwhile to have checked whether the odds were quite so good as we had thought in the beginning, but no one felt it was right to question the motives of our visitors. They seemed so willing to help us increase our treasury!"

"I bet they did," I smirked. "Did they take all your money?"

"Not all of it," Wensley hastened to assure us. "Well, most. We could still scrape by. I think they felt sorry for us. So they sold us this." From inside his tunic he brought out a D-hopper. It looked functional but in poor condition. "A marvelous device," he said enthusiastically. "Everyone wanted to have a chance to try traveling to other dimensions—imagine, before the Deveels came we never knew there *were* other dimensions! I think perhaps we would have been better off never knowing, because, well, travel can be so expensive, you know..."

I nodded.

"Your people saw all kinds of new things and went on a buying spree. It happens."

I knew, because when I first went into the Bazaar at Deva I wanted to buy everything I saw, too. It was lucky for me that I didn't have any money to spend. I still ended up with a baby dragon.

"That's right," Wensley confirmed. "And the payments we owed for our purchases and the D-hopper turned out to be more than we could handle. To be honest, Wuhses have never been very good at negotiation. Among ourselves we agree all the time."

"So you're on the run from bill collectors?" I asked.

"No, no! We always pay our debts. That wouldn't be fair, to cheat someone out of their hard-earned wages...well..." Wensley paused, "...out of what we owed them. It's not their fault we weren't experienced enough to handle such..."

"Cheats?" Bunny suggested.

Wensley blushed to the roots of his pale hair. "Oh, let's not call them that. But we ran out of money. Almost completely. We needed help."

"I'm not a financial advisor," I stated.

"We don't need a financial advisor," Wensley pleaded, his eyes huge with woe. "We found financial advisors. Now we need help getting rid of them."

Bunny and I looked at one another, then back to our guest. "Why don't you just ask them to leave?"

"We...can't," Wensley quavered, dropping his gaze to the ground. "You just don't tell the Pervect Ten to leave."

I raised my eyebrows. This was starting to sound interesting. "Perfect Ten? They're beautiful women?" I started to picture myself the heroic intercessor between the Wuhses and their lovely foes. They'd be so grateful that I stepped in to clear up a misunderstanding. I didn't need to study *all* the time, did I?

Wensley made a face. "I suppose they are beautiful ...though I have to admit that I might be prejudiced against green scales and yellow eyes, and then there are the big teeth...really off-putting, but I might not understand the aesthetics of..."

My ears pricked up. "Wait a minute—not *perfect*, Per*vect?* You went to *Pervects* for investment advice?"

"Really, it started out as a consulting contract," Wensley said desperately. "They came highly recommended. Ten of them came in and within no time ripped out the entire organization we had in place. They assessed our debt structure and our earning potential, and pu—steered us onto a new course. Under their guidance we started small businesses, and they sold the goods to other dimensions. Pretty soon they made us open factories and controlled our expenditures. Within a couple of years we were out of debt again. But now they're pretty much in charge of everything. We can't get them to go away."

"Ten...Pervects?" I uttered, faintly. *"Ten...Pervect...women?"*

"Yes, well. I...then, one of the Wuhses who had braved the wilds of Jahk came back with stories about you and how you bested the Jahks and won their Trophy. We were so impressed! Here was the very person or persons who would free us from the yoke of oppression...well," he stopped, and gulped, "from a relationship that has accomplished rather more than we assumed it would."

"You do need help," I began. "But I'm not the one to do it."

"But, Master Skeeve!" Wensley wailed.

I stood up decisively, and the Wuhs jumped to his feet in reaction.

"Let me take you to a friend of mine. He's an expert on Pervects. I'll explain everything. You won't have to say a thing."

"To Aahz?" Bunny asked, linking her arm with mine.

"To Aahz."

# Chapter 2

*"I'm puttin' the band back together."*
J. Blues

"We're off to see a wizard?" Wensley asked, as we pushed our way through the crowds of merchants and shoppers thronging the lanes through the tents of the Bazaar at Deva.

Our visitor clung to my upper arm with limpet-like determination. His eyes were wide as he took in the variety of dimension travelers bargaining with Deveels and other sellers of goods and services. I had to admit that I'd gotten so used to the place that seeing the reactions of a newcomer reminded me how much of a racket filled the air. Among tents ranging from a tight fit for a Gnome to a canvas-covered space large enough to hold an Imp family reunion, red-skinned Deveels of all sizes, ages and shapes bargained with one another at the tops of their voices, denigrating one another's merchandise, parentage and general appearance, until they made a bargain, after which they'd be all smiles ... but their voices would still be ear-bleedingly loud as they offered one another brief compliments before parting. No Deveel stuck around long after having bought or sold. There was always another sale to be made, and customers waiting. Folk of hundreds of other dimensions walked or glided or blundered through the shoulder-to shoulder crowd, in search of that elusive item they had to have. If it wasn't for sale on Deva, or couldn't be obtained by legal or illegal means, then it was a rare commodity indeed.

Smells filled the air, too. Some of them, like spices, baking and cooking food, were pleasant, but they were overbalanced by an equal number of real stenches, like the wagon we passed full of rotting vermin. I was afraid to guess whether the pathetic corpses were destined for the trash heap, or the kitchen of a local restaurant. I'd learned to eat almost anything during my thin years as a would-be thief and apprentice, but my palate would never accommodate such foods as Pervish cooking or Deveel snacks-on-a-stick, guaranteed to give you a stomach ache you'd never forget, if you survived digestion.

A Trollop with plenty of green-tinged cleavage showing over the top of an inadequately-laced tunic started to give Wensley the eye, but I caught her gaze and shook my head. Recognizing me, she gave a sultry smile, tossed her moss-green hair, and turned to the next prospect, an Imp wearing a loud suit and flashing far too many rings and neck chains for a pickpocket-heavy ambience like this one.

"Not a wizard. He's my best friend," I corrected Wensley. We were lucky to hear that Aahz was on Deva. Tananda, my friend who was, coincidentally, also a Trollop as well as a trained Assassin, was at home in our old headquarters. Bunny assured me Aahz also made it his *piéd-a-terre* whenever he was in the dimension. Tananda had steered us toward a beer garden offering seasonal brews, some rows over from our office.

Oom-pah-pah music assaulted my ears as we walked into the tavern. I'd been by myself so long on Klahd that I forgot it was Weisenheimerfest on Deva. Deveels in lederhosen, with perky little green hats tilted on their heads between their sharp little horns and kegs on their shoulders, made their way between the broad wooden tables. Decorated pottery or metal mugs hung from pegs all the way around the wooden gallery. Below, people from all kinds of dimensions sat on the benches, some holding up their tankards for a refill, many taking a snooze under said benches after their long-awaited annual overindulging (Weisenheimerfest only came once a year). Others swayed from side to side in time to the music played by a trio of musicians who sat on stools at one end of a dance floor. No one was dancing in the heat of the noonday sun, but there was some serious drinking going on.

Aahz was there, alone at the end of one table, tossing down foaming draughts from a mug as big as a bucket. I had never been so glad to see him in my life. He almost looked beautiful to me, but nobody could call big, green, batlike ears or teeth as long as your fingers beautiful. Though he stood a little shorter than I, he had the air of power and ease that any Pervect commanded. (Some, less knowledgable dimensional travelers called the denizens Per*verts*, but that was all a matter of deliberately bad PR those who lived in Perv spread about their homeland.) I recognized his clothes as one of the outfits he called his "casual Friday" wear, though why a day of the week should make a difference in how one dressed I'd never worked out. A pale-green shirt open at the collar blended nicely with a pair of trousers the color of a sweet I had come to like called "butterscotch." His scaly, green, clawed feet bore no adornment and needed none. He'd tried to educate me about dress sense, but it was really Bunny who had taught me how not to look so much like a...Klahd.

He looked startled as he glanced our way. It had been a while since the last time, and I was the one who was responsible for our parting. But I thought that our mission was of sufficient importance to interrupt my self-imposed exile, and I knew Aahz would feel the same urgency.

"You want me to do what?" Aahz gasped, spitting a mouthful of beer clear across the open dance floor. The tuba player gave him a chiding glance and turned his instrument over to empty it. "Ten female Pervects? A dimension full of Wuhses? The Deveels cheated them out of their last dime, and the Pervects got it back for them? And now they want us to throw the Pervects out? Mmm, mmm."

He slammed his mug down. I recoiled slightly at the violence of the gesture. His lips twisted. His shoulders started to heave.

"Mmm mmm mmm. Ha ha ha ha. HAWHAWHAWHAW HAW!HAWHAWHAWHAWHAW!"

He laughed until the building rang with the sound of his voice. The other patrons watched him nervously as he slapped me on the back, stood up, slipped to his knees, and slid down the trestle of the table until he was sitting on the floor laughing.

Soon, he recovered and climbed up to his feet again. He took my hand in a crushing grip.

"Aw, part—Skeeve," he gasped, wiping tears from his yellow eyes. "I've missed you, kid. That is one of the best jokes I've heard in months. Really did me good. Fraulein!" He held up a hand and snapped his fingers. "A round for my friends!"

"But I'm serious," I insisted, as a Deveel maiden whose pointed tail stuck out beneath the frills of a tight dirndl skirt slapped a mug into my palm and held out her own for payment. I felt in my belt pouch for a coin.

Aahz drank deeply from his own mug. "No, you're not, kid. Nobody is going to march into a dimension taken over by Pervects and politely ask them to leave. At least, I'm not. That would be as pointless an exercise as asking a shark to give back the arm he just chewed off your shoulder."

"What's a shark?" I asked.

Aahz grinned, but there was a touch of sadness in his expression. "Just like old times, huh, kid? Well, if you're serious about it and you really want my advice, you'll scratch this one. I wouldn't do it for all the tea in China, and don't ask me where China is. I'm not in charge of your education any more. You don't really need me to explain to you why this is a bad idea. If you've already made up your mind to go and you're talking to me *pro forma*, good luck. Just make sure you leave burial instructions with Tananda, okay? I'll miss you. Nice to see you, Bunny. Tell your uncle I said 'Hi.' Sorry, Curly," he turned to Wensley, "but when you guys grow the backbone to take care of this on your own you'll find it a lot easier than you think."

"I'm afraid your friend didn't comprehend the serious nature of our...situation," Wensley bleated in my ear as we left the beer garden.

"I think he understood it just fine," I replied, glumly.

Now that I'd said it out loud it did sound like a suicide mission, and it *would* be one, without the aid of someone who really understood the way Pervects thought. I'd already tried to get in touch with Pookie, a female Pervect who'd worked with us before, but she was off on a mission with another one-time associate named Spider and couldn't be reached. Most likely she'd give us the same advice Aahz had: give up and let the Pervect Ten leave when they felt like it. The Wuhses certainly weren't worse off than when they'd arrived, but I agreed with Wensley that it was better to stand on your own. Pareley deserved to be freed from their yoke.

I felt in my belt pouch for the D-hopper, but to tell the truth I wasn't ready to go back to Klah yet. I didn't have an idea how to proceed. Wensley looked at me with those big sad eyes of his. I just couldn't let him down.

Bunny hadn't said a word. She probably agreed with Aahz. That made me all the more resolute to figure out a way to solve Wensley's problem. That would show everyone that I didn't need a dozen shoulders to lean on, that I could take care of a sticky situation on my own.

"As long as we're here, we may as well get some lunch," I decided, drawing inspiration from the dusty, aromatic air. "It would be nice to have a change from home cooking."

Bunny smiled. "How about kebabs at Ali Ke-Bob's?"

I crooked my elbow so she could put a hand through it. "Sounds delicious. How about you, Wensley?"

"Well," our guest began, very tentatively, though I could see the avid gleam in his eye. "If it's not too much trouble..."

"I'm next!"

"No, I'm next!"

As we came around the corner into the next street, a crowd all but filled the avenue. Men and women from every dimension I had seen were trying to get into a tent where I knew manuscripts and books were sold. A sign next to the door said "Autographing Today!" One after another, each person emerged from the throng triumphantly clutching a gaudy hardcover book. I peered at the title as a stout Troll went by with his book open in his huge hand. He studied something on the title page, and a tear rolled down his hairy cheek. I had to jump out of the way because he wasn't looking where he was going.

"*Imps Are From Imper, Deveels Are From Deva*," I read from the cover. "Well, that's obvious. Imps *are* from Imper. And Deveels *are* from Deva."

"Zol Icty!" Bunny cooed suddenly.

"What?"

"That's the author! He writes self-help books. They're wonderful! I have all of them. Just wait here a moment, Skeeve. If he's *here* today I have to have a copy signed by him."

"Sure," I agreed. Bunny dived into the crowd pushing in at the door. I pulled Wensley out of the way of the excited shoppers to a safe vantage point across the street. As more people came around the corner and saw the sign, they shoved eagerly into the throng, blocking those who were coming out from inside. Yet, strangely, no one seemed to be angry or impatient. Usually if there was a desirable item for sale, teeth, claws and handbags were the weapons of choice to make sure one got one's hands on it. I felt the air for lines of force, but no perceptible magik was in use in the tent. Something else had to be going on to keep everyone in such good spirits.

About an hour passed before Bunny emerged. She had a starry look in her huge, blue eyes. The prized book she held clasped to her chest, which was heaving with sighs of joy.

"Oh, he is so wonderful!" Bunny squealed, breathing deeply. "Look, Skeeve! See what he wrote in my copy: 'To Bunny. I can tell just by looking at you that you are sensitive and generous. Keep making the best of your splendid attributes so the whole world will benefit. All my dearest wishes, Zol Icty.' I'll treasure it forever!"

In the face of her obvious delight I didn't make the gagging sound that the fulsome dedication evoked from me.

"That's really nice," I offered. I know my voice sounded a little lame, but Bunny didn't seem to notice.

Wensley turned the book over to reveal a portrait of the author, a little gray man with huge eyes, a thin mouth, a small turned-up nose, delicate little ears, and fine, wavy black hair. I recognized him as a denizen of Kobol, a dimension that had produced notable mathematicians and a technical profession that Aahz called "come pewter programmers." Kobolds were known to be very complex thinkers, far ahead of their time. I thought they looked like embryos, except for their coloration. Bunny kept talking about meeting him, the words tumbling out like water going over rapids.

"...And he's studied the people in hundreds of dimensions. He knows all about every one of them, Gnomes, Imps..."

"Pervects?" I said, a thought suddenly striking me.

"Yes, of course," Bunny said, halting in mid-flow. "I'm sure he mentioned them. Why?"

"We need an expert," I said. "Maybe we can talk to him."

"That's a wonderful idea!" Bunny beamed at me. "I'll see if we can take him to lunch!"

With that, she dived back into the fray.

Another twenty or thirty minutes went by, but after the crowd thinned out, Bunny emerged from the book tent with the author in her grasp. The little gray man's head only came to the middle of her ear, but she held on to his arm as though he was the most important man in her uncle's entourage. (Bunny had been brought up to be a moll, but she was wasted in that, er, position.) She performed introductions with the air of a magician presenting her very best illusion. The author's eyes widened as she spoke my name.

"Skeeve the Magnificent," Zol Icty said, holding out a long, narrow hand to me. "My, my, I've heard so much about you. And I must say that you live up to my expectations."

I wasn't wearing the terrifying illusion that I normally did when seeing clients, so all he saw was the blond youth whose face I shaved every day. "What do you mean?"

"I've heard you're a man of compassion and thorough-ness," the Kobold said, beaming up at me. "I can just see the generous nature glowing from every pore. I am honored to be in your presence." I was torn between wanting to throw up and feeling infinitely flattered. Aahz never noticed my com-passion or thoroughness. Most of the time he was upset that I *didn't* grab everything on the table when my opponents were at a loss. "So what can I do for you?"

# Chapter 3

*"Let's take this show on the road!"*
M. Rooney

I tried to live up to the reputation Zol insisted I had while I outlined our mission over lunch.

We were in a private booth in a very small, dimly lit diner I knew, at some distance from the bookstore, but it was still difficult to have a private conversation. Hundreds of people, one after another, came up to our table with a book held out and a simpering expression on his or her face. Because I was supposed to be compassionate, I tried to hold my temper at each interruption, though it got more and more difficult when I could only squeeze out three or four words before the next one came.

With my position in the Bazaar I could usually depend on a maitre d' to fend off intruders while I dined, but even he, a Deveel in his middle years, was starstruck at the sight of our guest, and did nothing to prevent the crowd of passionate Zol Icty fans from getting in the way of the service of our drinks and food, and of my narrative flow.

The Kobold blinked up wryly at me from the book he was signing for a Gnomish woman whose blue face was flushed a becoming sapphire at the sight of her idol. "You've been very patient, Master Skeeve," he assured me, "but you needn't worry. This is the last one. I only sold 8,736 copies today, and including this, I have now signed them all."

I gawked at him.

"You counted all of them? You kept track?"

He shrugged modestly. "Second nature for a Kobold. It's said we have a mathematical bent that inclines at a perfect 90° angle. Now, if you would be so kind, pour me some tea, and let's talk about your problem."

Impressed at last, I complied.

"Pervects," he mused, sipping from his cup of tea. "Pervects are very interesting. They have every advantage, coming from a dimension that uses both magik and technology with equal ease. Their physical attributes are such that they are saved from harm in circumstances that would kill weaker beings. Their skin is natural armor, their teeth and claws formidable weapons, yet their species evolved superior intelligence. They have so much confidence in their own expertise that it's difficult to prevent one from carrying out his or her plans."

I met Wensley's eyes and nodded. (Bunny was still staring at our guest, though I could tell she really was listening.) "That sounds like the ones I know," I said.

"The key here is secrecy. Don't ever tell a Pervect what you want from him, or he'll do his best to thwart you. You can't expect someone with that kind of intelligence and ego to go along with the wishes of a lesser species, and in their view, we are all lesser species."

"That's what I was afraid of," Wensley droned sadly. "We tried to tell them to go, but they wouldn't."

"You were not speaking from a position of strength, Master Wensley," Zol admonished him. "With Pervects you must dictate."

Lots of luck, I thought. "I'd like to lay out my plans before you, Master Zol," I began. "Ten Pervects is an army. We can't force them out by strength, because as you point out, any one of them could tear us apart. We can't use threats, same reason. Blackmail would backfire on us, and besides, it's too dirty a scheme for me. It looks like the only thing we can do is see if we can find out what they're afraid of and scare them away. I know Pervects don't frighten easily, but even they *must* fear something. Or maybe we could trick them into leaving and not coming back, convince them there's a plague in the kingdom or something. I hope you can give us some advice on what we could use to pry them loose."

The Kobold regarded me solemnly. "Once you have that information do you intend to put these plans into practical use?"

"Well, that's my intention," I asserted. "I promised Wensley here that I would try to free him and his people."

"That's one of the finest things about Klahds," Zol observedcheerfully. "They always want to do the right thing. My advice is to dive right in. Let your intentions be your guide." In my zeal I rose to my feet. Bunny put her hand on my arm and pulled me down to the bench again.

"We'd like some *specific* guidelines," she enunciated, pointedly. "How can a Klahd and some Wuhses oust a party of determined Pervects?"

"Why, with the help of an experienced Kobold," he replied, patting her on the hand with his thin gray fingers. "I've gotten so interested listening to you that I simply must come along."

I glanced at Wensley, who was looking hopeful but forlorn. "I doubt that Pareley would be able to afford your fees, sir."

"My fees?" he echoed jovially, blinking his huge eyes at me. "The only fee I'd charge is being right in the thick of things. This is an opportunity I can't afford to squander. Call it research. You can pay my expenses, that's all. Travel, housing, entertainment..." He started to tick them off on his long fingers.

I saw stacks of coins begin to mount up in my imagination. My dubiousness must have showed on my face. The little man laughed and patted my arm. "I don't eat much, I can sleep anywhere, and I find entertainment in almost everything. Don't worry. we'll get this job done. You'll see."

I began to like him in spite of myself. "I want to enlist a few more of my associates," I added.

"If you'll listen to me," Zol insisted, pouring himself another cup of tea, "they'll be female. Set a thief to catch a thief, I always say."

"Not a thief," I corrected him with a smile. "An Assassin."

Tananda was in our tent packing a bag when we arrived.

"I'm just on my way out the door," she declared, glancing up. "I'm going to visit my mother on Trollia. Chumley's already there. Mums decided she wanted to change all the wallpaper in the house, and you know how she is when she makes up her mind. She has a list of home improvements she wants him to do. The next thing you know she'll want him to pull up the floors and lay terrazzo instead of the flagstone that she had him put down last time. I've got to go and act as a buffer between them. He just can't say no to her even if she has a bad idea. As long as I'm in between jobs."

I had never met the elder Trollop who was the mother of two of my most trusted and intelligent companions. If Tananda was anything like her, she must be a formidable woman.

I was dismayed. "I would like to hire you for *this* assignment," I explained.

"Is Aahz coming too?" she asked, tilting her head at me curiously.

"Uh, no," I mumbled. Resolutely, she picked up a stack of lace underthings to put them in her bag: tiny brief panties of wispy black or emerald green, brassieres whose rounded confines would hold Tananda's marvelous curves gently but still allow that bewitching jiggle.... For a moment I stood fascinated, staring, but I forced my attention back to Tananda's eyes. "He's...er...busy."

Tananda nodded. "He said he wouldn't do it."

I had to admit she was right. "Uh, no. But we've got another expert to help us. He is sure he can help us think our way around the Pervect Ten's defenses. May I introduce you to Zol Icty?"

I presented the Kobold, who came to wrap his hands around hers warmly. "Mistress Tananda! What a happy moment for me to meet such a lovely Trollop as yourself!"

"I wondered if that was you," Tananda cooed, cuddling up to the author in the more than friendly way she had. "Call me Tanda."

Trollops, I didn't need Zol to tell me, believed in close physical contact, even when meeting someone for the first time. The Kobold seemed to relish it.

"I'd heard you were in the Bazaar today, but I didn't want to risk the crowds. I'm delighted to meet you. I enjoy your books."

"The pleasure is all mine, I assure you," Zol mumbled from the depths of a first class embrace.

Tananda released him and turned to me. "I'm not crazy about what you're trying to do, but I trust you. Chumley will just have to fend for himself with Mums. Terrazzo floors will look pretty."

"Good," I sighed with relief. "Now to sign up a few of the others."

Even the presence of Zol Icty didn't assuage the fears of my other former associates. I next approached the pair of enforcers who'd been muscle for M.Y.T.H. Inc., and now had sole charge of the Mob's interests in the Bazaar. They'd taken over our office space in the former Even Odds gambling club. Guido, a huge man who dressed in dapper zoot suits with big shoulders and wide lapels, the better to conceal the pocket crossbow that he carried just inside his jacket, regarded me with a mixture of disbelief and sympathy.

"With all due respect, Boss," Guido imparted, "I don't feel safe tanglin' with no Pervect females. I know Pookie and I know Aahz, and I'm glad they're on our side—and I *know* which one o' them I'd rather have mad at me. I'd stand a chance at survivin' Aahz."

"I must also tender my polite regrets." Nunzio, Guido's cousin, a slightly smaller but no less formidable ally, was equally adamant. He also dressed in dapper zoot suits, and was just as heavily armed. "We can lend you armaments, but it would be impolitic, if not impossible, for us to participate in your enterprise. Even if we were still seconded to your command, Don Bruce would say 'No' to this one. He does not tangle with

Perverts if he can help it. Still, we would not want anythin' to happen to you, so if you insisted we would accompany you in spite of our orders." When I said nothing, he sighed. "We wish you the best of luck."

I returned to our tent and looked at my small army, much smaller than I'd hoped, and frowned. "Maybe we can recruit on Amazonia," I suggested.

"Nonsense!" Zol exclaimed heartily. "A Trollop, an intelligent maiden and a Klahd—between you you have experience, ingenuity and leadership that will far exceed your needs. Add to that the malleability of the Wuhs and my own expertise, and you have nothing to fear!"

I'd been in the adventure business far too long to take a comment like that at face value, but I did know the skills of my two companions. If it was a simple matter of figuring out the weaknesses of a given group, an Assassin and an accountant might well be all I needed. Besides, Tananda and Bunny were watching me carefully. I didn't want to let them down by showing them I didn't have faith in them.

"Surveillance first," I asserted, firmly. "Let's find out just how their operation is structured, and see if we can figure out their plans before we make a move of their own."

Bunny smiled. I'd said the right thing.

"Surveillance," Tananda mused. "Where are they based, Wensley?"

"Oh, in the castle," the Wuhs informed her. "The prince wasn't using it. He prefers to live in the suburbs, and it's just too centrally located. It's very sturdy, he said. Stone walls and tiled ceilings with big heavy beams. Very protective. We Wuhses like protective buildings."

"Good," stated Tananda.

"Good?" I echoed. "It's not like they're out in a field somewhere, where it would be easy to hear what they're saying."

She gave me an amused look. "That would make it impossible to eavesdrop on them. Have you ever tried to sneak up on someone in the middle of a field?"

"Of course not," I replied indignantly. "They'd see you coming for miles...oh."

"Exactly, exactly," Zol beamed. "See? You're already building on one another's strengths. So the Pervect Ten feel very secure and certain no one will sneak up on them. It should be a simple matter to find a good listening post and learn all."

# Chapter 4

*"One's biggest problems are almost*
*always of one's own making."*
V. Frankenstein MD

"Run those figures again for me, Caitlin, darling," asked the elderly Pervect in the flowered dress. She tapped the side of the console with her cane.

"Don't do that, Vergetta," snapped the very young female at the keyboard. She turned deepset amber eyes at her senior. "It upsets the gremlins in the motherboard."

"Well, they need waking up, if those are the answers you're giving to me," Vergetta remarked peevishly. "They shouldn't talk this way to anyone's mother. This is a wrong answer. It has to be."

"I think she's right," declared Oshleen, a tall, willowy Pervect, sashaying into the room with a slighter, shorter compatriot in her wake. She waited for the skirts of her floor-length silk gown to settle around her manicured feet. "I've done the calculations myself, and Tenobia has checked the store rooms. About ten percent of the treasury is gone."

"Again?" Vergetta roared. She slammed a hand down on the console, earning a glare from Caitlin. "What is it with these Wuhses?"

"I told you you ought to let me confiscate that D-hopper," sneered the narrow-eyed Pervect in black, who was filing her claws to razor points in the corner of the room.

Vergetta turned to her patiently. "It's a toy, Loorna. It gives them pleasure."

Loorna sprang up, her long yellow fangs bared. "Every time they use that toy they end up spending money! Money they don't have! Money *we* don't have. They're such idiots."

"They're Wuhses, what do you expect? They're going to pull business acumen out of the ground?"

"If they'd dig up some self-control, then I'd set every one of them up with shovels and tell them to get to it. As it is, if you yell at one of them, he folds up and points at everybody but himself."

"If I could get my hands on the Deveel who sold them that D-hopper I'd park it under his pointed tail," Tenobia growled. "I've tried to get them to put it back in the treasury and sign it out when they want to use it, but no. They don't want to let us hold it for them. We might not give it back, and that's 'uncooperative and unfriendly'. So it gets passed secretly from hand to hand, never in the same place for five minutes. If we don't control it, we can't tell them where they can and can't go. And they do: they flit off to any dimension that takes their fancy. And every time they go off they come back with a souvenir. *Every single time.* So suddenly *everyone* has to have one of the new gizmos, and we have a flood of imports. Then, because this stuff *isn't* free, they raid the treasury to pay for it. No one ever asks—they're not assertive enough for that. So they sneak it out. Every single one of them feels entitled to spend some of the money. No one has ever had the backbone to take all of it, but they might as well. The trouble is that they don't check, in case someone says no. Like us."

"We made a mistake telling them we were close to solving their problem," Oshleen sighed, polishing her nails on her sleeve. "They think the money shortage is over."

"It's not over!" Caitlin snapped. "I keep a spreadsheet going of input and output."

"I know that," Oshleen retorted. "I recalculate the balances every day, too, you know."

"On paper!"

"And if your gremlins stop working, what record do you have? Nothing!"

"Girls, girls," Vergetta chided them. "Enough!"

"It's natural to be interested in new things," Nedira inter-jected, soothingly. "They're curious. They like toys."

"It's not the toys that are the problem," Tenobia insited. "It's paying for them. They don't sell their used toys when the novelty's worn off. They just accumulate them, and think that the money's going to fall out off a tree."

Paldine drummed her fingertips on her lip. "If we could only head off the trend before it catches on kingdomwide, *we* could control the flow and make a percentage on the value. Not to mention making sure they're not being cheated. As it is, they *always* pay too much, then they can't admit it. Sooner or later one of them sneaks in with the janitors and abstracts the coins when we're not looking. I told you we should have put a wyvern in the treasury."

"So they're not so good at personal responsibility either," Vergetta shrugged. "That's why they hired us."

"They need keepers, not financial managers," Loorna coun-tered. "Shepherds, that's what, and maybe a bunch of border collies. Yes, that's it. Put them all in pens until we're finished straightening them out."

"If they would just have let us do our job," Oshleen drawled, bored with the never-ending arguments, "we could have been out of here six months ago. They're making it impossible. Paldine should never have agreed to a milestone-based con-tract, especially one that prevents us from taking any other consulting contracts in the meantime. It should have been strictly time-based."

Paldine, pristine and elegant in a two-piece skirt suit and flowered scarf pinned at the shoulder, jumped up from the couch and grabbed Oshleen by the neck of her silk gown. "If you say that one more time I'll rip your head off! Where were you when I was negotiating it? Sashaying around look-ing for more clothes? Strutting around on a runway?"

"I was humiliating myself for this group! We needed that device! We could have used the Bub Tube for mass hypnosis, and maybe broken the habit they've gotten into.

That Deveel created a nation of shopaholics!" Oshleen said with a dangerous scowl.

"And you couldn't get it. You failed in the one assignment that should have been a walkover."

"Ladies, ladies," Nedira interupted, pushing in between them. Her plump body made an effective buffer as the two taller Pervects glared at one another over her shoulders. Charilor came up quietly behind Paldine and detached her hand from Oshleen's throat with a sharp tug. Paldine glared and massaged her wrist. "Why are we fighting? What's done is done. What we need to do now is find a solution."

Oshleen rubbed her throat. "Every single time we get these fools out of debt, one of their precious committees spends the new profits, without letting us deduct expenses, or taking into account what any of the other committees are doing with the proceeds. They're spending it faster than we can earn it. We can't even request payment because of your contract. We have to get them on their feet and keep them there for a period of sixty days. That's what we agreed to! We can't even get paid. Our work would be undone completely if we request our fee—that would clear out the rest of what's left in the treasury. And if we leave without fixing the leak, we'll be blamed for it. Our reputation will be ruined throughout the dimensions."

"She's right," agreed Tenobia. "We've got to hang in here until we get them up and running, and make it stick."

Paldine groaned and clutched her head. "Oh, I just want to leave here and never come back!"

"What if we set up one big score that would net all the money the budget would need for the sixty days, including our fee," Caitlin suggested, a wicked look in her eyes, "but that the Wuhses would be responsible for? Then we could leave. The kingdom would be in excellent shape, financially if not socially."

"And what would happen when the creditors descended?" Nedira chided the little Pervect. "It would take them less than a week to use up two months' worth of money. Where can we increase revenue *legitimately?*"

"Well, there's no more money to be made out of Pareleyan exports," Paldine stated, firmly. "I'm already straining the markets for handweaving. Their books of poetry went over like a dead horse. We were doing pretty well in the factories that assemble housewares. If only Vergetta and Charilor," she glared at the stocky young female, who went to lean against the wall with her arms folded, "hadn't blown their caper on Deva we'd have had a virtually infinite customer base."

"And that was our idea?" Vergetta snarled. "Forget it. If I ever get my hands on that Trollop, I'll paint her wagon, just before I fix it for good."

"We did," Charilor smirked. "We smacked her and her two henchmen around fairly thoroughly. We paid in advance, if you look at it one way."

"Well, I don't!"

"Please!" Nedira shouted over the others' voices.

"I believe," Monishone spoke up for the first time from her work station close to the window, "I may have the solution."

The others turned to her. Of the group she was easily the best magician, though Vergetta believed she hated all technology, unnatural for a Pervect. "So what you got, baby?"

The slender, delicately built female came forward. Her blue silk robes clashed horribly with her green scales, but it was the traditional color for ceremonial magik. She pulled back her wide sleeve so the others could see the small device balanced on her palm. "This."

"Glasses?" Niki asked. "So you're leaving the Luddite contingent at last?" Where Monishone was the technophobe, Niki was the technophile. If something broke down Vergetta didn't bother to try and fix it herself; she always called Niki.

"Don't be stupid," Monishone stared at her haughtily. "They're storytelling goggles."

"Come again?" Niki demanded. "What's the difference between those and virtual-reality headsets?"

"Because they're magikal, wirehead," the smaller Pervect spat. "They work, unlike the crap you play with."

"All right, all right, no more fighting," Vergetta soothed them. "We just fixed the wall again last week." She swooped down and snatched the spectacles out of Monishone's hand. "How do they work?"

"Just put them on."

The elder female hooked the ear-pieces over her large ears and settled the frame on the bridge of her nose. "So what am I supposed to see?"

"Do you see the little books in the corner? Pick one and flick a tiny bit of power at it."

"And...?" Vergetta pressed. Monishone waited, a little smile on her lips. "Aaaaagggghhh!"

Niki leaped forward, and plucked the spectacles off Vergetta's face. "What's wrong?"

The elder Pervect grabbed them back. "Give me those! It's wonderful!" She put them back on.

"What's wonderful?" Tenobia asked, taking them away and propping them on her own nose. "Wha—wow!"

"Let me see," Oshleen insisted, hooking the eyeglasses with one long claw. She stiff-armed the shorter female with one arm while she put them on. "Fantastic! I could almost pluck those jewels off the walls!"

"Inconsiderate bitches," Charilor snarled, twisting Oshleen's arm up behind her back. With her free hand she felt around the other's face until she got the spectacles.

"Ow! You hit me in the nose!"

"Let me see!" Nedira demanded, pushing the others out of the way until she reached Charilor.

"Enough!" Vergetta bellowed. The stone room shook until the hanging lamps danced. Eight of the Ten stopped squabbling and turned to look at her. Monishone stood with her arms crossed, wearing a smug expression. "Give me those! Now!" She put out an imperious hand to Charilor. Very reluctantly, Charilor peeled the goggles off and put them on Vergetta's palm. "You all sit down, and you wait until I am finished with these, and then everyone may have a turn! Just because I'm the oldest doesn't mean I can't kick your behinds from here to tomorrow!"

Shamefacedly the rest of the Ten settled down into their favorite seats to watch her. The only sound was that of Caitlin's fingers clicking on the keys of her computer. Vergetta nodded and resumed the goggles.

Inside the glasses it was dark except for the tiny glowing bookshelf in the upper left edge of her field of view. It didn't take a master magician to manipulate the individual books. The merest touch of power caused each one in turn to open and display its title page to her. A pink one was entitled *The Rose in the Tower*, a blue one *Dragonfest*, and a black tome *It Came From Klahd*..."Horror, too?"

"Anything you like," Monishone confirmed.

*Dragonfest* looked good. Vergetta went back to it and opened it again. With the merest touch of magik she turned the first page.

Suddenly she was not seeing the tiny book, but a landscape that surrounded her completely. In the distance were three active volcanoes spewing smoke into the gray sky. Her feet shifted on the uneven ground. She looked down, and realized she was standing on a mountain of gold coins and jewels. She started to bend to pick up a handful of treasure.

"Hiyyaaaa!" a voice screamed behind her. The jewels scattered. She turned around to see a little being clad in shining silver armor waving a sword at her. He stood no higher than her knee. He plunged forward, waving the brand. It flashed down and hit her in the knee.

"Ow!" she roared. A jet of flame shot out of her mouth, narrowly missing the knight. "Hey! I'm the dragon! This is great!" She stopped to examine her hands. They were long, slender blue paws with gleaming red nails. "This clashes, baby."

Abruptly, a narrow band of rainbow light appeared next to her right hand. "That one," she decided, pointing at a stripe of burnt orange. "Always go for the complementary color." Before she'd finished speaking the nails had turned orange. "Very nice. Now, for you, you little *pesgunyik!*"

But the knight didn't wait around for her to revarnish her fingernails. He hauled his tin behind down the hill as fast as his fingerlong legs would carry him. It took no trouble at all, even walking dragon fashion on all fours, to catch up with him. Vergetta grabbed him by the scruff of the neck, rolled back on her long, scaly tail, and started slapping his face from one side to the other. "You don't pick on a lady like that! Didn't your mama tell you anything? Behave yourself!"

She had the knight blubbering like a baby in no time. When he had apologized no fewer than fifty times she let him drop to the ground. He picked himself up and started running. With a puff of breath she gave him a hot seat to remember her by. He vanished over the crest of the hill. She bent down at last to count the treasure in the hill.

When she took off the goggles her eyes were wet with tears.

"That vas beautiful, darling," she told Monishone. "Brilliant! You're a genius! It's a Pervect fantasy."

All eight of the others pushed forward, grabbing for the glasses. "Me next!" "No, me!" "Me!"

"Everyone gets a turn, in order of age. Caitlin?"

The little girl jumped down from her chair and ran up to Vergetta, her hands up. The older female held the spectacles just out of reach. She pointed an admonitory forefinger.

"What do you say?"

"Gimme, you old trout!"

Vergetta beamed and patted the child on the head. "Isn't she darling?"

The rest of the group watched Caitlin's face as it twisted and contorted. Her mouth occasionally gaped open to reveal gaps where a few baby teeth had fallen out and the adult fangs had not yet grown in. Of the Ten the next in age had almost twenty years on Caitlin, but they couldn't do without her. Something about computer technology only yielded its innermost secrets to the very young. She had a gift for data analysis that rivaled Oshleen's less-technical approach. The wisdom to make use of it would come with time. In the meanwhile, her total lack of fear let her wholeheartedly enjoy every experience. Under the goggles' spell she yowled and grunted and crowed, then let out a loud shout.

"Awesome!"

She whipped off the glasses with a look of triumph, and handed them to Charilor.

One by one the Pervect Ten took their turns wearing the Storyteller Goggles. Vergetta watched their faces. Every one of them that had tried them had a gleeful look on her face. When at last Nedira took them off and handed them back to Monishone, they were all wearing the same expression.

"Well, ladies?" Vergetta asked.

"It's amazing," affirmed Tenobia.

"It'd be a gold mine," insisted Paldine. "How many of them can I get, and how quickly?"

"How much do they cost to produce?" Oshleen wanted to know.

"I want to try them again!" announced Charilor.

"No!" Vergetta chided. "Not now! All right. All in favor of producing and distributing Monishone's invention, say 'aye.'"

"Aye!" The call was unanimous.

"Any opposed?"

Silence. Vergetta swept her eyes across nine eager green faces. She clapped her hands together. "All right, then! Chop, chop! I want a business plan laid out by ten o'clock tomorrow morning. This is our big chance to blow this *meshugina* burg and go home!"

The Pervect Ten burst into loud applause and cheers.

Outside, the Wuhses of the democratic kingdom of Pareley shivered and held one another. The terrifying females in the castle were asserting themselves again. And did they have to do it so loudly?

# Chapter 5

*"Sometimes you have to help people*
*whether they want you to, or not."*
J. Stalin

The transference from the Bazaar to Wuh was shocking in the extreme. From heat, noise and dust to we emerged to virtual silence, wan grass and a pale blue sky. Behind us on the cobblestoned avenue stood a curved row of small but very neatly kept houses, each with virtually identical shops in the front and gardens behind. At one end was a wide, grassy park with trees. At the other, an open green where animals grazed around the statue of a crowned Wuhs with both his hands stretched out, palm up. The local equivalent of pigeons roosted all over it, or pecked on the ground for forage. Gleep's blue eyes opened wide at the sight of the hairy-feathered birds. I knew he wanted to go chase them, but I held tightly to his leash. I'd brought him along with us over Tananda's objections, but I wanted all the potential muscle I could get. Since the day I'd accidentally attached him he had protected me, once saving my life, though the effort nearly cost him his own. Even Pervects thought twice before tangling with a dragon. He was still a baby, but he could breathe fire, a little. And he was very strong and nimble. Besides, no one else knew that Gleep and I shared a secret: he could talk. That made him invaluable as an additional gatherer of information. Gleep was disguised as a local pet, a curly-haired goatdog. The disguise didn't change his shape, though. I could feel his tail occasionally slap against my leg as he contemplated breaking loose to go chase birds. Tananda *had* managed to talk me out of bringing Buttercup. Even I agreed that there was little use for a war unicorn when we were facing Pervects. They'd either consider him a pet, or lunch.

Wensley gestured shyly at the tall building of tea-colored stone on the hilltop above us. From the high, conical towers plain beige pennants waved.

"Well, there it is," he announced with shy pride. "Our castle."

"It's not a castle," I pointed out. "Castles have fortifications."

"Oh, we couldn't do that," Wensley jabbered, looking shocked. "That would be unfriendly. We still call it a castle anyhow. It's a matter of pride."

Behind him, Tananda rolled her eyes. Well, at least we didn't have to worry about creeping through a shield wall or having to trick our way under a portcullis. Pareley Castle didn't have either. Nor did it have arrow slits in the walls. Every window was wide and bright, letting in plenty of light through clear, polished glass. I didn't see a single bar on any of them. A few of the sashes were thrown wide, and a gentle breeze caused the frilly curtains to dance. I squinted, but I couldn't see any movement. Were any of the Pervect Ten up there looking down on us? I'd been careful to pull a disguise over us, concealing my lanky height, Zol's dainty frame, Bunny's shining red pixie cut and Tananda's green hair. If anyone did happen to look out of the window, they'd see a quintet of Wuhses milling around like sheep.

The denizens of Pareley really did look like a flock of sheep. I noticed one of them, a large-bosomed female, lean out of the window of a house above a greengrocer's shop, then pull her head back in. I thought no more of it, as Wensley pointed out the memorial.

"That honors our retired king, Stelton the Agreeable. As you can see, he stretches out his hands to all in a gesture of equality. Things just haven't been the same since he left." Wensley sighed. "Not that I would ever want to criticize Prince Coulommier. He had to make the choice that was best for him."

Over his shoulder I noticed a group of his countrymen walking towards us with purpose, and huge smiles fixed on their faces. "Oh, look," Bunny pointed. "A welcoming committee."

The resemblance of Wuhses to sheep was very strong as their slitted eyes were fixed upon Wensley, or more specifically, upon the D-hopper in his hand.

Wensley blanched. "Oh! Come with me, please," he brayed, his voice down to a strangled squawk. "I have so much more to show you." Without looking back he started walking. We followed, but found ourselves having to increase our pace from an amble to a trot. Without breaking into a run, Wensley managed to open his stride until I was running to keep up with him. "Over here you see the baker's. Very fine breads, Cashel makes. Very fine! And there's the vintner's. And the healer's. Very useful after you've been at the vintner's."

"Wensley!" one of the big females in the lead hailed him. We could understand her easily because of the translator pendants we were all wearing. They assisted in helping us to comprehend nuance and emotional content as well, though I had no difficulty telling the state of the female coming toward us. She had a broad smile on her face, but even at a backwards glance I could tell it looked forced. "How nice to see you! Come and chat for a while. I'd just love to catch up with you."

"And so would I!" insisted a slenderer wench, edging around the matron and pumping her elbows so she picked up just a hint of speed. "I've been thinking about you! I've wondered how you are!"

"We've all been thinking about you!" called a male with gray curls.

Looking panicked, our guide pulled us hastily around a corner to the left, then dodged right, so we were heading into the thick of the city along a much narrower street. The balconies almost touched overhead, letting in only a slit of sky. Unfortunately, another group of Wuhses had also taken this less-traveled road, probably with the notion of heading Wensley off, to speak to him about his "well-being."

"You've been such a stranger, Wensley," a big male exclaimed heartily, his arms wide open. There was no getting past *him*.

"Yii," Wensley bleated, in shock, then turned us around.

The first group had not been fooled for long by our de-
tour. There they were, still power-walking towards us as
quickly as they could. They saw the other group, and increased
their speed to get to us first. We were trapped in between. I
braced myself, as all the Wuhses descended on us, smiling
and slapping our backs, all of them clamoring that they had
no other reason for seeing our guide except to pass the time
of day with him.

"And who are your friends, Wensley?" asked a young
male about my age. "They're from out of town, eh?" He
reached around to shake hands with me. As soon as I
relaxed my grip, his hand dropped, seemingly of its own
accord, onto the D-hopper in Wensley's. "Say, isn't that
the community travel wand? I've wanted to get a good
look at it for ages!"

"So would I!" a dark-fleeced female announced. "My
goodness, let me see it. *Please!*" The D-hopper became the
object of a three-way tug of war, with the youth on one
side, the black sheep on the other, and Wensley holding
onto the device in the center with both hands.

"Please be careful," he gritted through clenched teeth. "I
might lose my grip on it, and who knows what would happen?"

It didn't take a genius to figure out just what would happen: the winner of the contest of wills would take the D-
hopper and pop off to another dimension.

"Well, just let me see it a moment," the female insisted,
holding on with determination.

"I...did you meet my guests?" Wensley sibberred, desperately. "I brought them here with the wand. I will have to take
them back again this evening. Yes! This evening! Possibly earlier. So, you see, I can't let go of it for now. I'm devastated not
to be able to oblige you...ungh!" he grunted. With one tremendous effort he pried the D-hopper out of their grasp and
clutched it to his chest with both hands. "...But perhaps later?
Just a little."

The crowd looked as though they wanted to glare, but they glanced at one another out of the corner of their odd-pupiled eyes, and decided to paste on the big smiles instead.

"Of course we understand," the big, hearty male trumpeted. "So these are your guests? Welcome, welcome! You must have a tour of our beautiful city, and then dine with us. We must help Wensley shoulder the onus of hospitality. Believe me," he added, bowing to the women, "it is our great pleasure. Ladies, I am Gubbeen, committeefriend of the Committee of Public Safety."

"Committeefriend?" I asked, glancing at Wensley.

"It means, 'spokesperson among equals,'" our guide explained. "Gubbeen is taking his turn on behalf of the Safety organization that has done such an excellent job at making sure there are always handrails on stairs, and that bridges are safe and not slippery. You know."

I nodded. They did not even have the guts to risk offending the rest of the committee members by calling him the chairman. It had to have been the easiest thing ever for the Pervects to take over their government. Anyone who asserted himself on Wuh was as good as king. It must have been thousands of years since there had been a predatory species anywhere in this dimension.

"So, may we be so bold as to ask what brings you to beautiful Pareley?" Gubbeen asked, after gathering a sufficient number of approving looks from his fellows.

"We're here," I announced as positively as I could, as I dropped our disguise spell, "to help you. I am Skeeve the Magnificent."

At the sight of four outworlders and a green dragon, the Wuhses stampeded away in all directions. Wensley looked as if he would have liked to run away with them, but Tananda held on to his arm.

"Not so fast, handsome," she insisted. "You're carrying our ticket out of here."

"Eh? Oh, yes," Wensley babbled, patting the D-hopper in his arms. Making sure none of the others were around to see, he slid it into his boot. I had not let him see our D-hopper back at the inn or on Deva, using a pinch of blinding light powder to cover our transitions between Klah and Deva, and back again. I considered it our ace in the hole in case we had to depart quickly from Wuh. Tananda, a much more experienced magician than I, was capable of transporting herself up and back between dimensions without the use of a piece of philosophical equipment. Zol, too, assured me that he commanded sufficient talent. Only Bunny and I had to rely on a device. As a potential weakness, it was much better that it remained hidden. It so happened mine was in my boot, too.

One by one the Wuhses came creeping back, eyeing us curiously, at a distance at first, but approaching ever nearer until they surrounded us so tightly we couldn't move.

"Look," one of them gasped, peering into my eyes. "*Round pupils!*" Then, with a shocked expression in case he had offended me, "not that there's anything wrong with that!"

They seemed fascinated by our various skin colors, textures, heights and shapes. In spite of the fact they were of a different species, they admired Tananda and Bunny greatly, gazing at them shyly out of the corners of their eyes, or peering through their lashes, while circling them as closely as they dared. I had no fear that any of the Wuhses would take their admiration too far. For one thing, they were too timid, and for another, Tananda and Bunny were more than able to take care of themselves. None of the Wuhses would pet Gleep, for all he stretched out his neck and rolled his big blue eyes winningly.

"We had no idea you were different, good sir," Gubbeen stammered, putting out a tentative finger to touch my sleeve. "Please forgive my familiarity, Mmm-master Ss-skeeve the Mm-magnificent. What...what did you say you were here for?"

I felt that my dramatic gesture had been ruined by the outward stampede. I used magikal amplification so the whole crowd could hear me. "*We're here to rescue you!*"

"Shhh!" Wensley almost shrieked, signing to me to keep my voice down. "*They* might hear you!"

I guess no one had to be told who They were, because the entire crowd dropped their heads and looked around fearfully. No disaster descended from the skies, so the Wuhses relaxed, and moved in closer than before. I could have walked on their shoulders, if they had let go of me or my companions.

"You have heard of our plight, good sir," Gubbeen whispered, wringing my fingers in an excited grip. "Thank Ram you have come to help us. We were a free people, governed by our consciences and cooperation, until They came along. Now our lives are no longer our own!"

"Well, we're going to put a stop to that," I assured him. "Allow me to present my companions. This is Tananda. And Bunny. And the eminent scholar and author Zol Icty."

Though only a few of the Wuhses who had visited Deva had ever heard of me, at least half of them were acquainted with Zol Icty and his self help books. Zol produced dozens of copies of *Deveels Are From Deva* from the bag slung over his shoulder and autographed them for the crowd. After that, Gubbeen and his fellows couldn't do enough for us. They took us on an exhaustive tour of the city, pointing out every building larger than an outhouse. Three hours into the tour my feet were killing me from trotting over the uneven cobblestones. To the admiration of the crowd I levitated Bunny and myself so we floated just above and behind our hosts. Tananda stretched herself out on the air with her head propped on her palm, as though she was lying on a divan. Zol hovered crosslegged, his bright eyes darting here, there and everywhere. In greater comfort we finished the round back in the alley where it began. I enjoyed the glances of wonderment we received.

"And now, may we offer you some refreshment, you and your first Wuhs friend?" Gubbeen said, though his expression as he looked at Wensley was not as welcoming as the one with which he favored us.

"I appreciate your offer of hospitality," I accepted heartily. My throat had dried out every time they paraded us up and down the promenade that faced the castle. No one wanted us to resume our disguises, being proud of their extradimensional visitors. Only if the Pervect Ten maintained no lookouts at all could we possibly have gone unnoticed.

"Truly, we would enjoy that," Zol agreed. "I would love a cup of tea, and it would give me great pleasure to sample Wuhs cuisine."

That evoked a loud clamor from the crowd. All the restauranteurs begged us to dine in their various establishments. At a frantic signal from Wensley I realized that I'd cause a political backlash if I chose one inn over all the rest, but we couldn't eat in all of them.

"Good friends," I declared, smiling at the dozens of expectant faces, "we are strangers in your town. Would you choose for us?"

# Chapter 6

*"If you can't say anything nice, don't say anything at all."*
D. Rickles

The resulting non-argument about where to eat might have been entertaining to watch, but it stretched on for hours. By the time they decided who would have the honor of hosting us, night had fallen.

"That's it, then!" Gubbeen announced, waking us all out of the bored doze we had fallen into. He came over to us, rubbing his hands together. He was still smiling, but he looked tired. "We will all go to Montgomery's Tavern, where you will sample the average in Wuhs cuisine! You will be our guests."

"But if we are hiring them to help us," an earnest female in spectacles put in, "then properly, they are our guests, but the cost of meals ought to be accounted for as part of their fee."

Another overly polite discussion started. "Hold it!" I insisted, stopping the argument before it began again. "We'll pay for ourselves. We'll negotiate the fee separately, once we see how serious the situation is."

"You didn't set the fee up front?" Tananda asked me in a whisper, as eager hands reached out to pull us towards a brightly lit doorway up ahead.

"Uh, no," I admitted, feeling guilty.

A green eyebrow climbed up her flawless brow. "What if they don't have any money?"

"Well, we can't just leave them under the thumbs of ten Pervects!"

"Just watch me," Tananda asserted, flicking her middle finger against her thumb. "Nobody's dead. Nobody's starving. Your services have value. You can't just run a major freebie like that. If word got back to the Bazaar..."

I opened my mouth to say that I was retired, but that wasn't true either: I was on sabbatical, as I'd told Wensley...as I'd told everybody. Some day I would be finished with my studies...and I didn't know what I wanted to do then. Tananda was right: if I went back to the Bazaar and rumors had gone around that I was giving away my talents for free I'd be flooded with applicants wanting me to take on ridiculously petty tasks, or epic heroics with no hope of remuneration. It had happened before.

"I...I..."

"Don't worry, Skeeve," Bunny assured me, planting a palm in my chest as she passed by me to go first into the brightly lit restaurant. I stopped, the breath knocked out of me. Bunny works out. She is *very* strong. "This is my job. I'll take care of it."

Montgomery's Tavern would not have been called a tavern in any other dimension I'd ever visited. It served liquor and spirits, as well as a simple dinner menu, but since it suffered from a total lack of smoke, grafitti, bar fights or drunks, it put me more in mind of a tea room, the kind in the town near my father's farm that my mother visited when she and her fellow teachers held a meeting on a restday. Montgomery's was so orderly and neat I wondered how anyone could relax in it.

"It's a fern bar," Tananda observed, belting down one drink and signaling for another. "I'd love another one of these lemonades," she smiled at the innkeeper, a stout Wuhs with ruddy curls.

"I hope you're not finding our citrus martinis too strong," Montgomery said, filling her glass from a pitcher.

"Not a bit," Tananda said, monitoring her drink carefully. Montgomery stopped pouring. Tananda cleared her throat meaningfully. With a startled glance, he filled her glass to the top. "That's better. You might as well leave the pitcher. Thank you, you handsome man." When Montgomery went back to polishing the shiny wooden bar, Tananda shook her head. "They'd get thrown out of the Bazaar for watering their drinks. There's hardly any alcohol in these at all. I'll have to visit the necessary about six times before I ever get a decent buzz."

That lack made little difference to me. I was intent on nursing one beer throughout the evening so my head would be clear.

And I needed all of my clarity. Now that they had a champion to save them from their conquerors, the committeefriends of Pareley decided to hold a secret meeting to discuss how they wanted us to do it. Wensley introduced representatives from each of the kingdom's fifteen committees. For people who never fought these Wuhses sure managed to make agreeing sound like an unresolvable blood feud, even though they never spoke directly to one another, or uttered a single harsh word.

"My learned friend," orated Wigmore, the chairman of the Committee for Public Health, "probably didn't hear me very well when I explained my position. I know he would concur with all of my points if he had. The absence of influence of a legitimate democratic system in Pareley is deleterious to the well-being of every Wuhs. It is therefore a direct concern of the health system that we are being governed without our whole approval. Therefore, I and my committee ought to be at your side to consult about the course of action you might take in this matter. If you would concur, Master Skeeve."

"My learned friend from Public Health," intoned Yarg, the chairman of Public Safety, "can't claim I am anything but fair to him. He understands, as we all do, that having outsiders assuming functions that, while it is very kind of them to take such an interest, since we presently lack the ability to counsel them as to our wishes it suggests this case to be within the breadth of Public Health. We would like Master Skeeve and his party to consider having us just a trifle more in his mind than health. Not that health is not incredibly important, you see."

There were a few gasps from the assembled. These were strong terms for any Wuhs to utter. Every one of them was still smiling, still seeming friendly, but if their eyes could shoot fire like dragonbreath, every one of them would be scorched.

As Yarg retired to his seat another committeefriend leaped to her feet. The crux of her address was that Wensley should trust all of them and return the D-hopper to common circulation, specifically to her custody. In spite of the energetic gestures her speech was as mindless as the others had been. I felt myself starting to drowse. Gleep had already fallen asleep with his head on my foot. My head drooped over my half-full glass. Bunny nudged me awake in time to nod approvingly when Ardrahan sat down.

Each speaker had to have his or her turn. I felt like grabbing each one by the neck and telling them they had only one sentence to inform me what they wanted, or I'd take my entourage and go home.

Zol was perfectly at home in the midst of all this. A tea room was all he would ever need. He refused all offers of wine, beer, liquor, liqueur, intoxicants, narcotics or hallucinogens (not that any of our hosts would ever admit to partaking of the last three). The Wuhses seemed a trifle chagrined at first that he turned down their offerings in favor of tea, and tea alone, but they began to produce dozens of varieties of infusions, until they covered the entire table except where his modest little pot, cup and saucer sat. I began to see why the Pervect Ten had been called in to help the citizens of Pareley in the first place. Their extravagance had to have put a severe drain on the kingdom's finances. Some of the teas I recognized as the most expensive ever grown. They were for sale in the Bazaar at approximately a gold coin per ounce. For that much the tea would have to nourish a family of eight for a month, not be thrown out after making a mere six cups. Zol sipped from his cup and listened to the exchanges.

"Yes, it is good to explain what you feel," he kept saying. "Through sharing lies clarity and understanding."

I'd long ago finished my beer. I sat slumped with my fist holding my chin up off the table. I heard birds begin singing outside. Through the window the dark sky began to lighten. Morning was approaching, and no one had really said anything yet. My eyes were burning. I didn't think I could stand one more speech. As the eighth committeefriend stood up and launched into her tale of woe, I interrupted her.

"Tell me more about the actual *oppression*." I insisted, pulling myself upright. I turned to the assembly, most of which looked as tired as I felt. "You've all been talking about how your committees ought to be involved with their overthrow, but what is it the Pervect Ten have really done to you?"

"Haven't you heard what our friends have been saying?" Wensley asked. "They've taken over everything! No one can do what they want to do. They control every coin. They visit all the craft centers, the factories, the farms, and keep track of everything we make."

"They would take away everything that we've gotten from all the other dimensions, too, if they could," Ardrahan bleated. "We *need* it. We haven't got very much magik of our own. All these labor-saving devices are so useful!"

"And the items we bought to defend ourselves—not that we need defending, no!" Yarg insisted. "We have no enemies. Pareley is the safest place you could live. But...just in case...we bought a few things. We feel much safer now that we have them. The Ten want us to give them up!"

"We don't want to be cut off again," Wensley added. "All these centuries Wuh thought it was alone in the universe. Think what we've been missing! Perhaps we are not very experienced in the ways of other cultures, but how will we learn without going there?"

"Exactly!" a few of the committeefriends agreed with him. "Yes!" "They're being perhaps a little *too* cautious."

"If our exuberance about our travels circulates as far as the castle," Gubbeen explained uneasliy, "they come and personally invite the traveler to the castle. Just for a chat, of course!"

"They arrest people and take them in for interrogation?" I asked, aghast. "Has anyone been harmed?"

"Er..." The Wuhses looked at one another. "We can only say that the invitees often emerge with self-esteem issues."

"They ask very hard questions," Ardrahan put in, helpfully. "It shows how very intelligent they are. That is why we invited them here to help us. But, if I may speak hypothetically, if one has certain material needs, and they are not being met as fully as they were before certain people came along, then would you call that a disagreement?"

In spite of my muzziness I managed to extract the kernel from the center of her statement. "Shortages? What kind of shortages? It looks as though you have plenty of good food. And beverages," I added, gesturing at the wealth of tea surrounding Zol and the range of bottles on the wall behind the bar. "You're all well-dressed, and your homes seem to be in very good shape."

"We have no money!" Wensley wailed. "Barely a coin between us! Perhaps we do give the appearance of prosperity, but we have to beg for everything from Them. They store provisions for our shopkeepers, and release a day's worth of goods at a time. They lock up the warehouses at the factories. In the morning everyone has to ask for the stock to replenish their shelves. If a request strikes them as unreasonable they will not release the merchandise. And it's our merchandise!"

The others seemed at once horrified that he was speaking so frankly, and relieved that someone was saying what he was thinking. They were clearly terrified of the Pervect Ten, and afraid to speak openly.

"What's an unreasonable request?" I pressed. "More food?"

"Oh," Wensley began, a shade too casually. "Suppose a silversmith had a lot of very beautiful pendants that the Pervect Ten were minding for him, and he wanted them, say, to trade for other, more rare items?"

"I'd say it sounded like normal commerce," I shrugged. "Why don't both shopkeepers go to the castle together and negotiate the trade there? The pendants could be put into the other guy's bin, and the silversmith could have access to the stuff he bought."

"Uh, er...what if the other shopkeeper...didn't live around here?"

"Like in another dimension?" Zol asked. It was too direct a question. Not an eye met his. I nodded.

"You're afraid that they would cut you off from the rest of the dimensions."

"If they can! But they can't," Wensley insisted firmly. "Not as long as we have the D-hopper! We will be free to visit everywhere!"

"Shhh!" the others chided him.

"But so many things we never see again," Wensley went on in a whisper. "They are entitled to their fee, but we believe that they are supplementing it with very generous self-assigned bonuses."

Robbing the poor Wuhses blind. I was appalled.

"But, and this is the most difficult thing for us to say," Wigmore began, "Wuh is such a pleasant place to live that it frees one to think about expanding one's base of operations..."

"They're planning to use Wuh as a jumping-off point to conquer other dimensions? How do you know this?"

"You know," began Yarg, of Public Health, "they do speak so loudly. Some of what they say might have been overheard by the sanitation supervisors ('Cleaning staff,' Bunny whispered.) in the castle. Quite by accident, of course."

"Of course." I shared a glance with Tananda, Bunny and Zol. I could tell the others were thinking the same thing I was. The Pervect Ten had to go.

"All right, then," I agreed resolutely. "We all need a good night's sleep. Tomorrow, my company and I will begin our investigation and see if we can figure out how to kick them out."

"Er, eh..." Gubbeen began, raising a finger. "Master Skeeve, if I may be so bold, we've been giving you our input all evening."

I looked at him, puzzled. "You've been telling us how we can get rid of the Pervect Ten?"

"Well...perhaps not direct suggestions," Gubbeen coughed modestly. "That would be presumptuous. But we would like to be able to guide you in your approach."

"What?" I asked, then shook my head to clear it. I'd been awake far too long. "Let me try and sum up what I've been hearing: What you're all telling me is that you want to tell us how to run our operation, is that it?" I prompted them. "Hmm?"

I could hear wordiness bubbling up like soup about to boil over. I cut it off. "I'd like a one-word answer, please."

"I don't know whether the feasibility of a simple reply..." Gubbeen began.

"Yes or no?"

"Well," Ardrahan ventured, "er...yes?"

"No," I stated firmly.

"*No?*" The Wuhses all stared at me. I crossed my arms.

"That's right. No. We're the experts you called in. We will take all of your advice, but we have to run this operation our way. If you could have ejected the Pervect Ten on your own, you'd have done it by now, wouldn't you?" I looked around at my audience. They were fumbling for a reply.

Ardrahan cleared her throat. "Well, they know lots of magik, and we don't; we don't have the strength to reassert our interests."

"But you have the knowledge of how to deal with very magikal opponents?" I asked, pointedly.

Cashel pursed his lips. "We might have, if they weren't also extremely knowledgable about technology, too. Between the two..."

I cut him off. A rooster had just crowed outside. "So what you're saying," I began, holding up my hands to forestall any more interruptions, "is that you *don't* know how to handle them."

"Uh...well, not at present...."

"Good," I beamed. "Then you can leave the job to us. All right?"

"You'll, uh, let us know how you progress, won't you?" Gubbeen asked, very timidly.

"Of course," I smiled. "I'm not against consultation, but you have to understand I'm under no obligation to use your advice. With that in mind, then I think we have a deal."

"Well said, Master Skeeve," Zol applauded. "Well said."

To give them credit, the Wuhses looked relieved, especially Wensley.

"I think we all understand one another very well," Bunny said, favoring the big Wuhs with her sexiest blue eyed glance. "Perhaps," she purred, taking her cue from the traditional Wuh form of circumlocution, "we should depart from this subject? Master Skeeve has a long day ahead of him tomorrow. Why don't we let him and my other associates go to bed? But I would like to talk to you all for a little while longer."

"It would be our very dearest wish," Gubbeen exclaimed.

"Good!" Bunny grinned, showing all her teeth and folding her hands on the table. "Now, about the matter of payment...."

Gubbeen and the others shuddered. Suppressing smirks, Tananda, Zol, Gleep and I followed Montgomery towards the stairs to the sleeping rooms.

# Chapter 7

*"Have I got a product for you!"*
Prof. H. Hill

"Sorry I'm late," Niki apologized, closing the door behind her. "I had to check the assembly lines in Factory #5. The cutting machines jammed, and the damned sheep didn't know how to fix it."

"We just started," Vergetta replied. She and a handful of the others stood at a big table as Monishone demonstrated the features of her invention. Caitlin, as usual, sat at her computer keyboard, uninterested in the proceedings. Charilor hovered beside Vergetta, ready to run errands if the older female needed her to. "Come here a minute, darlink. Tell me, are they behaving themselves today?"

Niki grinned, showing every one of her pointed fangs. "They don't dare not to. But they gripe on and on in that mealymouthed whine so much that I want to tear their heads off."

"Never do they understand this is all for their own good," Vergetta sighed. "All right, Monishone, honey. So, tell it to me like Paldine's going to put it in the sales brochure."

Monishone tucked her hands into her long sleeves. "You put on the goggles, you become part of the story that you see. You can change the whole plot inside the setting just by using a tiny spark of magik to activate commands that will be visible on a scroll at the side of the illumination. As you've seen, it is a very realistic illusion, but it is no more than that: an illusion."

"Very nice," Vergetta said. She remembered how vivid the image had been, and how enjoyable it had been to plunge into it knowing she could depart from it just by taking off the glasses, not having to cast a dimension hopping spell. "But how about the variations?"

"No problem. The stories I've already bespelled are traditional fairy tales, or archetypal tropes. For a nominal investment we can hire bards and poets to tell new stories into the master spell, which will translate their words into pictures, characters, even scenarios. We can support this product almost endlessly. To change the stories it holds, one only has to take it for recharging to a qualified wizard who will get our new scrolls on a regular basis. The fee per tale ought to be nominal."

"It'll keep the punters busy for ages," Paldine gloated, making notes on a scrap of parchment. "This is perfect for Scamaroni. Their society is advanced enough so the inhabitants can understand the difference between fact and fiction, and wealthy enough so at least half the population has disposable income that can be used for hobbies."

"There's more," Monishone continued with a little smile that showed the tips of her fangs. "The spectacle can be shared. One can unite with others in a group quest, and take any or all parts of a drama. If one would prefer to be the banshee on the battlements instead of the heroine rescuing the hero, then one can. You can be the hero, the villain, a minor character, or just an onlooker."

"I like it," Oshleen declared. She was dressed for the day in tailored military camouflage with a black beret and boots and a white scarf tucked jabot style into the neck of her jacket. She swept a riding crop down and tapped the side of the goggles on the table. "Is that what the many pointed star is for? A sigil to join the wearers together?"

"Yes." Monishone demonstrated. "Just touch the star, then bring your finger to the star on the next pair of goggles. Anyone you touch becomes part of the group. Of course it means all of you have to have that story in your pair..."

"More recharging fees," Tenobia crooned, licking her fangs, "and no significant outlay except for royalties to the bards. We can make a fortune. They'll forget about every other personal entertainment device they've ever had! Hundreds of dimensions will be clamoring to get their hands on this!"

Paldine shook her head. "You'd be surprised. Of all the dimensions that support magik, only a few fall into the right niche. Many are too advanced for a toy like this, but many more aren't at the level to buy this or use it. I'd say thirty or forty at most."

"That would be plenty," Oshleen emphasized. She smacked her riding crop down on the desk.

"It's more likely to be ten or twelve...why are you dressed like that?"

Oshleen polished one of her brass buttons on the front of her jacket. "It puts me in the mood for strategy," she explained.

"Bah," Paldine snorted. "Like you know from strategy."

"Listen, fishface, you think that a winning smile will cause people to pour gold down on you..."

"Enough!" Vergetta roared. "Back on topic, please, darlinks. We can't talk among ourselves without arguing?" She paused and blinked. "Dammit, I sound like those wretched Wuhses."

"What will it take to manufacture these glasses?" Nedira wanted to know.

"I've made several dozen pairs on my own," Monishone informed her. She snapped her fingers and a box floated into the room and set itself down in the center. "If the test-marketing works out, we'll have the Wuhses make the rest."

"A better use for those factories than tea towels and bobble hats," Loorna said.

"What'll we do to keep them from walking away with a big handful of product?" Tenobia asked, sourly. "These are potentially a lot more valuable than tea towels."

"We'll put a whammy on the section working on it," Niki suggested. "They'll leave any conscious memory of the goggles inside. But the glasses won't be operational. They haven't got the talent to enchant them."

"It will take enchantment on our part to set the spell. It's quite simple, but does take a lot of power. We don't have to worry about anyone jumping in and duplicating these," Monishone grinned ferally. "No one can do what we do."

"All right, then," Vergetta stated. "Places, girls. Caitlin, get away from that thing. You'd think it was attached to you at the fingertips."

Reluctantly, the smallest female jumped down from her console and came to take her place with the rest of the Pervect Ten standing around the table. They joined hands.

"Shouldn't we lock the door?" Nedira asked.

"Why?" Charilor asked with a smirk. "No Wuhs would ever come in here unless we invited them. Besides, they'd be incinerated if they walked through our security spell."

"Reach for the line of force," Monishone instructed them. She closed her eyes and tilted her head back. "Draw all the power inside the circle."

"For these?" Niki scoffed. "We don't need *all* of it."

One hot yellow eye opened and glared at her. "It's a comprehensive spell, you mechanical imbecile! It depends on forming an atmosphere of power. We have to place all of the component spells in a cascade, and the structure can't exist outside of the circle!"

"How'd you do it, then?"

Monishone glared at her. "One pair of goggles at a time!"

"Oh," Niki yawned. She rolled her eyes. "All right."

"Shut up, then. Bring in *all* the power."

The major force lines that ran through Pareley didn't go underneath the castle, something that had proved to Vergetta that the Wuhses didn't know a damned thing about magik, which was all right, since they had little aptitude for it, anyhow. The closest one, a weak arrow, lay on the other side of the moat. A much stronger sky line, lying at perpendicular angles to the first was just a little farther away. In their minds they glowed soft green and bright yellow. Slowly, but with gathering intensity, the circle bounded by their arms and bodies filled with light. Their shadows, knife edged, crept up the walls until ten black shadows loomed over them like giants watching from the sidelines.

It had been by accident a few years ago that they had learned they could unite their talents. It happened in the middle of an end-of-year bargain sale, when all of them had been trying to get the only bronze alembic left in a bin. Vergetta had first tried to use main strength to toss her rivals out of the way. They hung on. Then, she started using magik, first subtly, then with all of her powers, dragging everything she could out of the local line of power. So had the other nine females all reaching for the same thing. To Vergetta's surprise, they all seemed to be evenly matched, from the muscular young woman at her side to the minute tot across the circle. But Vergetta had been determined not to let go of the alembic—it was 70% off! She pushed, they pushed; she pulled, they pulled. When the dust settled, they were all sitting on the floor, or what was left of it. The store walls had been blown down. All the other customers had been thrown hundreds of yards away in every direction, and the merchandise had exploded into its component ions, except for the alembic, which sat in the center of the circle shining like an atomic pile. There was nothing left for Vergetta to do but figure out a way to kill them all, or form an alliance to make use of the hundredfold magikal force the ten of them could raise. Being Pervects, they'd gone into business together. Even so, there were times when she still thought about killing all of the others.

"This is so camp," Caitlin whined.

"Shut up, gearhead," Tenobia snapped.

"Right," Monishone declared. At her nod the box opened and the goggles danced out into the air. The frames were blue or red or silver, and the lenses glimmered with all the colors of the rainbow. "The frames control the spell, and the lenses are like magik mirrors. With our combined will we can do all of them at once."

Like veils of color, the individual spells poured out of Monishone's fingertips. Each of them grabbed hold of an edge of each veil and stretched it out so that it covered all the hovering pairs of spectacles. The first, gleaming silver, was the master enchantment that held all the others together. Vergetta was impressed at the complexity of the structure Monishone put together. The girl was a master wizard. She was a credit to her parents, Perv, and the Ten. It troubled her a little that they were putting so much masterwork into trinkets, but it took a lot of pebbles to make a mountain. They needed the money. Some day they were going to sponsor her to research some wizardry that was really worthwhile.

Tiny threads of color began to embroider scrolls and books on the stuff of the spell: the stories going into the framework. Sparkles of gold energy twinkled in the light, sinking into the frames and making them glow.

"Ash-shoo!" Caitlin exploded, and started to pull her hand loose to wipe her nose.

"Don't let down the barriers!" Monishone warned.

"Here, sweetie," Nedira offered, floating a handkerchief out of her pocket and sending it across the circle to the little girl. Caitlin obediently put her face forward and blew her nose resoundingly in the white square.

"Ugh," Loorna grunted with a grimace. "Don't let that get into the spell."

Caitlin crossed her eyes and stuck out her tongue at the acquisitions manager.

"More power!" Monishone cried.

# Chapter 8

*"It looks like a trap!"*
F. Buck

"What happened?" Tananda whispered, gripping my collar. I clawed at the air, trying to get back on the ceiling with her.

"I don't know," I whispered back. I glanced down. It was a good thirty foot drop to the floor, and my magik had deserted me. I felt desperately for the lines of force I'd just been using, but they were drained. What spell needed that kind of power expenditure? I began to believe in the Wuhses' tale of the Pervect's quest for interdimensional conquest.

Tananda, maintaining her hold on the ceiling with an Assassin's trick that didn't rely upon lines of force, crept backwards, swinging me by my collar, until I was over the fireplace at one end of the big, dark room. Gently, she stretched down until my feet touched the mantelpiece. I heard a tiny 'clink.' I froze, hoping the Pervects in the room ahead hadn't heard it. Ten of them! I wasn't a coward, but I started to realize what a huge mess I had gotten myself and my friends into. If they opened the door just then...

"There's a row of knicknacks on either side of you," Tananda murmered, climbing down the wall like a spider.

I put my back against the big mirror and waited until she was on the floor again. I felt like a complete idiot. I might as well have been a knicknack myself. What a lesson to learn! The Great Skeeve, trapped like a fly in amber.

A tiny glow from her dark-lantern lit up the lines of her face, highlighting her cheekbones, nose and eyelashes. "Lift your left leg up to your knee, then swing it over. Stop! Put it down. Now bring up the right..."

Slowly, painfully, I inched my way through priceless *tchotchkes* until I had reached the side of the fireplace. Tananda

held the lantern down to show me the heap of cushions she
had piled up for me to jump onto. I had not felt so helpless in
years. There had always been some kind of magik wherever
we had gone. I wasn't used to relying on my own skills any
more. I vowed that when I got back to the inn I was going to
learn how to climb walls again. Garkin had talked me out of
being a thief (not that I had been *that* good at it), but some of
the skill set I had let go dormant would have come in very
handy right now. I wasn't used to being self-reliant. It was even
tougher to realize that I didn't even know what that meant. It
had been Tananda who had gotten us past the sophisticated
alarm system in the hallway, Tananda who had guided me along
the ceiling as I levitated so we wouldn't trip any of the pressure plates in the floor or the walls. ("Devious," she had murmured to herself.) True, I had blunted the lines of hot red light
that crisscrossed the final five feet of the corridor, but it had
taken her to remind me to look with my inner eye for such
traps. Someone who knew what she was doing had devised
the security system. The Pervect Ten were taking no chances
on being interrupted.

Outside it was broad daylight. Tananda, Zol and I had
slept into the late morning. Bunny woke me once about dawn.
I started up at the sight of the dark circles under her lovely
eyes, but she signaled me to lie down. "I got them to agree to
fifteen hundred gold pieces, but Wensley had to let them take
their turns with the D-hopper," she said, wearily. "I could have
gotten more if you had let me negotiate before you said you'd
take the job, but as you have pointed out *ad nauseam*, we really
don't need the money. I'm going to bed. Please don't wake me
for breakfast."

When we left for the castle about noon, I had left Gleep
guarding Bunny's door, to make sure no one bothered her. I
asked him to make sure, even if we didn't come back, he
would keep her safe. He promised, and laid his head on my
foot with worry in his big blue eyes. Zol also remained behind at the inn, getting more information from our hosts,

who also looked somewhat worn out...but whether from the all-night speeches or negotiations with Bunny I wasn't sure. Tananda and I had assumed the images of a couple of Wuhs housekeepers, trudging along in line with the others to begin their cleaning shift.

Once inside the real Wuhses went to work, while Tananda and I dropped the disguises and crept off in the direction of the Pervect Ten's wing of the castle.

I had to admit I couldn't see much evidence of the endless greed Wensley and the others had told us about—I mean, more than usual. Aahz, my best example for how Pervects behaved, had always felt there were two kinds of wealth in the world: his, and that which wasn't his yet. Still, Tananda and I poked through the ten suites the Pervects had claimed for their own. The furnishings belonged to the castle. Little of the clothing in the presses seemed to have been made on Wuh: the Pervect Ten hadn't gone in much for the handmade fabrics and modest styles that were prevalent in this dimension. Far from it; a few of the outfits we found even made Tananda whistle in disbelief. And every room was relentlessly clean. The possessions that the Ten were supposed to have confiscated weren't among their personal goods.

I found the dining room by smell. The aroma of Pervish cooking reminds passersby of a stableyard compost heap, only slightly more likely to linger in the nostrils. I could never stand watching Aahz or Pookie eat their hometown grub. I had been hungry in my day, but I could never picture a situation so desperate I wouldn't rather risk starvation than eat Pervish food. Our eyes watered painfully at the stench, but we went in, anyhow.

A forlorn Wuhs in a white tunic and hat stood by a gigantic cauldron. In one hand he had a huge spoon for stirring, and in the other a hammer. He wore protective goggles and nose clamps. He hadn't noticed us; he was too deep in his own misery to pay attention to anything but his job. A pseudopod of purple goo rolled over the lip of the cauldron and started to crawl towards him. He brought the hammer down. *Clang!* The

tentacle-like blob stiffened, then slid back into the pot. Tananda
and I had backed carefully out of the room.

Forcing my thoughts to return to the present, I rolled off
the heap of cushions and got down on all fours to follow
Tananda to the giant wooden doors that led into the room the
Wuhses said was the Pervect Ten's headquarters. No Wuhs
was ever allowed in there even to clean. A line of blinding
light leaked from beneath the portal, lighting our hands and
feet. I heard voices inside, but they sounded far away. I leaned
down to try and see under.

"It's ajar," Tananda whispered. She pointed to the crack
between the doors, which showed an irregular angle of light. I
nodded resolutely. We could try to slide in. If the Ten noticed
the movement we would have to roll into the shadows and
hope they thought it was just an ill-fitting old door creaking
open by itself. After all the deterrents they'd set in the hall,
they had to believe no one could reach them in this last room.
I slipped my fingertips along the smooth stone floor and started
to pull. To my relief the hinges rolled back silently, no eldritch
screech of rusty iron announcing us.

Almost on toetips and fingertips, I crept into the room. I
wished I could have the power of illusion at that moment,
because I faced the most terrifying thing I had ever seen: ten
Pervect women, their long teeth gleaming as they chanted
something in unison. Since Aahz had lost his powers even before I met him I'd seen very little Pervect magik, but even I
could tell this was something extraordinary. The Ten were
working a vast, powerful enchantment right before my eyes.
The room was full of golden light that I could feel burning all
the way through my body. I cowered in the shadows at the
base of the wall. In the reflected brilliance I could see
Tananda's eyes wide with amazement.

"...And they all lived happily ever after!"

The web of golden light gathered itself up, tied a knot in
the top as if it was a sack of potatoes, squeezed down into a
mass the size of a bucket, and dropped into a box on the

table. The lid slammed shut. I felt a rush, not a physical sensation but a magikal one, as they released their hold on local sources of power. They'd been draining two entire lines of force. By themselves!

"That's it," a petite Pervect announced in clipped syllables, releasing the hands of the two females on either side of her. She dusted her palms together. "We're finished."

"Vonderful," gushed a plumpish one in a flowered dress. "This is all we need. It vill be so easy, bubchen!"

I heard a gasp from Tananda beside me. Pervects have far keener hearing than Klahds or even Trollops. All twenty green ears swiveled in our direction.

"What was that?" asked a young female in a leather miniskirt. She started toward the door. I realized we no longer had the shadows to conceal us. Hastily, I formed the image in my mind of sections of wall and wainscoting, and pulled the illusion over Tananda and me. The female came close, peering around the door. I held my breath, praying she couldn't hear my heart pounding.

"Don't worry," the older one reassured her. "We have those Wuhses so scared they'd wet their pants even thinking of coming in here."

The younger one shut the door firmly. "I don't want them seeing what we're doing, that's all."

"How could they? Come back here and listen to Oshleen's plan."

Oshleen! I knew that name. But from where?

A tall, slender female in military uniform strode past the older Pervect. I peered at her. She looked familiar. Where had I seen her? Maybe when Aahz and I visited Perv? She smacked a riding crop into her palm, then pointed it up at the wall.

"Caitlin?"

The smallest Pervect I'd ever seen jumped up on a chair and poked at some buttons on a board. A huge map appeared on the wall. I didn't recognize the country. It wasn't Wuh, or

Klah, or Deva, or any of the other dimensions where I'd been, but there was an infinity out there.

"Now, here's my plan," Oshleen proclaimed, indicating a city on the map. "Taking over only a portion of our factory output we can still cover the initial point of insertion. We can start pushing into this territory here, here and here." As she swung the crop, tiny red arrows appeared over the places she pointed to. "Expansion should be easy. They will fall to their *knees* before us. How could they resist? With our charm and business acumen, there's no way they can withstand us. It'll be a walkover."

"Yes," agreed Vergetta, holding up an object. My eyes were still dazzled from the spell light. Was it a pair of spectacles?

"They'll be ours, all ours," gloated the Pervect in the miniskirt. "Their eyes, their minds, will belong to us."

I was horrified. The Ten went on talking over my head, but all I could think was that Wensley and the others were right! The Pervects *were* trying to take over other dimensions. They had some sort of evil device they planned to use to brainwash them.

"Well!" the older female breathed, clapping her hands. "That took a lot out of me, I gotta tell you. Lunch has got to be ready, already."

"I'm hungry!" the little one announced. "Let's eat."

A stylish Pervect in a skirt and jacket snapped her fingers, and the box on the table leaped into the air. "I'm off to start gathering converts," she explained. "I'll report back as soon as I have them." She and the box vanished.

The remaining nine Pervects marched past us. The last one, the strong one in the short skirt, stopped to look around the room before she slammed the door. A blast of white light filled the room. I felt, rather than heard a hum. As soon as I was sure they were gone, I got to my feet and let the wall disguise slip. Tananda was already standing beside me, a grim expression on her face.

"What's the matter?" I asked.

"I've met two of them before," she mused.

"Are you sure?" I asked.

"Could you miss that flower-print dress?" Tananda demanded. "They were trying to take over a part of the Bazaar a couple of months ago."

"What?"

"Running a protection scheme. Don Bruce sent Guido to ask me and Chumley to get rid of them. It wasn't easy. They were starting small, but as you can see, they had bigger plans. They've taken over Wuh, and now they're going for another dimension."

"Ten Pervects," I shuddered.

"Ten wouldn't be enough to take over the Bazaar. Deveels are used to dealing with Pervects. But an unsuspecting dimension, unaccustomed to magik..."

I slammed my fist into my other palm. "We've got to prevent it."

"How?" Tananda asked. "We don't know where they went."

I started for the door. "Let's ask Zol. I bet he could help us figure it out."

"Hold it!" Tananda ordered, just before I touched the knob. "Look!"

To the naked eye, the door seemed like what it was: a door. But I knew what she meant. Letting my eyes go half-shut, I looked for magik. The blue glow was so intense I had to clap my eyelids shut.

"What is it?" I asked, rubbing my eyes.

"An incineration spell," Tananda replied. "We're locked in."

# Chapter 9

*"I'll be out in a second!"*
H. Houdini

"Can't we just pop out?" I asked, squinting at the wall. Now that I had stopped to look, the door, the walls, the ceiling, and even the windows were covered by a flickering blue haze. I backed into the center of the room, as far from the perimeter as I could get. "One of them did. The others just walked out."

"They know what spell they set," Tananda pointed out. "We don't. We might manage to transport ourselves and still get fried."

"What can we do?" I asked, trying not to sound as panicky as I felt.

Tananda looked at the magik field thoughtfully. "Polarity," she stated at last. "It's supposed to keep people out, but not necessarily in. We could try to push it outward."

"Okay," I explained, slowly. I had pried open a few magik traps in the past. I wished Aahz had been there to offer his advice, but it would probably be along the lines of "you know what you're doing, kid, do it!" Which was no help at all, under the circumstances. If I knew Pervects they wouldn't linger over their food. They could be back any minute.

I rubbed my hands together as I stared at the blue fire. But what was I waiting for? I had to find a way out.

Now that the Pervect Ten had finished with their sorcery there was plenty of magik around. I could feel the pulses of minor spells, like the flutter of leaves in a forest. I pictured the lines of force in my mind. Here the lines deep within the earth were green. It wasn't very strong, but it was close. I drew as much of it up into myself as I could.

When working with magik you had to think in very positive terms to keep control of forces that were greater than you. Lose your concentration while you were constructing a magikal framework, and the resulting backlash could tear you to pieces. Lose your focus while defusing a trap, and *smack!* You did your opponents' work for them. I summoned up the image of a huge pair of hands, and imagined them pushing at the blue force blanketing the door. It moved! The whole curtain shifted backwards about five paces.

"Hold it!" Tananda ordered. "Look behind you."

I halted the progress of the hands, but kept them in place as I glanced around. The curtain shielding the far wall had *also* moved forward five paces. Very, very carefully I pushed the spell back to where it started. In my mind I formed four big pairs of hands and pushed outward. This time the walls moved but the lid of the spell started to come down on us as its supports were moved further apart. I tried pushing in all the directions. I succeeded in stretching the spell every which way but never finding a hole in it through which we could escape.

"I've never seen one that moved before," Tananda mused, peering at the force field curiously. "That's really interesting. It dragged over the table but didn't burn anything. These are still intact." She picked up a pair of gaudy-framed spectacles that lay on the wooden top.

"That's what was in the box the Ten were putting a spell on," I declared, excitedly. "It's a clue. We'll take them to Zol. He'll help us figure out what they are."

"When we get out of here," Tananda reminded me. "We can't wait here for them to come back, then ask them pretty please to remove their security spell because we got trapped in it."

"Then we won't," I stated, grimly.

"What? What are we supposed to do with a huge cage of burning blue fire?"

"We'll take it with us," I explained. "It doesn't hurt inanimate objects. All we have to do is shrink it around us and walk out of here. As soon as they get back and notice it's gone, they'll dispell it and start over. We'll just have to make sure that neither we nor anyone else touches it until then."

A slow grin curled the side of Tananda's mouth. "That's so ridiculous it's brilliant," she nodded. "I'll help you. We have to hurry."

I dismissed my invisible pairs of hands inside the room and reconstituted them outside. "All together now, push!"

The spell became very tall and narrow. I hoped when the top of the now rectangular shape vanished through the ceiling that it wouldn't hit any poor, innocent Wuhs working on an upper floor. Tananda and I held onto one another as we shuffled in the center of the narrow square, walking out through the antechamber, into the hallway, past the defensive spells that Tananda disarmed then rearmed as we passed. To my relief we did not run into any of the Pervect Ten. Before we reached the main entrance I put the disguise spell back on us, but if any of the Pervects had looked out the window, the tower of magik would attract their attention long before the little figures inside it did. To prevent any Wuhses from approaching us to pass the time of day I created the illusion of a couple of wheelbarrows full of rotting offal.

"That looks so bad I can almost smell it," Tananda grinned admiringly. "You really know your illusions, handsome."

It took us some time to get back to the inn. We stood at the open door, reluctant to go inside lest the spell towering over us kill anyone in the upper storey.

"Zol," I called, seeing the author sitting at a table chatting quietly to a couple of Wuhses. Bunny peered around the side of the booth and smiled with relief. Gleep, curled on the floor beside them, raised his head from the floor. His eyes widened with joy, and he sprang to his feet.

"Gleep!" he cried, charging over to greet me.

"No, Gleep!" I shouted. "Stop! Go back! Don't touch the..."

There was a blinding flash of light as he galloped through the spell's boundary. When my sight returned I dropped to my knees beside my poor, fallen pet. I cradled his head in my lap. He had probably been charred to death by the incineration spell. He...he was still green. The mustache under his long nose was still white. And his eyes...

"Gleep!" he exclaimed. His eyes flew open. He tilted his head back so he could lick my face with his long, forked tongue.

His eyes were still blue. He was all right! I hugged him, and he slurped my face again. I gagged. His breath was as stinky as Pervish cooking.

Zol and Bunny hurried over to us with Wensley scurrying nervously behind.

"What has happened?" the author asked.

"Don't come any closer!" I yelled.

"Yes," Zol pondered, throwing out an arm to prevent Wensley from stepping right into the edge of the spell. "I see it now. My goodness, where did you find that?"

Now that we were safely around the corner of the inn facing away from the castle, I plunged the bulk of the spell down into the earth. Tananda and I sat down, and I told the others what we had seen. "And once they let go of the power all of these active spells began working again, including this one. Now we can't get out until the Ten turn it off and take it home."

"Yes, you can," Zol agreed, peering at it closely. "Mistress Tananda was right about the way the spell is constructed. It is a case of polarity. You were inside when it resumed operating, and the Pervect Ten left the room. If you had gone with them, you wouldn't have felt a thing. If you examine the individual tongues of flame that make up the walls, you would see that they have a blunt end and a pointed end. The pointed end is the dangerous one. When you arrived back just now, they were pointing in. This kind of spell works like a door on a two-way hinge. First it swings *out*, then it swings *in*."

"Oh!" I exclaimed, as enlightenment dawned. "And Gleep swung it in. So the points are facing away from us?"

"That's right! So now all of you can come out."

Very nervously, Tananda and I rose to our feet. I bent down and looked Gleep in the eye.

"You jump out at the same time we do," I ordered, sternly.

"Gleep," he stated blandly, but I noticed his eyebrow ridges rise. He understood me. I wrapped my arm around his neck.

"One, two, *THREE!*"

We bounded out. Another brilliant flash of light blinded us for a moment. I could feel my hair crackle on my head, but no blaze of fire tried to consume me. When we let go of one another I patted myself down to make sure nothing was burning. Gleep's long neck snaked all around me as he looked to make sure I was all right. Tananda brushed her hair back, and pulled her tunic down so her décolletage returned to its normal buoyancy.

"That's a nasty one," she remarked. "I'll have to remember that trick."

We'd barely straightened up when I heard another crackle from behind me. I spun around just in time to see the column of blue light collapse and vanish. The Pervect Ten were calling their safeguard spell home.

"A very sophisticated use of magik," Zol Icty agreed, leading us back to the table. Montgomery, our host, brought us a tray full of food and beer. I fell on the food as though I'd been starved for weeks. Tananda served herself more daintily, but she filled her plate as high as I did mine. Being terrified and nearly incinerated did help us work up an appetite. "We are up against very intelligent opponents. You say they had a computer in the room?"

"Yes," I affirmed, washing down a mouthful of cheese with a swig of beer. "The little one was reading from an almost infinite scroll. I think it would be the longest scroll in the history of the world, but I couldn't see where it was rolled up."

"It's in virtual space," Zol explained, smiling. "A kind of magik. I could teach you, but that is not the best use of our time now. Can you get me in there?"

We looked at Wensley. He writhed uneasily.

"They're in there all the time except when they eat or sleep or come to supervise us."

"Tonight is time enough," Zol assured us. "I am awake a good deal of the night anyhow."

"You don't want to go back *again?*" Wensley squawked, aghast.

"How do you want us to figure out what they're doing?" I demanded. "Ask them?"

The Wuhs had no answer to that.

Once again we found ourselves sneaking into the great room of the castle. The Wuhses on what anywhere else would have been guard duty carefully looked the other way as we passed, with all the subtlety of a child counting to 100 in a game of Hide and Seek.

Apparently it had not made the Pervect Ten suspicious that their security spell had been stolen that afternoon. The gleaming blue cage was back in place, this time tethered with lines of force to the walls of the castle, preventing it from moving again. That didn't worry me, because now we knew how to pass in and out of it without being killed.

The little flames were pointing inward when we reached the room, a sign that the Ten were not in it. Very carefully I used a tendril of magik to ease open the door wide enough to peer through. As I hoped, the room was dark and silent. I signaled to the others. We tiptoed in.

I had left Gleep at the head of the corridor curled up under a couch set in an alcove. If he saw any Pervects heading towards us he had instructions to cry out. At the sound of "Gleep!" we were to run into the anteroom and pop back to the inn. He would meet us there as soon as he could get away from them. They'd be unlikely to suspect an innocent-looking baby dragon of subterfuge. I hoped.

"Now, Pervect code is very hard to break," Zol explained, as he sat down in the child's chair and flexed his long fingers. I noticed with surprise that he fit into the seat fairly well. "They tend to like permutations of complex numbers as their secure logarithm."

Bunny sat on the desk beside her hero, watching him raptly. I felt a twinge of jealousy, wondering what I would have to do for anyone to admire me like that. Tananda came up and wrapped her arm around me.

"Don't worry, hot stuff," she told me, with a little smile. "She'll snap out of it. She likes you just the way you are."

I flushed. Bunny was my friend. I wasn't trying to impress her. Was I? Embarrassed, I moved off to take a look out the door. I hoped none of the Pervect Ten was going to get up in the middle of the night to work on their plans for conquest. The hall was empty. My breathing was the loudest thing at this end of the room.

Zol wasn't doing so well. Using all his fingers and thumbs he was pushing the buttons on the board so fast they chattered. I noticed that there was a small symbol in the center of each button. Since I had seen written and printed Pervish I knew they stood for letters of their alphabet, though I couldn't read them. In the screen images and words flashed. I couldn't tell what any of them meant, but one kept coming up time and time again: a big X.

"What's that mean?" I said, pointing.

"Well, in some languages it means do not enter," Zol began, his fingers dancing along. "In Pervish and a few others it is an archaic way of writing 'ten,' which in this case would be appropriate, but I believe it also has the added meaning of 'the unknown variable,' this being the key to the library of documents locked within this computer. There are quite a lot of them. That is one of the few facts I can glean. The rest is protected by the password, which the X indicates. Since I don't know it I have been putting in my guesses as to possible keywords. I've tried over a thousand words in every combination of capital and small-case letters, plus permutations and combinations of profit/loss formulae, which are familiar to every Pervish college graduate, but I've been unlucky so far. Still, there's hope. I'm bounded only by the number of keys here on the keyboard, and there's a finite number of combinations..."

I glanced nervously at the door. "How long do you think it will take you?"

"Oh, well, this is not like cracking a safe, you know," Zol stated, cheerfully as ever. "I might stumble upon the correct key any moment now."

"And the longest it could take?"

"Oh..." Zol paused a moment to think. "Two or three years. At the outside."

"We don't have three years," Wensley whispered. "My people are already suffering because these Pervects won't leave!"

"Naturally not," Zol agreed. "You Wuhses are sensitive souls. You would see the Pervects as nonparticipants in your cooperative lifestyle." His hands never stopped moving, but suddenly images began to pour out of the magik mirror, wreathing the Kobold in colored smoke. I saw faces: Pervects, Imps, Deveels, Klahds, Wuhses, and plenty of races that I didn't recognize. "I'm trying to unlock any files that may have been left upon the desktop."

With a skeptical expression I let my eye fall upon the otherwise clear table. Zol smiled. "Just like the books from which you saw the little Pervect reading, there is also a desk, though it exists only inside here."

"Ah," I breathed, enlightened at last. "Magik."

"Yes, indeed," Zol declared. "We Kobolds thrive upon this kind of magik."

The longer he worked, the more agitated the specters surrounding him became. The faces grew ugly and hollow-eyed, threatening him with claws and fangs. They distorted into big blobs with hair scattered on their surfaces.

"Stay away from me now," Zol warned. "Those are viruses. I've been inoculated, but you haven't. If they touch you they will take over your mind. Ah!"

Suddenly the whole end of the room lit up. I recoiled from it, narrowly avoiding a cluster of the blobs.

"That's the map," I confirmed, eyeing the circling blobs.

"It's the only thing in the files that's not password protected," Zol informed me. "But what does it represent?"

"It's not part of Wuh," Wensley stated.

"I don't recognize it, either," Tananda frowned. "It's certainly not Trollia or Klahd."

"I'll have to compare it with maps of the other dimensions I've visited," Zol remarked.

"How?" I asked. "You can't memorize something like that."

"I don't have to," the Kobold assured me. "Coley will remember it for us." From his shoulder bag he removed a silverbacked book. When he opened it I saw it had no pages. It was a computer, but in miniature. He held the shiny screen toward the map. I peered at the bright surface with interest. Unlike the computers I had seen on Perv, this one featured color images as well as words. At the moment it had a picture on it of shutterbugs, those tiny denizens of Nikkonia who could capture images on the translucent cells of their wings. They looked so real I reached out to touch them and found my hand stopped by a clear barrier. The shutterbugs looked up at me and gestured impatiently for me to get out of their way. I dodged to one side. One of them held up his thumb, squinted one eye shut, then began fluttering his wings. Zol watched it until it looked up at him to signal that it had finished.

"And a backup, please."

The second shutterbug stepped forward, framed the scene with its hands, then began fluttering. In a moment it, too, was finished. Zol clapped the covers of his miniature computer closed and put it back in his satchel.

"Now, to Kobol!"

# Chapter 10

*"Interface is a breeze!"*
W. Gates

"What a lovely place," Bunny breathed, gazing all around her as Zol led us toward a round building I could just see above the tops of the trees. It was daylight in this part of Kobol. We had arrived in a garden surrounded by high hedges. Arched doorways carved directly into the dense green bushes led from section to section. Every plant, every tree appeared to have been planted and tended with mathematical precision. I couldn't see a leaf out of place. Even the flowerbeds were neat, not a dead or faded bloom in sight. Wensley felt nervous in such utter tidiness. He stayed by Tananda, who seemed perfectly happy to cuddle close to him. I had my hand on Gleep's collar so he wouldn't go running off through the maze. I would get in trouble if he destroyed the precise perfection of this placid scene by punching holes through the hedges.

"Yes," Zol smiled, guiding her along the shady lanes on paths of clipped green grass. "We always have gardens, not that most of us spend too much time in one, but they are here for our mathematicians to take mental health breaks. Numbers can become all-consuming, you know."

"There really was no need for me to come with you," Wensley babbled, looking around him in dismay. "I trust your judgment. You know I do. I...someone needs to keep watch on the castle. I can do that while you are away. It would be very nice if I could go back, just for a while..."

"Don't you want to help in your own dimension's defense?" I asked, fixing him with a gaze that made him wriggle like a worm on a hook.

"Well, of course," Wensley managed, "but is this a matter of Wuh? It would seem to me that my people's concern is mainly with the well being of our own dimension. Not that others are unimportant, of course. Wuhses have compassion for others. We might just be concerned that you are dividing your attention. That's your business, of course. I would never be the one to tell you that you are not doing the job you promised us you would do."

That was the most direct statement I had heard him almost make. "This is connected to Wuh," I assured him as positively as I could. "We're trying to figure out a place where they are vulnerable. Now, they're stronger than we are, they're experienced, they're better magicians, they understand technology and they have all of you under their control. Does it sound like we have any lever to pry them out of Wuh?"

"Er...not that I could discern," Wensley admitted.

"Right! That's what we're doing here. We're looking for a weakness, and in the meantime saving another species who don't know what's hitting them."

"Bravo, Master Skeeve!" Zol cheered. "Well said! And we of Kobol will do our best to facilitate your aims. Count upon us!"

Wensley looked discontented, but he stopped grumbling, especially when Tananda melted a little closer to him.

We passed a niche where a Kobol female sat on a bench. She wore a long, shapeless white garment with a high neck and wide sleeves. In her fingers she had a single blue-petaled flower which she raised to her nose occasionally to sniff. Her large black eyes, fixed in the distance, came back into focus as she acknowledged Zol's cheerful greeting.

"This is Ruta," Zol introduced us, "one of our most talented programmers."

"☺," she replied, her cheeks turning a deep gray. "Too kind, Zol."

"What did she say?" I asked, as we passed.

"She smiled at us," Zol answered.

"Why didn't she just smile?"

"She did, in our language."

The round, flattened building had a silvery gray shell not unlike the book in Zol's satchel. It loomed over us as we stopped at a curved, translucent panel. Zol placed his open hand on a pale blue square beside it.

"Zol Icty and four visitors," he announced, beaming at us. "Excuse me. Five visitors." He winked at Gleep. A humming sound erupted out of nowhere. I felt as if someone was touching me on the back. When I jumped around to see who it was, the touch moved to my front, but no one was there. Gleep swiveled his long neck to peer over his back and under his belly. By the expression on their faces Bunny, Tananda and Wensley had also felt it. Only Zol looked calm. He gestured as the translucent panel slid sideways. It was a door.

"This way," our host directed us. He led us down an immaculately clean, white-walled corridor. Oddly, this surprisingly clean place reminded me of the Bazaar, because loud, unintelligible noises, music and shouting poured out of every door. Tananda, Gleep and I stuck close together, on guard in case anything jumped out at us. Bunny walked with Zol, hanging on his every word. "I confess I am a trifle peckish after all that work. Would you like something to eat while I and my friends analyze the map?"

"Yeah!" I replied avidly. Zol smiled and pushed through one of the identical doors. The room beyond was filled with Kobolds, all staring into screens like his and playing upon keyboards as though they were pianos. At the far end of the room was a long table filled with brightly colored packages.

"Help yourselves," he offered. "The amount of nourishment in each bag is approximately equal to one-sixth of a Kobold's daily needs, therefore Master Skeeve will need twelve, Mistress Tananda nine, and Mistress Bunny eight. Gleep can have as many as he likes."

The packages were easy to tear open. The food inside was mostly what was sold in taverns at the Bazaar as snacks to eat with beer: sweet or salty, crunchy morsels. I munched on golden twists that smelled faintly of meat. Gleep ate the packages wrapper and all, licking his chops happily. Tananda picked through the packets and chose bags of tiny cookies and some pork rinds. Bunny waited and selected what Zol did.

"Take as many as you like," Zol invited, tearing open a bag of cheese pretzels. "And here! Have something to drink."

He filled mugs for us from a keg set in a cradle at the end of the table. I took a deep draught, and nearly choked. The beverage looked like ale, but tasted sweet and fizzy, filling my nose, lungs and stomach with bubbles. I lowered the tankard in a hurry, and let out a tremendous belch. I smacked my lips, waiting for the familiar sensation of warmth and well-being. It was not forthcoming.

"Not very strong, is it?" I asked.

"Oh, this isn't liquor," Zol explained. "Liquor is consumed on Kobol, and it's very good, but you cannot do complex mathematical calculations if you are drunk. We wait until after we log out."

My mother had taught me the basics of arithmetic when I was a child, and I'd picked up a lot about bookkeeping, percentages and commissions in my years working in and around the Bazaar, but nothing I had ever done or seen remotely resembled the work I observed going on around me.

"What are they doing?" I inquired.

"They are helping to maintain our reality. Field agents such as I gather up factual information. These analysts translate it into formulae that we are working on to explain how everything fits together. They help us decide what crops to grow, what professions to take up, what parcels of land to develop...oh, everything. We call it the Unified Field Theory."

I gazed around me. All the noise I had noticed coming in was not coming from the Kobolds, but rather from the computers. While line after line of tiny characters spun out on the shining surface of some, other Kobolds were using their mirrors to spy upon the actions of travelers such as my own companions. Where those travelers encountered opposition, say meeting up with other-dimensional beings, bloody battles always seemed to ensue. None of the parties I saw ever tried to avoid conflict, instead drawing sword or raising wand against one another immediately. I watched being after being die, until I was nearly weeping for the unnecessary loss of life.

"Don't worry," Zol assured me, touching my arm sympathetically. "Those aren't real. They are only make-believe characters in a game. Kobolds use such things to relax their minds when they are not working. It's only a game."

"A game?" I reiterated, shocked. "Why don't they play a *real* game, like dragon poker?"

"Too easy," Zol shrugged. "The odds are fully calculable, and that's not relaxation to a Kobold."

"Too easy?" I sputtered.

"Why don't they just go and relax...when they want to relax?" Bunny said, her eyes fixed on the busy Kobolds.

"They seem to like it," Tananda commented. "Look, they're all smiling. They get pleasure from these devices." She eyed the nearest Kobold up and down with a speculative eye. He was grinning vacantly at his code. His fingers seemed to stroke the buttons on the board sensuously. Tananda moved closer to him.

"Mistress Tananda, I have always said that the folk of Trollia understand physical sensation better than any other dimension," Zol smiled, admiringly. "It is true. And the computers enjoy the contact as well. Kobolds become one with their machines, joined at the fingertips. The more a Kobold interacts, the better the computer understands him or her. There is an important symbiotic relationship between us and our computers. In fact, we can't leave them for long, Master Skeeve. If one doesn't pay a great deal of attention to one's unit, it becomes lonely, in extreme cases taking its own life. The others mourn, and sometimes suicide in sympathy. And a Kobol left alone after its computer dies is a sad and terrible thing. It takes intervention by such social researchers as myself to bring them back and introduce them

to a new unit. Still, you never forget your first computer."
Zol sighed reminiscently.

A fetching unit with a red case alone on a table started
blinking its screen at me. I moved closer to look. In the mirror
I could see my reflection, only my image's hands reached out
and started to fondle the button board. Hypnotized, I began to
follow suit.

"Don't do that!" Zol ordered. I halted, my fingers in mid
air. The screen signaled frantically. "Not unless you're planning to make a lifetime commitment to it."

"A lifetime...? Oh! Like attaching a dragon." Gleep, hearing the word, trotted over and leaned his head against my leg.
I moved my hands away from the keyboard to pet him. A sad
face appeared in the screen.

Zol shook his head. "No, much more comprehensive than
that. You two wouldn't be able to live without one another."

"Me and a machine?" I was aghast. The face in the mirror
became even sadder.

"It's a natural symbiosis. Your creativity interacting with
the computer's. It's really very fulfilling. We've been interac-
tive for centuries."

"What about marriage?" Bunny asked, curiously. "Don't
men and women marry on Kobol?"

"Oh, of course! When a couple of Kobolds have compat-
ible systems, they can have a long and happy life together,"
Zol explained. "Computers don't interfere with personal relationships. They *can* enhance them."

"It would make accounting a breeze," Bunny murmured, looking at the red-cased computer. The face didn't look at her. In fact,
it cut her dead. Occasionally, when it could catch my eye, it gave
me dreamy looks like the ones with which Bunny favored Zol.
"Can it be adapted to work in an all magikal environment?"

"Naturally," Zol replied. "Mine is fit for travel. It's a dual-
power system. When lines of force are available, it uses them.
When only electricity is to be had, well, then, it plugs in." He
smiles. "I can see it intrigues you."

I frowned as she regarded the author with adoration. "I'd love one!" she cooed.

"Bunny, I don't think you ought to...er, get involved...with anything strange."

She turned to me. "Why not? Zol wouldn't let anything hurt me. Would you?"

"Of course not," Zol exclaimed. "Master Skeeve, I see your concern, but it is groundless. Come with us! I will take you to the adoption center. If Mistress Bunny can find a computer that wishes to bond with her, it will be perfectly safe. But, I must caution you," he said to Bunny, "not to be disappointed if you don't form a relationship today. It is possible that the computer for you hasn't been manufactured yet."

"I'll take that chance," Bunny declared. Resolutely she straightened her spine and tightened her hands into fists.

"She's acting like she's in a spell," I whispered to Tananda, as we followed them back into the wide hallway.

"If it looks like there'll be trouble, we'll jump her out of here," Tananda whispered back. "Hang in there, tiger. This may turn out to be handy."

# Chapter 11

*"Completely user-friendly."*
I. Mac

The adoption center looked exactly like the last room we'd been in, down to the fast-food buffet, except for a huge round table in the middle of the room. On it lay dozens of silverbound books, magik-mirrors-on-a-stick, multicolored, handsized round objects like powder compacts, and one big silver scroll. I eyed them the way I had learned to shop in the Bazaar: look, but stay well away from touching. As I had learned my first visit to Deva, looking is usually free, but you never know what constitutes touching until the stall owner comes up and forcibly tries to extort payment for what he refers to as "used merchandise."

Zol brought his little book out of his satchel and handed it to another diminutive Kobold, whom he introduced as Asciita. I was struck with how much all of them, male and female, looked alike, with their gray skin, dark hair, long hands and huge eyes. She, or perhaps he, set Coley down on top of her own book. The two computers glowed brightly for a moment. Suddenly the books adjacent to the first two burst into light, then the next ring, like ripples spreading out in a pond. The Kobolds sitting before the magik mirrors burst into activity, tapping and stroking the button boards with eager looks on their faces.

"There," Zol concluded, retrieving Coley and tucking him into his satchel. "They are all working on it now."

He escorted Bunny to the huge table. The books, mirror and compacts, seeing that someone was paying attention to them, began flapping and blinking eagerly like puppies in a basket. Bunny wore an expression of delight, overwhelmed by the number of choices before her.

"Now, just let yourself choose," he told her. "They're all very impressionable at this stage. But use your intuition. You will know if you are making the right decision."

The entire concept of deliberately letting oneself be tied for life to any creature made me nervous. True, I had permanently impressed a dragon, but it had been by accident. If I had known it could happen, I would have stayed away from the stall. But then, I thought, putting my hand on Gleep's head, I would have missed all the joy and fun of the companionship we had shared. Apart from the yearlong chore of housebreaking, of course. Dragon dung is second only to Pervish cooking in terms of all-time gagging stenches, and dragon breath comes in third, I mused, as Gleep snaked his head up to slurp me affectionately on the cheek.

Bunny nodded. "They're all beautiful," she murmered, softly. Her hands ran over the surface of each of the books. I thought I saw the gleaming shells quiver at her touch. I understood that; I had felt the same way. She unrolled the big coil of silver and discovered that it was almost as wide as she was tall.

"That is really an item for an artist," Zol put in. "You'd mount it on a wall or a big table to work."

"Oh! I couldn't leave it in plain view," she explained. "It's too technological for Klah, and in the Bazaar I'd be afraid someone would be able to see what I'm doing. So much of my work is confidential."

Zol gestured toward the tiny ones. "Then you want a compact. It will do all of the tasks you have mentioned so far: bookkeeping, spreadsheets, projections, expense breakouts, and it will fit in a handbag or a belt pouch. See if you like any of these." The little round mirrors began to clack at her like castanets, all vying for her attention.

"Oh, they're perfectly darling," Bunny cooed.

The Kobold beamed. "How very intuitive of you! That's what they're called, Perfectly Darling Assistants, or PDAs for short."

The little objects, seeing that she favored them, began to jump up and down like fish snapping at bait. Bunny looked them all over carefully. Their jewel-like colors were very attractive. Each of them seemed to grow brighter, hoping to attract her attention. But as she came close to a red cased compact, it opened wide to show its miniature screen. Bunny's blue eyes were reflected in it. She reached out, and it almost jumped into her hand. Bunny brought it close to her and began to stroke the smooth, gleaming shell, murmuring to herself.

"Goodness," Zol stated. "That one really likes you, Mistress Bunny. I've seldom seen such an enthusiastic response."

The feeling was mutual. Bunny kept turning the little object over, examining it, touching every inch of its surface. It leaped up to get the full benefit of each pass of her hand, and emitted a cacophony of sounds that was a combination of music, chirps, sensuous purrs and whistles.

"Awwww," Tananda crooned. "How cute!"

"It is," Bunny agreed. "I think I'll call her Bytina."

"How do you know it's a she?" I asked, skeptically.

"Well, just look at her," Bunny insisted, holding the little device out to me. It snapped its covers shut as I leaned down to examine it. "Oh, you've scared her."

"*I've* scared her?" I echoed. "What did I do?"

"Now, now, Master Skeeve, the relationship has to build naturally, one connection at a time. Put her here for a moment, Mistress Bunny," Zol suggested, patting the top of Asciita's book, which extended a silver pseudopod large enough to hold Bytina. "Good! Now she, and you, will have connections to networks to which you are invited." Instantly dozens of books and mirrors on-a-stick all around the room began to blink. "See! They all want to get to know you."

Bunny glanced down into the minute magik mirror, which no longer reflected her face. Instead, we could see the image of a polished wooden desk. I understood the "desktop" concept now, because hundreds of envelopes of every size and

shape began to fall onto it with the swishing sound that real paper would make. "There. You've got mail already."

Bunny tapped the mirror with her fingertip. "How do I open those envelopes?"

"There is your hand," Zol replied, pointing to a hand-shaped button. Bunny touched it, and the very image of her hand appeared in the picture.

"I can't open envelopes one-handed," she objected.

"Touch it with the other hand, too."

Suddenly there were two little hands in the mirror. It was good magik. The disembodied images picked up the first envelope, opened the flap and extracted an engraved card. Bunny peered close.

"I can't read it."

"Expand the window," Zol instructed her. Before Bunny could ask how, Bytina stretched and stretched until she was the size of a dinner plate. The first missive was now easily read.

"'Welcome,' the card said in swirling blue letters. 'u r v beautiful i would like to be your friend do u like pizza (g)? rofl Kas Nostat.'"

Bunny smiled, bemused. "I like pizza very much," she said. "Who is Kas?" A unit in the far back of the room started blinking blue. Bunny's compact started flashing silver. "Oh! Are they talking?"

"Yes. They all speak their own language. This is very convenient, because it will provide me with a means of communicating with you if we are not together."

Bytina's mirror filled with more envelopes, all of them flapping around like hysterical butterflies. Bunny opened them all with pleasure. Before long she had been introduced to everyone in the room. Further invitations were pouring in from farther afield. Zol identified some of the signatures as coming from entirely different countries in the dimension.

"How can it do that?"

"We harnessed natural forces," Zol explained. "You know how quickly a rumor can spread, for example? A story that you thought was private going to the ends of the earth before you know it? Well, we tagged one, let it loose, and followed how it made its way all over the world. Those information pathways are the basis of our system. So our rumor-nation, if you will forgive the term, is now able to ruminate upon our little problem. And Bytina is part of the solution."

"Well, I like her," Bunny declared, happily. "She is just darling, and she's a genius." The compact in her hands seemed wildly happy, flipping its mirror open and closed. Gleep came close for a sniff. Bytina closed her lid with a snap that nearly took off one of his whiskers. Gleep retreated behind me with his head peering over my shoulder. "You'd really like having one," she told us. "It's wonderful. I feel like I'm connected to so many people now."

"Not for me," Tananda insisted. "I have complicated enough relationships of the breathing kind."

"How is this worldwide connection doing on finding the dimension the Pervect Ten went to?" I asked, peevishly.

"I'm glad you asked," Zol smiled at me. "I believe I have an answer for you."

Our host led us to yet another huge white room filled with Kobolds and computers. The Kobold scribes were too busy with their keyboards to look up at us as we entered, but they had noticed us. Several of the screens offered flashes of welcome. A vast silver curtain filled the wall opposite the door. On it was a complicated design that looked like a web. I would have hated to meet the spider-bear that had woven it; it was *gigantic*.

"There are an infinitely large number of dimensions that can be reached directly from Wuh," Zol lectured, gesturing up at the curtain. A pale beige light erupted close to the center of the web. "As you can see on this screen, we are here," he pointed to a small silver light immediately adjacent to the pale dot. At another gesture the whole chart burst into brilliance as the first-generation connections lit up. "Based on research I and other field researchers have already gathered, these are the other dimensions we know of that are on a first-jump basis with Wuh. Now, Pervects have a tolerance for far more poisonous atmospheres and less salubrious terrain than, say, Klahds and Trolls, but we can begin to eliminate numerous dimensions from the total. First of all, we can ignore the ones that don't use magik. And the ones whose level of civilization is insufficient to accept the presence of demons, particularly ones who resemble Pervects. You must admit their appearance takes a little getting used to."

"You can say that again," I asserted fervently. Tananda elbowed me hard in the ribs.

"Skeeve!"

"Moreover, we need one whose denizens can make use of a sophisticated philosophical device, one that has a good deal of disposable income, respects wizards openly and has two eyes in a fairly narrow head."

"How did you figure that out?" I said, genuinely curious. While Zol could be a bit of a pain, there were times when I was overawed by his applications of logic.

"Why from the object that Mistress Tananda abstracted," Zol explained, holding up the spectacles. He put them on his own nose. The ear pieces slid down the sides of his head, having no visible ears to clip onto, but the spectacles were still too wide to fit. "It must be put on willingly; there is no spell, strap or adhesive to adhere it to the wearer's head. Once donned it is bespelled to speak directly into the wearer's mind, and to transmit a good deal of data therein."

"What kind of data?" I asked suspiciously.

"Fantasies," Zol frowned. "Nonsense. Mind-filling trash that numbs the emotions and dulls the calculating faculties."

I was horrified. "They're going to take over another dimension by brainwashing the inhabitants. Who is it? Where is it? We've got to go there and warn them!"

"We have reduced the number of possibilities to thirty-five dimensions," Zol calculated, peering into the magik mirror of his book. "It will take some time to narrow our target further."

"We can visit each one," I offered. "As soon as one of us spots these glasses, we'll know we're there."

"It would be easier to wait for the data," Zol suggested. "Don't exhaust yourselves searching unnecessarily. Let our fingers do the walking."

I glanced at my companions.

"I have to admit it makes sense," Tananda shrugged. "Dimensions can be big places. This isn't like a house-to-house search."

"Okay," I agreed at last, though I was itching to go in search of the Pervect Ten's latest victims and liberate them. "We'll wait."

Paldine paused until Vergetta and Oshleen materialized beside her on the steps of the First General Savings Bank of Scamaroni, Volute branch. Volute was a medium-sized town within a day's ride of the capital city. Merchants, mostly those who had big holdings in dry goods, kept their factories here, where they could oversee them from their vast and handsome manors. Privilege oozed out of every pore. Even second, third and fourth children had their own carriages. Babies were tended by captive or indentured Genies and Brownies. Even the working class had good clothes, whole shoes and a general air of cleanliness. Theaters and other entertainments abounded, including magikal revues and small venues for performing wizards. They'd ascended far enough above peasantry to be the ideal market for the storytelling goggles. Scamaroni was not unlike Perv, Paldine mused, of several hundred years before— if that unnamed Pervect had not discovered electricity and realized it was good for more than a really hilarious practical joke. A statue to that long-ago inventor still stood in the capital, lightning jolting upward from its outstretched palm, though the name had been excised centuries ago, probably by the families of jealous rivals who would like to have taken credit for such a revelation, or by outraged consumers because he had tried to extort a royalty every time someone plugged in a vacuum cleaner. A greedy bastard after Paldine's own heart.

"And we're here for what, this early in the morning?" Vergetta asked, as Paldine pulled them into the alley between two buildings to avoid being seen by the locals. "Take it easy on the material, darling."

"To see the evolution of our marketing empire," Paldine gloated, pointing. "See there?"

"It's a shop. I've seen thousands."

"It's our first outlet. I signed him up yesterday. The shop owner, who, by the way, owns ten stores in Volute alone, loved the goggles. His mate loved them. Their children loved them. They thought they were fabulous, the best entertainment they had ever seen. Once he got over being awed at my appearance, he bargained like a Deveel..."

"What, that badly?" Oshleen asked with mock innocence, polishing her nails on her designer dress.

Paldine ignored her. "...for an exclusive license to distribute on Scamaroni."

Vergetta grinned, a sight that made the vermin in the alley flee, squeaking. "For which you made him pay through the nose, of course."

"If you call that outrageous protuberance in the middle of their faces a nose, yes," Paldine replied. "He would have promised me anything to get his hands on them. He thinks he can sell a thousand a month in this town alone, and plans to expand to the capital as soon as he has merchandise. I already notified Niki to get the Wuhses to start manufacturing more."

"Isn't that putting the cart before the horse, to use a backward expression for a backward place?" Oshleen sneered.

"Listen, window-dummy, he was wetting himself! At one point in the bargaining I pretended to get insulted at his offer and started to leave. He threw himself in front of the door! In front of a Pervect! The kids fought over the sample unit until one of them broke its arm." Oshleen's face slowly split

into a grin. Paldine nodded smugly. "Yes, you believe me
now. We've got a winner, ladies: we're feeding an addiction.
We're scratching an itch." Lines of force were plentiful on
Scamaroni. The marketing specialist reached into the ground
for a handful of power. With no effort whatsoever she drew
a blanket of nothingness around herself and her two companions, rendering them invisible to the crowd on the street.
"The goggles are about to go on sale. It could be a bloodbath. Let's go see the fun."

# Chapter 12

*"This must be the place!"*
C. Columbus

It took three days of number-crunching and data-wrangling while the Kobolds worked on reducing their original list of thirty-five dimensions to the Pervect Ten's most likely destination. Zol saw to it we were housed comfortably, in a little podlike house that looked like an egg laid by the big building. We were all starting to get indigestion from the local food, but none worse than Gleep. Between the starch and the grease of the processed packets, his digestive system was producing stenches beyond all previous efforts, some of which were legendary. In the end I took him out miles out beyond the manicured gardens and let him hunt for his own food in the fenlands. Once I had been assured there was nothing sentient out there, I didn't worry about Gleep. Dragon digestive systems are notorious for being able to find nourishment in almost anything.

Gleep dug happily in the marshes, scaring lizard-frogs and marsh slugs while he looked for something to eat. He emerged from one particularly nasty bog clutching a football-sized, gray-shelled creature that had far too many spiky legs and eyes. I winced as he crunched on its carapace and slurped down eye stalks, all with relish. At least he never seemed to eat anything cute. Or if he did, I mused, I'd never seen it. I chose not to worry about the concept. He licked his moustache back to fluffy whiteness and trotted over to me with a pleased air.

"Come on," I urged, hooking my hand through his collar, though I stood about as much chance of keeping him next to me if he didn't want to be as I did harnessing a tornado. We stalked back to the pod-house, shedding mud as we went. The whole Kobold system seemed to be in harmony with cleanliness and order. By the time we stepped inside we were both as clean as if we had had baths. Gleep pranced up and collapsed next to Tananda to groom his scales with his long tongue. She sat in an easy chair with her feet up on the table, cleaning her nails with a long knife. Wensley paced back and forth. A groove in the silver-gray carpet proved he had been engaged in that activity for some time.

"Where have you been?" Wensley wailed, coming over to wring his hands at me. "What are we waiting for? Every minute, the Pervects could be digging their claws more deeply into our backs. Wuh is in danger, and we are *sitting* here."

"Just how much money do you owe them?" Tananda asked. "Couldn't you just work out a solution and pay them off?"

"We have nothing to pay them with," Wensley whined. "No liquid assets worth speaking of. We would prefer not to deed them the equivalent in land, and our people chafe at the notion of working off the fee as involuntary personal assistants."

*Indentured servants*, I translated. I gave a moment of thought to being personal valet to a Pervect, and the pictures that sprang to mind made me shiver.

"As it is, they control all our manufacturing. We have no tourism. 'Come and see our historical castle, currently under permanent occupation by an outside consulting firm.'"

"Listen, cutie," Tananda began, stopping her manicure to point the knife at him. "The Great Skeeve is taking time away from his very important studies to help you. Do you want him to back out? I'm sure he'd be thrilled to go back to the work he was doing when you interrupted him."

"No!" Wensley exclaimed. He came over to wring my hand, his eyes wide with horror. "Forgive me, Skeeve. I wasn't thinking. Of course you must do what you think is right...I hope you still consider our problem worthy of your attention. Please, don't abandon us. What would we do?"

Why couldn't I come up with retorts like Tananda's? I wondered. I glanced over at her. She threw me a broad wink.

"Of course I'll help you," I confirmed. "It's just gotten more complicated than it started out being."

"I understand, I understand," Wensley babbled gratefully. "Forgive me for not comprehending the time involved in a comprehensive plan such as the one that I know you have formulated."

I wish I had his faith. I was saved from having to come up with one by a glad cry from outside.

"Results!" Zol announced, coming down the path waving his notebook. Bunny came in behind him, her eyes shining. "The very place! I am sure that this must be the solution to the enigma. The map matched the terrain within 89% plotted points of similarity, and the spectacles would fit the inhabitants." He flung open his book to show us the name. "Scamaroni!"

My eyebrows lifted. I should have realized when I had first examined the list of dimensions whose denizens met our criteria that the Pervects would have homed in on that one. Even in the Bazaar the name had become a byword for easy marks. To have been "Scammed" was to have fallen for a great selling job, such as the Deveels were masters of. But plenty of other demons and merchants had made their way to Scamaroni over the centuries. Unlike the Wuhses, who realized they had gotten in over their heads and asked for help, the Scammies never seemed to learn. It sounded like the Pervect Ten had lit upon Scamaroni as the next link in their chain of conquest.

Just to make sure we landed in the right dimension, we diverted back through Wuh. As soon as the pigeon-bearing statue under the familiar gray-blue sky appeared Wensley bolted. Tananda, Bunny and I looked at one another.

"Gleep, fetch!" I shouted, pointing in the direction of the fleeing Wuhs. The ground thundered as my pet set off in pursuit. I ran after them, but Wensley outdistanced me, dodging around a corner in the middle of town. With an uneasy look over my shoulder at the castle looming over me, I sprinted down the narrow lane. The sounds of bleating and whimpering let me know which alleyway to turn into. Wensley lay on his back as Gleep dragged him by one leg back in the direction they had come.

"Oh, please, Master Skeeve!" he begged, as soon as he saw me. "Please, please don't make me come with you. I'm not good in fights. I'm not clever enough to figure out how to liberate a dimension." Gleep hauled him to my feet and let the leg drop. He sat up on his haunches and begged for a reward. I felt in my belt pouch for a packet of crisps and flipped it to him. He caught it and gulped it down, licking his chops. The Wuhs scrambled to his knees and tugged on my tunic hem. "Let me stay here. I'll gather information for you. I'll conduct interviews. I'll do analysis. I'll scrub lavatories. Just don't make me go with you." He burst into tears and blew his nose on my sleeve.

"I don't understand," I remarked, as Tananda, Zol and Bunny came running up behind us. "You didn't mind traveling by D-hopper to Klah or Deva."

"That was shopping," Wensley sobbed. "This might be confrontation."

"Please consider it, Master Skeeve," Zol suggested. "Wuhses aren't very assertive. Pushing him into difficult circumstances won't help break him of his fears. He might collapse when you need him most."

That could be disastrous for us. I looked at the others, but Tananda and Bunny waited for me to make the final decision. I wished, not for the first time, that Aahz was here, either to pick the sorry Wuhs up by his shirt front and shake him or to let him crawl away and hide.

"All right," I agreed at last. "Try and find out where the spectacles are being made, and if your friends know anything else. We'll be back as soon as we can." Wensley was blubberingly grateful.

"You are as wise as you are mighty," he gasped out. I stepped back and wrung out my soggy shirt. By the disgusted look on her face, Tananda wasn't going to snuggle up to him any time in the future.

"Very well," Zol stated. "We have the coordinates. Will you do the honors, or should I?"

"Allow me," I said, reaching into my belt pouch for a pinch of magikal flash powder to cover up the fact that I was going to use our D-hopper. Wensley clambered to his feet, staying far enough away that we would have had to lunge to get him into the sphere of the device's influence. He waved a brief farewell, then took to his heels again with the expression of a deermoose surprised by lightning. The light blazed up, imprinting an image on my retinas of the Wuhs with the expression of a deermoose surprised by lightning.

"Sad," Tananda tsked, as we gathered around the D-hopper. "I thought we were getting somewhere with him."

Bunny fondled Bytina, who now rode in a color-coordinated pouch on her belt. "Maybe he needs a computer."

"Maybe he needs a personality transplant," Tananda suggested, dryly.

"Those can have some nasty side-effects," Zol frowned. I looked from one to the other, wondering how one went about transplanting a personality. Would it be like possession? What if the new mind didn't like the body it was put into?

But I had no more time to speculate upon higher philosophical processes. At the press of the control stud we found ourselves on a main street in a prosperous-looking city under a blazing hot sun. People, dressed in dark colors in spite of the day's heat, crowded the wooden sidewalk that ran past the gray stone-fronted buildings, pushing by us without a word of courtesy. A huge Scammie in a coat that reached his knees rammed right into me and kept going. Caught off guard, I teetered for a moment on the curb, waving my arms furiously for balance. With a cry I stumbled off into the path of a beast drawing a carriage, bearing down on me at a gallop. The animal, a six-legged, barrel-chested, long-tailed creature that looked like a cross between a rat and a horse, pawed the air with three-toed feet and let out a loud squeak of alarm. The driver hauled back on his reins, sniffed hard at the air, wrenched the animal to the side and kept going. He didn't say a thing. His expression remained unperturbed, as though he hadn't seen me, or even observed that his dray animal had nearly had an accident. I noticed that he was wearing dark glasses against the brightness of the day. Perhaps the Scammies had poor eyesight, and their psychometric talent or keen sense of smell allowed traffic to flow along as well as it did.

Tananda grabbed one of my arms and hauled me back onto the curb and up a flight of stone steps where Bunny and Zol had retreated to get out of the crush. We found ourselves on a hilltop overlooking a main street. Above us was a solid-looking government building of some kind, with prosperous Scammies coming and going through the molded bronze doors.

"I think it would help if we blended in," Zol noted.

I agreed. I stopped to study the Scammies. They tended to be taller than Klahds, with greeny-bronze faces and hands, all the flesh that was exposed by their garments, long-sleeved robes that swept the ground. The faces were inverted triangles. A round mouth down near the sharply pointed chin was nearly concealed by the most distinctive feature of the Scammie physiognomy: the nose. The average nose, ridged and glistening like a segmented worm, was longer than my hand, more like a junior trunk. The huge nostril, for there was only one, ran upward from just above the little mouth to right between the eyes. Those I could not see well, because nearly everyone on the street was wearing dark glasses.

"The spectacles!" I exclaimed, pointing.

"Disguise first," Zol cautioned me, as a uniformed Scammie, clearly an authority figure of some kind, turned his trunk in our direction. He started sniffing. Quickly, I formed a mental image of the five of us, then erased our features and superimposed Scammie mouths and noses, surmounting them with glasses to disguise our eyes. It helped that the natives, too, were upright creatures with their eyes on the front of their heads. I had little time to do more than clothe us all in identical robes before I bent down to take a good sniff of the nearest passerby. I wasn't that proficient at non-visual illusions, but if fitting in here meant disguising our natural aroma, I was certainly going to try. Their body odor was pleasant, like oranges with vanilla overtones. The police officer stopped sniffing. He tilted his triangular head with an air of confusion, then turned back to directing traffic.

"Mmm," Tananda smiled, lifting a wrist to her nose. "Nice. You can design a perfume for me any time, handsome."

Gleep stared at me with puzzlement in his round eyes. They were now black like the rat-horse's, with the rest of his form to match, because it was the only nonverbal creature I'd seen yet. He was troubled because not only did I not look like me, but I didn't smell right.

"It's okay, Gleep," I reassured him, petting him behind the ears. He looked dubious, but my voice was still familiar. I put my hand on his head and took a really good look around.

It had been only four days since we had lost track of the Pervect Ten, but they hadn't wasted a moment. It had not simply been the man in the carriage wearing dark glasses. Everybody we could see, in every direction, was wearing colored spectacles exactly like the pair I now had in my belt pouch. The reason the Scammies crowded one another so rudely on the sidewalks was that none of them was paying attention to where he or she was going. They bumped into vehicles, walls and one another, but no one seemed to get angry or upset. It was eerie. I had never seen traffic accidents resolved without swearing before.

"They all seem to be very happy," Bunny observed.

"They are under a spell," Zol confirmed, his voice rising with concern. "Their minds are under the control of the glasses. Tell them, Master Skeeve! Take your case to the common Scammie. Help them! Only the truth can save them now! Speak to them and set them free!"

His alarm galvanized me into action. I saw before me another world on the brink of falling under the influence of the

Pervect Ten. We had been too slow to stop the infiltration, but those demons wouldn't keep the Scammies under their thumb, not if I could help it. I ran to the top of the stairs, spread out my arms and cried out to the people of Scamaroni.

"Take off your glasses!" I shouted. "They're part of a plot by a group of females from Perv who want to enslave your entire dimension. They're enchanting you! They are poisoning your minds!"

# Chapter 13

*"Do you really want them eating off your hand?"*
P. Benchley

My voice died away. I looked around me for the thousands of eager, raised faces, grateful that someone had come to liberate them from their involuntary thralldom.

The trot-trot of rat-horse feet, the rumble of carriage wheels, the trudge-trudge-trudge of thousands of feet did not come to a halt. In fact, no one paused for a moment. I couldn't believe it. Nobody understood what kind of danger they were in! I gawked at the resounding wave of apathy that greeted my announcement. Didn't they care?

"Take the initiative, Master Skeeve," Zol urged me. "Use that Klahdish determination!"

That steeled my resolve. What I needed was an authority, an important citizen, to set an example by casting off the Pervect Ten's device. I cast around me.

There was the very person: coming out of the big building at the top of the peak was a stout, prosperous male with a heavily embroidered coat over his robe. He wore the glasses, too, but he was being led by the hands by a couple of muscular young Scammies whose eyes were uncovered. Their protuberant brown orbs turned toward me as I dashed up to the male they were escorting.

"He's being brainwashed!" I exclaimed. "Make him take off the glasses. He'll see reality, not fantasy."

"It's just jealous," the escort on the left sniffed to the other, pointing its trunk in my direction. "It hasn't got any."

"A have-not," snickered the escort on the right. "Sad, really. He'll never know how great they are."

"Probably not," agreed his companion. The male in the middle said nothing. His mouth gaped open, and drool collected in the corner.

I should have known Scammies would think that anything worth having was worth bragging about. I tried again. "Look at him. Help him. His mind is under its control. It could happen to you."

"I hope so," shrugged the escort on the right. "I've started saving up for my pair. Senior Domari says he loves them so much he's never taking them off."

They didn't understand. I would have to take matters into my own hands. I reached for the pair of pink-framed glasses perched on the male's snout. The escort on the left reached for my throat with a huge hand. The little round mouth bristled with sharp teeth. He lunged for me. I dodged back. If they were going to play rough, I was more than a match for them. At a safe distance, I used the reverse of my levitation spell to send him flying backwards. The other escort let go of his employer's arm and came hurtling at me, only to go hurtling in the opposite direction as I threw a chunk of power into his chest. With a flick of magik I snatched the glasses off the face of the portly Scammie. He let out a bellow, and clutched his eyes.

"Where did they go? Give them back!"

I swept my hand downward, and the spectacles dashed to the ground. The lenses splintered into a hundred pieces. "You're free!" I exclaimed. "Reclaim your mind!"

"What?" the stout male trumpeted, focusing his protruding eyes on me. "Those cost me twenty gold pieces! How dare you! This is an outrage!"

"No, it's liberation!" I explained. Twenty gold pieces! The Pervects were making the victims pay for their own conquest? That was a wrinkle even Aahz would have had trouble stomaching. "Your minds were being clouded by evil sorcery. You can all thank me later." I turned to the next person feeling her way blindly down the stairs while wearing Pervect Ten spectacles. With a spark of power I whisked the device off her nose and hurled it down. She shrieked as she was set free, possibly for the first time in days. One after another I picked the Ten's malevolent glasses off their victims and destroyed them. The vacant looks on their faces changed to more normal expressions, such as surprise and enlightenment. Another three pairs went flying past me, off a slender female hauling a couple of youngsters by the hands. The children began to cry. I turned to offer a thumb's up to my companions, standing at the side of the stairs. Tananda grinned back at me. She and Zol were getting into the act, helping me break the people out of the demons' spell.

"*Thank you?*" demanded the first Scammie I had helped, his trunk rampant with fury. He held up his fists. "*Thank you? You're mad! Guards! Guards! Arrest this...this fool!*"

At the cry, the officer directing traffic turned his face up towards us. Throwing both hands up magnificently to halt the flow of vehicles, he stalked off his pedestal and started up the stairs in the direction of the shouting Scammie. It must take time until the brainwashing began to wear off. The portly male still carried on as if he was angry that the stream of nonsense the Pervects' device fed him had been halted. It looked as if we had better clear out of the immediate area until all of them were in their right minds again. I had been the target of mobs before. I knew I didn't want to have that experience again.

"Come on," I gestured to my friends. Gleep came charging through the crowd of Scammies converging on me, bowling half of them over and sending them rolling down the stairs. Tananda leaped down to help me clear a way for Zol and Bunny.

"Get us out of here, Gleep!" I yelled. I released the illusion masking his natural aroma. At the sudden wave of lung-constricting smell, Scammies threw themselves out of his path, cannoning into one another, shrieking in fear.

"Gleep!" my pet yodeled, turning his nose downward.

We plunged down the steps in his wake, stripping spectacles off Scammies as we went. To my surprise mild-mannered Zol threw himself into the liberation effort with gusto. With a wave of his hands the little gray man flipped glasses off dozens of people at a time. Tananda, too, lent her magikal abilities to the cause. Bunny just held tight to Bytina and did her best to stay with us.

The crowd behind us grew as we ran. What had gone wrong? I started to wonder if just removing the spectacles was enough to break the hypnotic trance the Pervect Ten had set on their victims. They were still shouting at us and shaking their fists long after I would have thought the impact would have begun to wear off.

"After them!" shouted the stout male.

"They broke my glasses!"

"They broke my children's! What will we do?"

I sprinted down the middle of the main street. Rat-horses reared and gnashed their big front teeth as I swung under their noses. Scammies operating pedal-driven vehicles halted and swore. People not wearing the Pervect goggles stopped to point and stare. We were definitely attracting too much attention.

I looked around for a place to duck into so I could operate the D-hopper, but every inch of the street was filled with shouting, angry people. I glanced over my shoulder. Zol, for all that he stood a foot shorter than I, managed to stay just behind me, but Bunny was getting lost in the crowd. I'd lost sight of Tananda. She could dimension-hop on her own with a chant and a wiggle, so I didn't have to worry about her, but my assistant was not a magician. I had to get back to her.

I saw her hand go up before it was blotted out by a mass of Scammies bearing down on me.

"Gleep!" I called. "Go get Bunny! Protect her!"

"Gleep!" my pet responded. He stopped clearing the way ahead for me, looped around in his length, which caused several of the pursuers to trip on him, and came galloping directly back toward me. I threw up my hands to halt him.

"No, Gleep!" I cried, just before we collided.

"Now, now, now, what's all this, then?"

When I opened my eyes, everything was in a haze. As my vision cleared I found myself staring at the protuberant brown eyes of a Scammie police officer whose face was only inches from my nose. He reached for my arm. I started to pull it away, then realized that the ground was preventing my elbow from moving back. I was lying down. How had that happened?

It all came back to me as the roar of furious voices rolled over my ears again. Gleep, in his zeal to take the shortest path to Bunny and carry out my instructions, had crashed into me and knocked me flat. I didn't know if the bruises I felt on my chest were his footprints, or those of some of the Scammies standing around me, one of whose foot was still planted across my neck. I had probably been knocked unconscious when I hit my head on the ground. How long ago had that happened?

I gasped for breath. The person whose boot was impeding my airway removed it, and the policeman hauled me to my feet. His trunklike nose twitched. I sniffed, too. I must have let the nasal illusion slip. In the mélange of vanilla-orange I smelled like a pigpen by comparison. It was too late to disguise my normal scent. Half the Scammies caught my stink and edged away from me, or pinched their big nostrils shut with their fingers. The policeman's eyes watered, but he was made of a better mettle than his countrymen. He kept my arm clamped in his hand, and felt my face. When his fingers met my ordinary, and very small (by comparison) nose, his brow ridges went up.

"Who are you, and *what* are you?" he demanded.

I tried to choke out my name, but only a squeak came out, thanks to both having the air knocked out of me and the foot in the throat. "I'm Sk—" I gasped.

"All right, make way!" Another police officer came bustling up. The first one held out a palm.

"Magik dispeller," he demanded. The second officer slapped a wand into his hand. The first officer pushed a small stud on the handle and leveled it at me. I saw the faces of the crowd change as my disguise was stripped from me.

"A Klahd," the officer sniffed in disgust. "What do you think you're doing here?"

"My name is Skeeve," I croaked. "I'm here to save you."

"Crazy, too," the second officer opined.

"No, really!" I protested. "You're all in danger."

"Save us, eh?" the officer in charge queried. "Is that why you stood on the courthouse steps screaming like a fool? If you have evidence that Scamaroni is in some kind of peril why didn't you go to our government and make your case?"

"I..." I was starting to wonder that myself. I couldn't tell him that Zol Icty had told me to. I was beginning to think it had been a bad idea after all. But I couldn't make this officer think I was a bigger twit than he already did. I eyed him. "If you can ask a question like that, you've never tried to change anything by getting the government to help," I pointed out.

It looked as though Officer Two agreed with me privately, but the Officer One was not amused. His voice was even and calm, as though he was talking to a very small child. "So tell me why you caused a riot."

"The glasses," I began, feeling a little foolish. "They're part of a big plot."

"So you said."

"The people who made them want to take over your dimension."

The brow ridges went up again. "And you have proof of this?"

"You have to take me seriously," I insisted. I gestured at the angry people around me. Tananda, Zol and Bunny were nowhere in sight. I hoped that they had jumped back to Wuh or Klah and weren't going through an interrogation like this somewhere out of sight. "Really. You'll lose control of your own lives! I'm a magician, a great magician. I've seen it happen in another dimension. I don't want it to happen to you!"

"They had these glasses?"

"Well, no...but it's the same ten Pervects. They've conquered one world, and yours is next!"

"Uh-huh," the officer said, still in the same patient voice. He exchanged a look with the other officer, who tapped his chin with a forefinger. It must be the local gesture for "nut case." I started to protest.

"...And I had mountains of treasure! Gold! Jewels! Silver! But I used that cheap stuff only to scratch my back," added the female Scammie, escorted into our little circle by a third policeman, "until *that imbecile* destroyed my storytelling goggles, and I got yanked out of my beautiful dream!"

"You see?" I stated, indicating the female. "It's clouding your minds."

"So what?" the female asked, her trunk rampant with disapproval. "I was loving it!"

"But what about your productivity?" I said, beginning to feel desperate. They didn't understand. "What about your normal lives?"

"This is much more interesting than my life," the woman told me impatiently. "I have five children. You think I can't use a little escapism?"

"The makers of these things want to control you, maybe bleed you dry," I insisted.

"Twenty gold pieces is steep," the woman admitted, "but it's worth it! I've wandered in beautiful places, free as a *greblich!*"

"No, it won't stop there," I warned, looking about at all the hostile faces in the circle. "They'll take over your dimension while you're not looking."

A male Scammie poked me in the stomach. "So what? If we're happy, how bad could that be?"

The first officer put his free hand on his hip. "Have you ever even tried these things yourself?"

"No," I admitted. "But I know what they can do..."

"Well, here." He plucked the goggles off one of the by-standers. The owner's eyes flew wide in alarm, but calmed down when he saw a law officer holding them. He started to put them on my face.

"No!" I protested, throwing up my hands. "They'll enchant me!" The cop shrugged and handed them back. The owner went to put them back on. I couldn't let him be dragged back into the spell. I raised my hands and made a twisting motion. The owner cried out in alarm.

"You'll thank me later," I tried to say, as he went for my throat. All three police officers pulled him back. He shook his fist over their shoulders.

"You...you vandal!" he yelled, his nose-trunk erect in out-rage. "Aargh! That's the last time I help the police!"

"Look," I said, desperately, "You don't know what they're doing to you. Today it seems like you're just enjoying harmless fantasies, but before you know it you'll be their slaves. I'll reimburse everyone for their glasses—wholesale cost," I amended hastily. If I'd learned anything from Aahz, it was never pay the full price for replacement of an item. If I had ever agreed to give anyone the retail value of an item I had broken Aahz would have rolled his eyes right around inside his head. "They're harming you. Trust me."

The more I protested, the more faces I saw becoming thoughtful.

"Maybe he's on to something," a narrow-faced woman mused, tilting her head. "I never considered it more than a toy...but you never know what extra spells might be tucked in there. I've heard all kinds of things happen to people. You read about it in the news all the time."

"Hah," a young male sneered. "He's just jealous that he doesn't have his own goggles. Can't afford to buy one for your-self, Klahd?"

"I bet he works for a rival toymaker," an elderly female shrilled. "He doesn't like theirs, but we should buy yours, isn't that right, stinky?"

"No, it's not like that at all!"

The first policeman held up his hands. "All right, all right, calm down. We'll get to the bottom of this. We'll have the goggles inspected to make sure they don't cause any harm to any of you. In the meantime, give your names to Officer Koblinz, and we'll notify you when we've finished our investigation. Move along! Move along! Clear the road!"

The Scammies, grumbling, obeyed the first policeman's commands. Officer Two, Koblinz, took a pad of paper out of his pocket. Names magikally limned themselves down the index. He nodded and put it away.

"You can better believe we're going to get to the bottom of this," he promised.

"That's a relief," I breathed. Very quickly traffic returned to normal, and the complainants departed. "Well, thanks a lot." I spotted an alley where I could retrieve the D-hopper out of my boot in private, and started towards it.

"And where do you think you're going?" Officer One asked, grabbing me by the back of my collar. I struggled to pry myself loose, even using a flick of power, but he had a good grip on me.

"I've got to get back to my work," I told him. "I told you, those Pervects have a grip on another helpless dimension."

"You're not going anywhere!"

"What? Why?"

Officer One looked at me as though I was an idiot. "You're still under arrest for destroying personal property."

"But, gee, I said I'd pay for them," I protested.

"Nothing doing," he said, hauling me by my collar down the sidewalk to a waiting rat-horse cart. "Restitution will be part of the sentence. You're still being held for assault on sixty or eighty persons, destruction of property, causing a nuisance on the public highway with that sick rorse of yours, creating an affray..."

"A what?" I asked.

The officer sighed, as if he had never met such a stupid being in his life. "Causing a riot, if you prefer it like that. The judge is really going to throw the book at you."

"What's the usual penalty for causing an affray?" I asked.

"Oh, thirty or forty days. But with all the other charges added on you're likely going to spend the rest of your life in here."

"Perhaps I could talk to the judge," I offered, stumbling as I climbed into the cart. "Arrange a payment schedule, and apologize to the Scammies I have offended?"

"I doubt it," Officer One said, gesturing his companion to whip up his animal. "Senior Domari was the first person you assaulted."

# Chapter 14

*"Maybe I should have kept my nose out of it."*
C. de Bergerac

I paced from one side of my small cell to the other. It looked just like your average cell, but it smelled good for a change, like roses and new mown grass. Except for the fact that there were bars on the hand-sized window, iron bands wider than my torso on the door, and, oh, yes, walls of big rough stone in between them, I could have been walking in a delightful garden.

Officers One and Three, whom I now knew were called Gelli and Barnold, had left me the D-hopper and all of my other magikal paraphernalia, including the sample pair of glasses we had picked up in the Pervects' headquarters.

"The whole place is magik-proofed," Officer Gelli informed me, at my puzzled expression when he handed me back the D-hopper. "You can use that as a backscratcher, or whatever you like, but you're staying here until your arraignment."

"Do I get a lawyer?" I said.

"Sure. Who can we call to get one for you?"

But there was no answer to that. My companions had escaped. I was thankful for that: there was no point in all five of us being locked up. Thanks to the disguise there was no way they could be identified as fellow perpetrators if they returned. *When* they returned. I knew my friends. They would not leave me here to rot.

The cell door had a huge, primitive key lock, the kind I had practiced opening hundreds of times back when I thought I wanted to be a thief. My fingers were small enough to reach the tumblers, but not strong enough to turn them through the keyhole. If I could only have summoned up a thread of power

I could have shrunk the shaft of the D-hopper to use as a lock pick, but nothing doing.

It wasn't as though magik was scarce. Strong lines of power abounded on Scamaroni. I could see a huge blue arrow running directly underneath the police station, but it was as untouchable as the shutterbugs behind the glass of Zol's little magik mirror. I tried a thousand times to reach that power, or the bright golden one I could see arching like a monochrome rainbow over the main street of the city, or the paler green one that crossed the blue one at some distance from the jail. Some big, tough wizards had created the containment spell around this building, wizards hundreds of years older and far more accomplished than I was. There would have had to be sixteen of me to make any dent in it. I certainly tried.

I pictured a magikal crowbar prying out the grille over the window. Sweat poured down my face as I constructed the spell over and over again. The bars didn't even grow warm. I pictured a magikal rope tied around the door dragging it off its hinges. Not a creak, not a quiver. I sat down, exhausted. I was just going to have to wait until someone came and let me out.

It didn't take a genius to tell me that I had made a mess of my opportunity to free the Scammies. Zol Icty may have had the utter adoration of every self-help book reader in every dimension, and know everything that there was to know about everyone who lived in them, but his advice was awful. I blamed myself. I had gotten caught up in his plausibility, and believed whatever he said without judging for myself whether what he told me to do made sense. I promised myself from then on I'd listen to whatever he had to say, then do the opposite of what he advised. If I'd done that, I could have been home by now.

I paced back and forth until my feet hurt, then I spent some time looking out the window. My cell faced the street. It seemed to me that at least half the people out there had Storyteller Goggles on, wandering blindly as their keen sense of smell kept them from running into obstructions, and most of the other half looked envious. But I thought that I had done some good: a few of the passersby looked disapproving at their fellow Scammies who were wearing the Pervect Ten's device. Maybe I'd gotten through to a few after all.

A clattering at the door announced the arrival of my dinner tray, pushed through a panel at the bottom of the door, which was firmly closed and locked as soon as the following edge of the tray was inside. A covered dish, a jug of wine and a jug of water lay on the wooden trencher, along with a candlestick, two candles, and flint and steel. By my calculations the candles would burn from sunset to midnight. I supposed I could try to set the room on fire, but there was nothing to burn except my clothes. The necessary was a covered metal bucket shoved underneath a wash stand consisting of a china bowl and pitcher on a stone shelf in the corner. The bed was a stone shelf, too. Not very comfortable, but then, nothing to attract insects, either. I didn't really need a blanket; the room was warm. I looked under the plate cover. The Scammies may have thought I was crazy, but they treated their prisoners well. The food looked and smelled as good as anything at the best restaurants in the Bazaar. I ate my supper, then spent the rest of the remaining daylight clutching the bars of my small window and watching the people go by. A few of them spotted me; with my Klahdish looks I had to be about as inconspicuous as a porcupine on a silk rug. They made faces or obscene gestures. With those flexible noses, obscene gestures took on new impact.

The sun woke me just before another tray was shoved under my door. I sprang up and pounded on the heavy wood.

"Hey!" I cried. "Let me out of here!"

I heard no other sounds for a long time, until there was the scrape of a heavy bolt moving on the other side of the door. It creaked open, and Officer Koblinz came in. He pointed at my pendant.

"That won't work in here," he spoke, haltingly, as he took his notebook out of his pocket, this time with a pencil, "but I speak Klahd. Let's hear your side of the story. Start at the beginning."

"Well," I began, settling down on my blanketless bunk, "I was working on my magik studies when this Wuhs popped in…"

In between meals I had nothing to do but peer out of the window. Shortly after lunch I saw Officer Koblinz and Gelli talking on the drawbridge that led from the prison. Gelli threw him a half-salute and marched down to street level. A female, probably Mrs. Gelli by the way their snouts reached out lovingly to touch one another, met him at the bottom. They started talking and walking along the river front. When they met another female, this one wearing a pair of the Pervect Ten's enchanted spectacles, they halted to speak with her. She listened with growing alarm, then took off her goggles and threw them away from her. They landed in the river, and sank in a circle of growing ripples. The Gellis passed on, and the now worried woman rushed over to talk to a cluster of young people with spectacles on. A few of them ignored her, but a couple must have listened, because they took the glasses off and looked at them closely. I cheered.

"What do you mean, you don't want the shipment?" Paldine demanded in disbelief. Bofus, the shop owner, cringed behind his counter, his long nose pressed against his face for protection. "We have an exclusive contract! You were going to sell a thousand a week!"

"Dear madam, I believed it! I was absolutely convinced you were right," Bofus protested, his back against the wall. He felt along the edge for the curtain that led to the back room, and probably a handy alley on the other side. Paldine wasn't going to let him escape that easily. She spread her hands out and spat out a chant that caused the cloth to stiffen harder than wood. Bofus prodded it with the tips of his fingers, then gave her a sickly smile.

"If you don't want to get the same treatment," Paldine snarled, showing all her teeth, "you will take these boxes and give me the money we agreed on. Then I will leave, and come back next week with your next order."

"Please, madam, don't!" Bofus begged. "You don't understand! There won't be another order. I haven't sold out the ones you gave me. In fact, people have been bringing theirs back!" He plunged his hand under his counter and came up with a dozen pairs of Storyteller Goggles. Paldine glared at them, then realized some of them had been mangled.

"What in hell's kitchen has been happening here?" Paldine said. "Didn't you sell them the way I told you? You had all the sales literature."

"I did! I told them everything you told me. I let them try a pair—once anyone put them on I couldn't pry them off—I sold every single one you brought! But yesterday there was a riot. A prophet spoke, some said," Bofus explained.

"A prophet? Not unless it's my prophet," Paldine said, raising the shopkeeper by his tunic front. "And what did this prophet have to say?"

"He s-s-says these aren't toys at all," Bofus stammered. "They're b-b-brainwashing tools."

"What? You people haven't got enough brains to wash! What kind of stupid twit would come up with a notion like that? Who is he?"

"I d-d-don't know! He's n-n-not from Scamaroni. He's f-f-from one of the sm-melly dimensions."

Paldine raised an eyebrow. "That narrows it down to almost all of them. Any distinguishing features that I could use to identify this prophet?"

"N-n-no. He walked like one of us f-f-for a while, until a policeman unmasked him. I...you demons all look alike to me. N-n-no offense."

The Pervect tapped her teeth with a manicured fingernail. A magician from some other dimension, one capable of shapeshifting or illusion. Who would want to queer their deal on

Scamaroni? *Everybody* took advantage of the Scammies, at least twice a year, so moral dudgeon had to be lacking on further outrages. The irony was that this time, the Pervect Ten were giving them actual value for their money, so the outrage was all hers. She bent to look at the damaged glasses. All that work, pissed away by ignorant peasants. Out of the corner of her eye she spotted Bofus wiggling his fingers in a spell to try and deossify the curtain.

"Not so fast," she cautioned him. He sagged. "You weren't so afraid of me a few days ago. You and I both know that what they're saying about these toys isn't true. What else have they been saying?"

"That you use s-s-slave labor to make the G-g-goggles, and you are planning to make us slaves so we can build goggles for other dimensions that will b-b-become p-p-part of your empire." Bofus swallowed hard.

Paldine's eyes narrowed. "That's the first I've heard about an empire, honey." For a moment she wondered if Oshleen or any of the others had been around to talk to him, then decided that was wrong. They might fight each other to the death over trivia, but they would do it openly. This would have been cutting one of their own off at the knees, and, worse yet, slashing their own income, something no Pervect would ever do. Bofus looked ready to faint, his long nose sagging like a discarded sock. Paldine decided to change tack. She turned on the charm, moving toward him with a sinuous wiggle.

"How can I find this prophet?" she purred, fluttering her green eyelids at him.

Two uniformed guards arrived in my cell with swords drawn. I sprang up in alarm. Very solemnly, they marched me into a corner and stood facing me. I peered up at their solemn faces.

"Are we going into court now?" I asked hopefully. "I'd like to get this all cleared up so I can go home."

But they didn't say a word. Their reticence made me nervous. In my experience, no news was not necessarily good news. I heard footsteps in the hallway, accompanied by the sound of metal clanging and creaking sounds. I frowned. Was this my release? Or more trouble? Did they torture their prisoners?

To my wondering eyes, the newcomer was an elderly female Scammie, dressed in drab brown and gray. Her hair was gathered up underneath a triangular scarf of the same gray fabric. A big clip held her single nostril closed. Not looking up at me, she pushed a bucket on wheels into the room. My shoulders sagged. A cleaner!

While the guards held the terrifying wizard (me) at bay in the corner, the cleaning woman swabbed the floor with a big mop. They moved me around the room from time to time so she could get into every corner without having to walk past the big dangerous criminal (me). I wondered about the chances of overpowering one or both of my captors, then fighting my way out of the jail using the cleaner as a living shield. I calculated my own body mass, even adding in a factor of 150% for all the dirty infighting tricks that Aahz had taught me over the years, and came up at least 400% short.

"Nice day," I observed, instead. The Scammie guards didn't reply. They both looked as though they would have liked be wearing clips on their noses like the old woman.

The cleaning lady continued to potter around. She removed my chamber pot and replaced it with a new one, emptied, rinsed out and refilled my washing pitcher, picked up the used dinner trays and laid a wrapped candy on my stone bunk. The guards waited until she had clanged and squeaked her way out again, then withdrew, bolting the door.

Depressed, I stumped back to my bed and sat down heavily upon it. I picked up the candy, unwrapped it, and immediately spat it out again. Licorice. No news was indeed no good news.

# Chapter 15

*"Darling, your slip is showing."*
G. Rose Lee

"This has to be your fault," Oshleen accused, striding alongside Paldine up the main street of Volute. "How could you blow something as perfect as the deal we had on those glasses?" Vergetta trotted to keep up behind her two young associates. Five of the others trotted in their wake.

Caitlin had refused to come.

"Straightening out other people's messes is not my bag," she had snorted, and gone back to working on her program to translate the specs of every Wuhs they knew into computer game characters for a game she called "Pretend Pushovers".

Niki, who distrusted anything in which Monishone and/ or high sorcery was involved, offered to stay behind and keep an eye on the Wuhses. Vergetta had to agree. They started *doing things* when the Ten were not in residence. And she had begun hearing rumors of unrest.

That was all right; eight of them was more than enough to straighten out a misunderstanding. One should have been. She didn't know what had gotten into Paldine, carrying on like that. Brainwashing, indeed! They were businesswomen, not voodoo economists.

"I didn't do it, I tell you," Paldine protested. "Everything, everything I did was according to our plan. We ought to have been raking in the gold pieces by now. This item ought to have netted us ten thousand this week alone."

"Well, that's five percent of what we need," Oshleen snorted.

"You think I don't know that? Bofus, that imbecile, claimed a group of strangers bounced in here, and started talking nonsense about how we were planning to rule the world, starting with everyone who bought our toy. *Non*-Scammies. Everyone believed it. They are so gullible."

"It's those Wuhses!" Loorna growled. "I told you we have to find that D-hopper and confiscate it. Then I'm going to tear all of them limb from limb. When I think of all the hard work we've put in trying to pull their fat out of the fire, I could just scream!"

"It can't be the Wuhses," Nedira stated, flatly. "To stand up in front of a crowd of strangers and make a speech like that? It's just not in their nature, dears. Wuhses couldn't do it."

"Who else?" Loorna demanded. "Who else knew we were selling merchandise to the Scammies?"

"I still want an explanation for why the fire barricade went for a walk the other day," Tenobia added. "Monishone saying that it ought to have been tethered down all along still doesn't ring true."

"The Wuhses can do some magik," Monishone suggested. "Perhaps we have overlooked a real magician among them."

"I still tell you they couldn't be responsible for this," Nedira protested, trotting ahead to catch up with Paldine. The marketing specialist opened her stride.

Vergetta threw up a magikal barrier to stop them all from outdistancing her. The younger ones ran into the barrier and bounced back several feet. She hauled them up one by one.

"Slow down, darlinks. Nedira is right. Don't go charging in making accusations. We ask this Bofus, quietly and calmly. And then we tear down his shop around his ears."

"We'd better not go charging in at all," Charilor exclaimed, brushing herself off. She pointed in the direction of Bofus's store. "Look at that!"

Vergetta rendered the group of Pervects invisible with a hasty chant. "Over here, darlinks," she urged, grabbing the two tall females by the hand. "We don't want them smelling us, either. We have to pick the only place in the known universe where their you-know-what don't stink."

The eight of them stopped. On the main street a protest was under way. Hundreds of Scammies marched in an oval, carrying picket signs that read "Our brains are our own!" and "Down with dictaters!"

"Their spelling stinks, too," Charilor growled.

"I can't believe they fell for the rantings of some wandering nutcase," Vergetta grumbled.

"Maybe we've got a rival," Loorna remarked darkly. "The Deveels probably want to open up their own shop and freeze us out."

"Already?" Oshleen asked. "We haven't been operating for five days yet."

"You know what they're like! Master merchants. We could learn a thing or two from them."

"Yeah, I'd have liked to," Charilor said, "but that interfering Trollop got in our way. Now we can't ever go back to the Bazaar."

"That's all water under the bridge," Vergetta reminded them. "What do we do about this? Never have I seen such an overreaction. They bought in to what this person or persons said, without ever checking with us, and the story seems to have been grown since this morning. Here comes a sign that says "Protect our children's future!" From a toy! Can you believe it?"

"Face it," Paldine pointed out, "we picked them because they'd be easy to sell to."

The crowd grew and grew. A Scammie carrying a voice-amplifying cone faced the door.

"Come out, traitor! Come out, Bofus, and face your neighbors! You monster!"

"Hmmph!" Vergetta snorted. "I can't imagine why he won't come out, with a nice, friendly invitation like that."

"Get the traitor!" shouted the Scammie with the loud-hailer.

"Yeah!" the mob cried, shaking their fists. "Get the traitor!" They rushed toward the door.

When the first line of protesters got within two paces of the door, they suddenly bounced and went flying backwards.

"Riot control," Oshleen observed. "Very good. Oh, look, here comes the cavalry."

As they watched, dozens of uniformed police officers in helmets and armor came pouring out of the store front like clowns out of a magikal circus car. Chanting a phrase that was indistinct at that distance, they pointed wands at the gathering Scammies, shoving them all back until they were behind an orange line painted on the sidewalk.

"Now, there'll be no more of this," the officer in charge bellowed, taking the megaphone away from the lead protester. "We're conducting the investigation. You all go home, now. Anyone who's still here by the time I count three is going to spend a week in jail. One...two..."

Most of the Scammies started running away, but a couple of bold young males came forward with a basket and a torch. The first tipped out the contents on the ground: several dozen pairs of Storyteller Goggles. The other one thrust the burning brand into the center of them.

"No!" Monishone yelled furiously. "You imbeciles! All my hard work!"

"Shh!" Vergetta hissed. Too late.

Police officers were leaping forward to stop the two males and to put out the fire, but the chief officer's head flew up.

"Who said that?" he demanded.

"It came from over here!" a female voice shrieked.

Vergetta turned around, and realized that more Scammies had filled in the rest of the steps overlooking Bofus's.

"There's someone invisible. Up here!"

"They smell!" added a hoarse male voice. "Outlanders! Demons!" Though the Scammies couldn't see them, they crowded in on the clot of concealed Pervects, hands out, feeling the air. One errant male's hand patted Oshleen on the rear. Her eyes flew wide in outrage.

"How dare you!" she shrieked, slapping his face. The blow knocked the male off his feet and sent him flying over the heads of his compatriots.

"Invisible invaders!" the crowd cried.

"That's enough," Vergetta declared. "Everyone, into formation! Start chanting."

"Chanting what?"

The elderly Pervect looked around. The speaker stood behind her: a Scammie about her age, dressed in a uniform with plenty of ornate braid around the collar and wrists. He was looking her straight in the eye. In fact, everybody was looking at them.

"What happened to the cloaks?" she demanded. Then, seeing the stunned look on her allies' faces, she realized it wasn't their idea that their spell had slipped. "Let's go!"

"Oh, no, you don't, madam, or whatever you are," the uniformed Scammie said.

"That's them, officer!" Bofus explained, appearing beside him. "They're the ones who sold me those glasses! I swear I had no idea that they meant for me to betray my own people."

The cop turned to her. "Is this true?"

"Of course not!" Paldine protested. "It's all a misunderstanding!"

The officer's face was imperturbable. "We'd like you to come down to our headquarters for questioning." Glancing over his shoulder, Vergetta realized that he was accompanied by about a hundred other officers, probably the force sent to deal with the riot.

"So sorry, bubchen," she apologized, patting him on the cheek. "Can't do it. Join hands!" The Pervect Ten minus Two tried to unite.

"They're trying to get away!" the crowd howled, and mobbed them, knocking their hands away from one another's. There were other ways to dimension-hop. As dozens of pairs of hands reached for her, Vergetta started chanting one of the old, more power-intensive charms.

"All right, all right, all right," the officer shouted, pushing into the midst of the crowd. "They're not going anywhere!"

And they weren't. Vergetta chanted again. And again.
No matter how she phrased the syllables, or delved for
power from the lines running all over the town, her spell
didn't work. Her surprise was echoed seven times on her
companions' faces. Scammies must be operating dispellers
strong enough to dampen even a Pervect's talent. Who in
the nine levels of Marshall Field's State Street had sold
them those?

Their momentary shock was long enough for two officers apiece to take them by the arms. The touch brought the
senior Pervect to her senses. She threw the first police officer high over her head into the crowd. The second two
retired from the fray clutching sensitive parts of their
anatomy that had been viciously kicked. But gradually,
enough police joined their brethren and sistern in bearing
the eight Pervects to the ground.

"This is no way to treat ladies," Vergetta grunted, as thick
irons were fastened around her wrists.

"You are under arrest for corruption of public morals, operating unsafe devices within the city limits and," the officer
added, wincing, "assaulting officers of the law." He gestured
to his army. "Take them away!"

"But, bubby," Vergetta explained, holding out her manacled hands
to the black-robed judge, "this is all a big misunderstanding.
Look at me. I'm just an old lady. I wouldn't hurt a fly."

A sharp inhalation of breath came from behind her, probably from one of the officers she had kicked on the way in. He
was lucky she only wanted to disarm him and get away. It did
cramp a lady's style when she intended to be merciful. The
other Pervects sat behind her on a hard wooden bench. Not so
comfortable on one's old nether parts. She was more comfortable standing.

"We have had two riots in two days," the magistrate
intoned, leaning over his tented hands toward her and the
others. "In both cases demons were involved. We have had

numerous situations in the past where outworlders have caused a lot of trouble. Now, I am trying to be lenient, but the evidence against you and your...companions is overwhelming."

"What evidence?" Vergetta said, bluntly. "We sell toys. That's all we're here to do: make people happy. Have you tried our product? It's fabulous. You would enjoy it so much. It would take your mind off your so very responsible job, and I can tell an important man like you could use a break once in a while, if you get my drift." She gestured toward him and the chains jingled. "You think maybe you could take these off, sweetie? They're a little tight."

The judge paid no attention. "Your account does not agree with what our other witness said, madam. He claims that your toy has more sinister motivations."

"Motivations, shmotivations! I heard what the crowd said, but it's not true! We're just businesswomen." Vergetta tried a friendly smile, but the sight of her teeth made the judge's bronzy-green face pale to polished brass. "Look at it from my point of view. Here I am with all my friends, coming in to see how well our new venture with our good friends on Scamaroni is going, and the next thing I know, I'm arrested! Now, how do you think that makes me feel?"

"At present, it makes me think that you're going to be here for a long while, madam," the judge replied. "According to our witness..."

"Yes, your so-called prophet!" Paldine exclaimed. "We want to see him!"

"I know Scammie law," Loorna snapped. "We have the right to be confronted by our accusers. Trot him out. We want to hear from him why he thinks we're..."

"Brainwashers," the officer supplied.

"Right. Thanks....Brainwashers."

The judge nodded, his color restored. "A reasonable request. It so happens that he is also enjoying our hospitality. We'll be happy to let you see him." He turned to the bailiff. "Go get the other prisoner."

Vergetta waited. It was sure to be some kind of misunderstanding. What's more, it would be straightened out easily enough once she had a chance to wring this other person's neck.

In a moment, the bailiff had returned, his face as pale as the judge's had been a moment before.

"The prisoner! He's gone!"

# Chapter 16

*"Give 'em the old razzle-dazzle!"*
B. Flynn

Loud clattering on the other side of the door made me jump in my eternal circuit around the cell. This time I was going to knock the guards unconscious and run for it. Very quietly, I lifted the now empty washing pitcher out of the bowl and tiptoed over to flatten myself against the wall next to the door. Slowly it opened and pushed inward. I raised the pitcher.

"There you are, handsome!"

Tananda threw herself into the cell and mashed me against the wall, pressing her lips into mine. "Mmmph! You must really have missed me, Tiger. Is that for me?"

She plucked the pitcher now hanging unsteadily over our heads from my nerveless fingers.

"Forgive the delay," Zol smiled, entering in Tananda's whirlwind wake with Bunny.

Behind them trailed a huge Scammie guard, his eyes fixed dreamily on Tananda. His breastplate was slightly twisted to one side, and his tunic was rucked up inside it. I also noted that his hair under his helmet was mussed.

"Things have been a little unsettled in the city. We had a little trouble entering this building. I am very impressed by the magik-dampening field! It certainly did not originate in this dimension, but it serves them well. Such a thing ought to be put into use in the Bazaar at Deva. It would cut down on some of the misunderstandings that occur there every day."

I smiled at him, mentally noting that if anyone in the future should happen to want to import the same kind of magik-dispeller in use on Scamaroni, I would campaign against it with every ounce of my influence. I'd been taken plenty of times in my day, and though I didn't enjoy it, I'd never change the way the Deveels operated their most impressive establishment. If you weren't savvy enough to shop in the Bazaar, you shouldn't shop in the Bazaar. Taking the challenge out of it was approaching the problem from the wrong angle.

"I'm glad to see you! How did you get in to see me?"

"Oh," Tananda twinkled, with a grin at the guard, "I have my ways."

"I bet you do," I agreed, a trifle embarrassed, as she and Bunny exchanged sisterly winks.

Only one of Tananda's talents was being a successful Assassin. Another came from a Trollop's natural proclivities, and all I can say is that circumstances have always seemed to prevent me from finding out about them myself. I was grateful they'd managed to get in to see me, but troubled that she had had to do something like that to accomplish it.

"We are ostensibly your legal counsel," Zol told me, "but Mistress Tananda has managed to convince our escort to allow us privacy."

"I'm sorry if you had to...do anything to rescue me," I stammered, attempting to censor my thought in mid-speech.

I think I blushed. Tananda laughed and put her hand on my arm.

"Don't be. It was fun. You won't *believe* what they can do with those noses."

"I don't want to know!" I yelped. I glanced past them into the empty hall. "Where's Gleep?"

"Back on Wuh with Wensley," Bunny replied. "He's taken quite a fancy to the Wuhses. They've gotten over being afraid of him, I *think*. They pet him whenever he asks, they feed him treats, and they never scold him, even when he damages their houses."

"I'll bet he likes that," I groaned, wondering if they were undoing years of obedience training with their indulgence. "I *have* to get out of here."

"You bet, Tiger," Tananda agreed. She turned to the guard. "Now, give me the key."

Slowly, the big hand rose and deposited a huge iron key in her hand. She patted him on the cheek.

"Good! Now, go away and count to a thousand, and don't look! I'll come back again and find you again later. All right?"

"All right," the ravished-looking Scammie echoed.

He rotated slowly around and ambled toward the cell door. On the threshold he paused and looked longingly at Tananda. She shook her head and twiddled her fingers at him with a rueful smile. He let out a disappointed sigh, and shuffled off into the hallway.

"How can I get out of here?" I asked. I explained my problem with the judge. "You can't convince every guard to go count to a thousand."

"Can't I?" Tananda challenged me.

"No need," the little gray man interjected. "Scammies believe anything they are told, so all we have to do is convince them that the person leaving the building is not you."

"It'd be better if you didn't look like you," Bunny added, looking me thoughtfully up and down.

"The whole place is magik-proofed," I informed them. "They use a lot of magik in this dimension, and it's the only way they can avoid having jailbreaks. No disguise spell will work."

"No problem," she stated. She excused herself. In a few minutes she was back with an armload of rags. "Put these on," she said, holding out a shapeless skirt and blouse.

"Those are the cleaning lady's clothes," I observed.

"Good idea," Tananda grinned at Bunny. "No one ever notices the staff."

I was concerned. "She'll tell someone about the exchange."

"She's retiring," Bunny reassured me. "I gave her enough gold to buy a cottage. She's already on her way out of town. She threw in the bucket and mop for free."

As my distinguished counsel, Zol was permitted to depart from the building without trouble. The little gray man led Bunny and Tananda out of the prison and down to the street, where they waited at the far end of the bridge for me. All I had to do was potter my way along until I was past the magik barrier, go invisible, and leave this dimension forever—or until the memory of the riot faded away.

I fancied myself a pretty good actor. Once swathed in the cleaner's sorry rags, I bent my spine so all anyone could see was the top of my head scarf, and shoved the pail on its creaking wheels along the hallway with hands wrapped in strips of cloth so the color of my skin wasn't visible. My progress was slow, but I couldn't hurry. I had only been along this hallway once since my incarceration, but it wasn't hard to guess which way was out.

A Scammie with a court badge on his tunic passed me, whistling through his nose as he tossed a big key in the air and caught it. He was heading for my cell door! I continued my amble, picking up the pace as much as I dared. He passed me on the way back, shouting for the guards. My disappearance had been discovered. I ducked my face farther down into my blouse. I had to be careful. Moments later, a small troop hustled past, swords drawn, to investigate my empty cell. They started searching the immediate area, coming up with Tananda's "friend," whom they pulled out of the corner where he was hiding.

"Eight hundred ninety-six, eight hundred ninety-seven..."

"Where is he?" the others shouted.

The Scammie looked abashed.

"I dunno," he muttered.

"Find him!"

I was only yards from the exit now. A few more steps and I would be free.

"Hey, you!" a voice growled.

I froze. Had they seen through my disguise at last? My shoes were concealed under the hem of the skirt. Loud footsteps rang on the stone floor. I found myself looking down at a pair of guard-issue boots. A hand gestured to my left.

"Mandrilla, come over here! We've got a spill for you to wipe up."

I groaned to myself. Of all the rotten luck! I had no choice but to play along. They thought I was the cleaning lady. If I protested they might look closer at me. At the moment my disguise was fooling them. Walking at a tottery pace I trailed behind my guide, who stopped in front of a wide, carved door and drew his sword. I blanched, but he stepped up and opened the portal for me.

"Wine's on the ground over there," he pointed. I muttered something, and minced inside.

I almost turned and fled out of the room.

There was no disguising the smell. I had woken up near it or in the same building with it for years: the aroma of agitated Pervect. The Ten were here! Or, I counted, peering up through the frayed edge of the headscarf, eight of them. Big and green and scaly and...looking for me?

"This is almost funny," the eldest one in the flowered dress said, peering up at the judge. "You've got a witness, but he's not here. I suppose you have other evidence? If not, we've got other appointments, honey."

"The fact that he is not here is immaterial," Senior Domani blustered.

The Pervects weren't convinced. I wouldn't have been, either.

Something prodded me in the back. I nearly jumped through the ceiling.

"Go on, clean it up," the guard reminded me, shoving me toward a broken carafe and a pool of spilled wine on the table near the Pervects. "I'll protect you from them."

It was brave of him, because he didn't sound at all certain that he could. In fact, I was pretty certain he couldn't, magikless though they were at the moment.

"He did say he was a wizard, Senior," Officer Gelli reminded the judge. "If he's more powerful than our containment spells, he could have killed all of us. Instead he chose to warn us. And he did pay for the goggles he broke."

"And there's Bofus's statement, too," Officer Koblinz added, removing his everpresent notebook from his pocket.

"He claims to be an innocent dupe of these demons. He's given us every detail of how they approached him and convinced him to spread their instruments of evil."

"Yes, Bofus," Domari's eyebrows rose. The tone of his voice boded no good for Bofus, whoever he was. Growling from the Pervects informed me that if this Bofus escaped official punishment he had some coming from them. "This is a serious case, one that involves the well-being, and indeed the security of Scamaroni..."

Cautiously I approached the pool of wine, the creaking of my bucket's wheels covering the chattering of my knees. I couldn't let the Pervects see my face. I hauled the mop out, slapped it onto the floor and began swabbing up the mess.

The tallest Pervect, the one in the form-fitting camouflage coverall, drew her knees in as I bumped past. I caught a glimpse of her out of the corner of my eye. She still looked familiar to me. I must have met her on Perv, or seen her coming out of a restaurant at the Bazaar (if you think I'd ever have been *in* a Pervish restaurant, you've never smelled one). I sopped up most of the wine, then took a brush and pan off the back of the pail to sweep up the broken glass.

"You missed a lot of the liquid, dear," the Pervect informed me, pointing a manicured fingernail. "Look. It ran away toward the wall. It's going to stain the fringe of that tapestry." I nodded, and kept brushing. "Hey!"

"Silence!" Domari roared. "As a result, I order all of you to stand trial on multiple charges of malfeasance and misfeasance, mental assault on hundreds, if not thousands, of citizens of our fair nation..." The judge paused in the middle of his pronouncement to lean over his desk. "Mandrilla, what have you been rolling in?"

The guard with the drawn sword cleared his throat. "She's been cleaning up after that Klahd wizard, sir."

"Ugh. Well, when you're done here, Mandrilla, go home and take a bath."

I muttered and nodded as I wrung out the mop and slapped it down on the floor.

"You didn't get all the glass, either," the young Pervect told me. "Take a wet cloth and pick up the particles. Then you can mop it down. You're just spreading the shards all over the place."

"This is ruining *everything*," said the shortest Pervect. "What are we supposed to do now?"

"There are plenty of other dimensions," the female in khakis told her. "Be patient."

"A Klahdish wizard?" the elder Pervect said, in a low voice meant to be heard only by her companions. "A powerful wizard who's a *Klahd*? They barely have an adequate magician once in a thousand years. Have you heard of such a thing?"

"I think I have," the angry one on the end replied thoughtfully. "Stiff, Stiv, Smee...something like that."

"We'll have to have Caitlin research it when we get back," suggested the elegant female in a skirt suit.

Hearing them talk about me made me nervous. They didn't know who I was, but the police could identify me if my disguise slipped. My hand trembled, sending drops of wine all over. The female sprang to her feet as I narrowly missed her ankle.

"Oh, for Crom's sake, female! I've never seen such an inept job in my life! Give me that mop! I could do a better job than you in my sleep!"

"Sit down, madam!" the judge roared. "Let our employee finish her work."

"I could have cleaned your entire courtroom in the time it's taken her to make matters worse," the elegant Pervect snarled back.

"You may end up doing menial labor," Domari warned her. "Each of these charges carries a penalty of a period not less than thirty days in jail, to be served consecutively."

"What?"

The combined outrage of eight Pervects was enough to knock me off my feet. Hastily I finished wiping up the last of the spill, scrambled up, and creaked out of the courtroom. Behind me, all of them were on their feet shouting at the judge. My guard escorted me to the door, then closed it behind me. I could still hear their voices echoing as I walked in increasingly long strides out of the building. A guard at the entrance gave me a strange look.

"My vacation starts tonight!" I piped, in a high-pitched voice. I didn't have to simulate the aged tremble; I was still shaking from being that close to my nemeses. The guard nodded and went back to staring off into space.

Unless I was very wrong, the Pervect Ten, or eight of them, anyhow, were going to be in a magik-proofed jail for years! Wuh's problem was almost solved. We should be able to handle the remaining two. I had trouble restraining myself from dancing a little victory hop as I left the courthouse and tottered over the bridge to Bunny and the others.

Bunny and Tananda embraced me as I reached them. I hid behind a pillar to shed the cleaning lady's garments and straighten my own.

"You had better restore our appearance," Zol reminded me. The disguises had been knocked out by the anti-magik field inside the building, but were restored the moment we stepped outside its sphere of influence. That was a sophisticated spell.

It took a less than a moment for me to reach down to the line of power I'd been staring at for over a day, erase the faces of long-nosed Scammies and restore their features. It felt so good to be doing magik again!

"Nice work, handsome," Tananda remarked approvingly, looking at herself in the mirror of Bunny's PDA. "You ought to get locked up more often."

"No, thanks," I replied. "I did learn something about concentration, but it does me no good unless I can actually practice my techniques."

"Down with the outworlders! Death to demons!"

I glanced up the street. A vast crowd of Scammies had collected in front of the courthouse. "What's going on?"

"They're protesting the loss of the goggles," Zol replied. "They should not be. Such time-wasting nonsense keeps one from the pursuit of truth and beauty. It is good that they have been taken away."

"It's not good! What will I do?" a female asked, clutching at us as she made her way forlornly toward the protest group. "I have to have my story! I loved it! I lived it."

"You must learn to do without it, my dear," Zol told her soothingly, patting her hand. "It isn't safe to fill your mind with falsehood."

"But I liked it! Can't I just have it for a while?"

"Oh, you must wean yourselves away from it. You should be as you were before, true to yourself!"

"How?" a male demanded hoarsely. "How can we do that? How can we do without them?"

"Help us!" a female pleaded, clutching my arm. "I don't want to give it up!"

"You need to be strong!" the little gray man shouted, his thin voice almost swallowed by the woe of those around him. "Believe in yourselves! That is all you need to do! Rely upon one another!"

"He knows what he's talking about," I told the Scammies who lifted tear-stained faces to me. "That's Zol Icty, the self-help expert."

"Zol Icty!"

Desperate for any kind of comfort now that the Pervects' false vision had been taken away from them the crowd swelled in upon us. People shoved in close to me, shouting questions. They were so distraught they were crushing me. I used magik to open up a little space, but there were so many people I was hurting the ones nearest me. Bunny let out a yelp of distress. Hastily I grabbed her around the waist and swung her up onto the span of the bridge, then jumped up beside her.

"Advise us, wise strangers!" a Scammie pleaded, reaching for us.

The protest had attracted the attention of the people in the courthouse. Police officers came boiling out of the entrance. Officer Gelli spotted me and pointed.

"The wizard! After him!"

In my haste to get out of the crowd, I had accidentally placed myself in plain view. I pulled the D-hopper out of my boot and set it for Wuh.

"Tananda! Zol!" I cried. They glanced up. I pointed at the dozens of policemen racing towards us.

Down in the midst of the crowd I saw Tananda starting her bump-and-grind transportation charm. Zol, in the thick of everything, seemed perfectly calm. He tipped me a wink. Reassured, I pressed the stud.

The coolness of Wuh's pale-gray skies rushed in on me like a welcome splash of water. I gasped for air and let go of Bunny's hand. We were safe and sound in Montgomery's tavern. Tananda appeared next to us and brushed back her magnificent hair with both hands.

"That was just a little *too* cozy," Tananda articulated, shaking her shoulders, a movement that hypnotized me on the spot. "I prefer to be introduced before I get that close."

"You are back!" Wensley cheered, rising from the table in the corner. "You are saved from Durance Vile! I rejoice!"

Gleep, too, noticed our return. He sprang up and came hurtling toward me like a cannonball. After the delicious smells on Scamaroni, his stench hit me before he did. I went down on my back with him slurping my face. I gagged, but I was pleased, too. The Wuhses might have been spoiling him, but he missed *me*.

"That was a close call," I stated, climbing back on my feet. I wiped the slime off my face with my sleeve.

Gleep looked sad that I was disposing of his token of affection. I grabbed his head and scratched energetically around his ears. He slitted his eyes and let his body fall sideways to the floor in bliss.

"But where is Master Zol?" Wensley inquired.

# Chapter 17

*"The only thing dumber than sticking your head
in the lion's mouth is doing it twice."*
C. Bailey

"Uh-oh," I groaned. I looked around. The Kobold did not re-appear. We waited. And waited. "Uh-oh."

"Perhaps he went home," Bunny suggested. "We didn't clarify where we should meet."

Another long pause, during which we just couldn't seem to talk about anything.

"He must have gotten arrested," Tananda said at last.

"Uh-oh," I reiterated. I got to my feet. "All right. We'll have to go back for him."

"*You* can't," Tananda reminded me.

"I can if I wear a disguise and stay away from their magik dispellers," I pointed out. "We have to go get him. No one knows he broke any of those mindbending goggles. They only saw me. He's part of our company. You wouldn't leave me in jail; I can't abandon him."

"Bravo," Tananda applauded, patting her hands together softly. Bunny regarded me with affection.

"But what about the Pervects?" Wensley babbled, ner-vously. "It would seem to me, though perhaps I am not see-ing the big picture, that your attentions have focused them-selves, probably with justification, upon a different situa-tion. Not that Master Zol has not been a great help, but we still suffer from the effects of that government not of our own choosing."

"You don't have to worry about most of the Pervect Ten," I replied confidently. "Eight of them were arrested by the Scammies!"

"What?" Tananda and Bunny chorused.

I explained what had happened when they had gone on ahead of me. "...And it sounded like they are all going to be stuck in jail on Scamaroni for a long time. A *magik-proof* jail. I'm not saying it'll be easy to pry out the other two, but once they know eight of their number are doing time in another dimension, I don't see them staying around long. And even if they stay, they can hardly thwart the wishes of a whole nation. You can run rings around them."

"Oh, Master Skeeve!" Wensley gushed. "You...you are the most average wizard I have ever met!"

I frowned.

"That's a compliment," Bunny reminded me gently.

"I know," I sighed. "It just doesn't sound like one."

Magik-proof the Scamaroni jail and courthouse might be; damage resistant they were less so. Tananda and I had planned to sneak back by ourselves and liberate Zol, possibly enlisting the help of the guard she had, er, bribed, but Bunny insisted on going along.

We hid underneath the drawbridge until the foot traffic in the street thinned out in the wee hours of the morning. The guards on duty marched just above us. I was waiting for them to sit down so they wouldn't fall when we hit them with the Assassin sleeping spell that Tananda knew.

But they never settled down anywhere. I wouldn't have, either, if I had had to listen to the banging and pounding that was coming from inside the station. Loud shrieks rang out, only lightly muffled by the twelve-foot thick stone walls.

"The Pervects aren't taking incarceration calmly, are they?" Bunny whispered to me.

Wham! The wall just overhead shook, as if a dragon had slammed into it. Male voices joined in the cacophony.

"Shut up or we'll chain you up!" a guard yelled.

"You and what army?" shrilled a female voice.

"Police brutality!" bellowed another.

"Let us out, or we'll let ourselves out!"

"Never! The Volute Jail has never had a successful escape!" a male announced proudly, but the sentence ended in a hesitation. After all, had I not departed unexpectedly only that day?

The footsteps overhead became more agitated by the moment.

"We're never going to get rid of them," Tananda murmured.

"Sure we will," I assured. "They're afraid of a jailbreak. We'll give them one."

From my long, slow promenade that afternoon I knew every inch of that drawbridge. It was no trouble at all to create the illusion of two heavily armed female Pervects dropping heavily to the stone path from above the door, then running down the bridge toward the town.

The effect on the sentries was electric.

"They're getting away!" one yelled. "Raise the alarm! Two of the Perverts got out!" Sprinting footsteps pattered away into the distance, along with the faint yellow light of the glowing torches they'd grabbed off the wall sconces.

"What? What?" came from inside. But the two guards were already in pursuit of my illusion. I listened carefully. The sentries' alarm had spread. Within moments, a troop of guards and police officers raced out and down into the street, following their fellow guards' lights.

Tananda grinned at me as she swung a hook over the side of the bridge. I levitated, pulling Bunny with me by her wrists. I lowered her lightly until her toes touched down, then swung in as far as I could into the darkened doorway. We all alit without noise, and tiptoed in.

As soon as we crossed the threshold I felt the chill sensation of the dampening spell. It didn't render me physically cold, but it stripped away from me all connection with the natural energy lines, something I'd come to associate with heat. As Aahz had trained me to, I had filled up my inner reservoir with as much power as I could hold, though it would do me no good in here.

The false escape had thrown the building into chaos. Half-dressed guards with veins showing in their protuberant brown eyes and their hair still mussed from sleep yanked on uniform tunics as they ran up and down the halls. No one seemed to know what he or she was doing. Following Tananda's lead, we flitted from shadow to shadow, ducking out of the sight of the hurrying guards. We made our way back to the cells.

Where I heard banging and yelling I knew I would not find our Kobold. I tiptoed to the first quiet door I could find and leaned close to the crack at the bottom.

"Zol?" I whispered.

"Who is that?" a voice bellowed from across the hall. The banging ceased for a moment. "*Who's out there?*"

I should have realized how keen Pervects' hearing was. "Zol, are you in there?" I repeated.

No answer. I heard a hiss, and looked up. Tananda was clinging to the keystone arch above the cell door. Bunny was perched on a rafter over her head. Tananda offered me a hand and helped me swing up just in time to avoid a patrol of three Scammies striding in, carrying lit torches.

"Prisoner check!" announced the lead guard, though he looked as though he'd rather face wild spider-bears buck naked. They started to insert the key in the first lock. A thundering blow from the other side shook the door so much the key almost hopped out.

"You let me out of here at once!" It was the eldest female. "You boys are going to be sorry you mistreated an old lady! When I tell your mothers what you've been up to...!" She left the threat unfinished, but it had its desired effect. The guards trembled and moved back. The sergeant, sweating, pulled the key out.

"That one's secure," he told them. They moved nervously along to the next cell.

By this time the other Pervects had heard the footsteps in the hallway. They were all clamoring to get out, threatening the guards with dire physical harm. I paid attention to the cells that the guards didn't visit. Either those were empty, or they contained non-Pervect prisoners.

Boom! Crash! Screech! The noise was the ideal cover as we went from one quiet cell to another. Once the guards had gone we were able to split up. In a few moments we met in a doorway.

"I don't hear him," Tananda whispered. "I don't think he's here."

"Where would they be keeping him?" Bunny asked.

We were interrupted by a bright *Prring!* like a doorbell being rung. Sudden silence descended. We all looked at one another. Wide-eyed with alarm, Bunny clapped one hand over her mouth, and the other over Bytina, in the pouch at her waist. The PDA had made that noise.

I didn't have time to chide Bunny for not telling the little computer to be quiet. Suddenly, the entire building burst into life. The Pervects started pounding on their cell doors again. Shouting erupted all around us. We may not have had access to magik, but we flew out of the cell block and headed toward the exit.

Luckily the confusion prevented anyone from paying close attention to us. Scammies ran up and back with torches, stopping one another at sword's point, and diving in and out of doorways. Whenever a section of hallway emptied, we traversed it, hiding in pools of shadow. The entrance, whose threshold I never thought I would have to cross again in my life, loomed up ahead of us. Beyond it, the sky was lightening. Morning had broken. An apron of light was just beginning to spread down the hall. Would we reach it?

As we were scurrying along the last few yards, a huge shadow loomed up in front of us. I froze. There was nowhere to hide. We'd been discovered. Any moment now, the guard would shout out the alarm, and this time we would all be locked in a cell next to the Pervects.

"Scootie!" Tananda squealed, throwing herself into the guard's arms.

"Tananda," the guard replied, torn between pleasure and embarrassment.

"Where have you been?" she asked, gesturing behind her back for us to keep moving. "I've been looking for you."

"Uh, I can't now," Scootie said, nervously. "We had an escape. Uh…I'm not supposed to say anything about that."

"Oh, I wouldn't tell," Tananda promised him, cuddling close. "You're so brave, chasing prisoners. I bet they were armed and dangerous!"

"Uh, not exactly…" We tiptoed behind the Scammie, whose entire attention was being commanded by Tananda.

"Scootari!"

"Uh, I gotta go," Scootie pleaded, extricating himself with some difficulty.

"Oh, must you?" Tananda cooed. By this time we were outside, plastered against the wall just beyond the door. I threw an illusion on myself and Bunny to make us look like the missing sentries. Tananda came sauntering out.

"Let's go," she chirped, straightening her belt and tidying her hair. "He couldn't stay."

I gave Tananda a Scammie face to wear, too, and added the flower-smell illusion that had initially kept us from discovery. The three of us found a quiet corner table in a local café to get some breakfast. I sat with my back to the wall, keeping an eye on the interplay in the room. The whole town was frantic about the purported escape of prisoners from the jail.

"I heard a wizard vanished out of the building, right in front of the judge," a female said, pouring opaque, pale blue liquid into her morning cup. She spooned yellow crystals in, and stirred the resulting green soup with a narrow metal stick, the local equivalent of a spoon that would fit into the small round mouths.

"I heard it was three of them, all green and scaly!" a big male exclaimed.

"That makes four," calculated the table server, a slender male in his early years. "That's almost an army."

"An army escaped?" asked an old female, coming in the door. "Preserve us! An army of demons!" She backed out of the door and scurried away as fast as her feeble legs would carry her.

I shook my head over my plate. These people really *would* believe anything. I was partly to blame for the mass hysteria brewing. I meant to undo as much of the damage as I could, but first we had to find Zol.

Bunny arranged herself with her back to the rest of the room, and opened up Bytina. She tilted the little magik mirror so the two of us could see it, too: there was one handsome parchment envelope visible on the desktop. In a twinkling Bunny tapped both forefingers onto the hand-shaped button.

"I shall be delayed quite a bit, dear Bunny," the message read. "I don't know if you are cross-dimensionally enabled, so you may not get this immediately. I hope you will not be too worried about me. As soon as I can get free I will rejoin you." The ornate signature was already familiar to me from the flyleaf of Zol's book.

"He's still got his notebook." Bunny breathed a sigh of relief.

"But where is he being held?" I asked.

"I don't know. How can we find him?"

Tananda aimed a fingernail at Bytina. "Does it ...or, should I say, *she*... have any ideas?"

"Do you, sweetie?" Bunny asked, stroking the little device with her fingertip.

Apparently she did. A blank correspondence card appeared in the center of the mirror. A long, fluffy quill dropped into view, dipped itself into an inkwell, and wrote upon the creamy whiteness, "Where are you?" The pen and ink vanished, and the card slid into an envelope marked "To Zol Icty." The sealed letter dropped out of sight, leaving the mirror blank. The PDA hummed as though it was proud of itself. Bunny petted it some more.

"Isn't she clever?" my assistant beamed. I rolled my eyes.

We were in the middle of a second round of doughnuts and hot drinks when the ringing sound came that we had learned to associate with engraved messages being delivered to Bytina. Bunny opened the little compact. We all crowded around the tiny mirror to see what it had received.

It wasn't a message. Instead, Zol's pale oval face looked at us out of the mirror. "Oh, how fortunate to see all three of you," he exclaimed. "I am here on Scamaroni."

"So are we," I replied, relieved that he looked well and unharmed, though there were deep circles around his huge dark eyes. "We're in a café just off the main street, about three blocks from the jail."

"I can't come to you right now," the little gray man responded, with a shake of his head. "I'm afraid I'm tied up."

"Tied up!" I echoed, ready to spring to my feet. "Well, we're here to rescue you. What kind of vile dungeon have they got you imprisoned in?"

There was a long pause, while Zol's whole face twisted strangely. I glanced at Bunny to see if Bytina was causing it to distort. It was a moment before he answered me.

"Good friend Skeeve, I think you misunderstand my circumstances, though I am proud that you have my best interests in mind. I must clarify: I cannot leave my present location because I have quite a number of people who need my services. Perhaps you can join me?"

I must have goggled. Bunny grabbed Bytina out of my hands. "Where?" she demanded.

"I'm in an open-air café down by the river, running a group encounter session to help wean the Scammies from those evil goggles. If you walk sunward from the corrections facility bridge, you will soon see me."

"Sure," I agreed, faintly puzzled. We paid our bill, then followed his directions.

# Chapter 18

*"Finding yourself takes a long time,*
*and costs a lot of money."*
S. Freud

Cresting the top of a hill on the street that led away from the jail, I could not immediately spot Zol Icty. There was too much of a crowd. Down near the small bistro were a thousand or more Scammies. They were all sitting or lying down on the blue-green grass on the bank, facing the center, where our little gray man sat at a table furnished with a tea pot, a cup and saucer, and lofty stacks of his latest book. Every one of the audience members seemed to be in a blissful trance, smiling vacantly. The thin voice of our companion rose and fell in a sing-song tone. The heads nodded in unison when he spoke.

"...Once you have really looked inside yourself and know who you really are, you can begin to understand the wonder that is you. You need no artificial stimulants or devices to enhance the very you-ness of you. You have but to face your reality, and be satisfied with it. It doesn't matter if your acquaintances have riches or opportunities that you lack—you have your identity, your uniqueness, and that is more precious than gold, more interesting than any false storyteller. Be true to yourselves."

Eyelids fluttering, Bunny let out a huge sigh. Groaning, I led my friends down toward Zol. If there was anything more painful than realizing his advice was off-kilter, it was listening to his mumbo-jumbo. In my opinion it was the verbal equivalent of illusions, disguising the reality underneath. But people seemed to respond to it. The rapt expressions were as fixed as anything I'd seen in hypnosis subjects.

Halfway down the slope I noticed that the site was surrounded by dozens of police officers. I skirted them nervously.

They, too, were smiling contentedly. I spotted Officers Gelli and Koblinz. They saluted me pleasantly when I caught their eye. I knew they could not recognize me in my disguise, but it made me nervous all the same. They, too, had become true to themselves once again. I couldn't wait for Zol to finish autographing copies of his book so we could get out of Scamaroni for good, and leave our problems behind—or at least 80% of them.

"Madam," Senior Domari repeated wearily, "we cannot produce that witness. I know you want to confront him. You can't. Now, I ask you again to explain how it is that two of your number escaped from this facility last night, but there were still eight of you in the cells this morning?"

"Sonny," Vergetta countered, "All I want to do is go home. What'll it take?"

"I wish I could pitch all of you into a bottomless pit, but I am required to follow the rule of law."

"Pitch us! It'd be better than spending another night in your pokey! I've been more comfortable in college dormitories!"

"Perverts," the judge muttered.

"Pervects," Vergetta corrected him. "We have a right to be addressed properly, your honor."

"I'm not sure the word doesn't apply," Domari retorted. "I've heard some ugly things about Perverts."

"It's an ugly universe," Vergetta replied philosophically. "You don't want us staying here, judge. Look at the condition of your jail. And if we can slip in and out of here without detection, well, you can't keep us here against our will."

That statement made the judge even more nervous. "Then why are you still here?"

"Because we want to reassure you that we're law-abiding beings. You've heard a lot of other things about Pervects, right? Don't tell me you haven't. I can tell by your face. Let's come to some kind of agreement. I know you'd really like to settle this. So would we."

Senior Domari picked up his stack of papers and began to straighten them again. Vergetta knew she shouldn't harass him any more. The poor boy was at the end of his patience, but so was she. She had too many questions, and no one knew the answers. Who were the two Pervects that had been spotted running away last night? Niki and Caitlin wouldn't have run away if you'd shoved a basilisk in their faces. She hoped they hadn't tried a stupid rescue. Their job was to stay on Wuh and keep the stupid sheep from bankrupting all of them in her absence. But who was responsible for landing them in jail in the first place? Who was out to destroy their reputation? Who had come in, unprovoked, and messed up their deal so their harmless little toy was considered to be the most dangerous thing since the do-it-yourself landmine kit?

The most puzzling thing was how a Klahd had gotten a hold of a pair of their goggles. It had turned up in the cell that had been vacated by the only real jailbreak. Monishone assured her that no units had ever gone to Deva or Klah. Paldine had been convinced at first that someone had created a knockoff and was planning to steal their market, but this pair was one of theirs.

"I must ask you again, er, ladies, which two of you led the patrol on a merry chase all over town early this morning, and then broke into the jail again. And why?"

None of them knew the answer to that question, but the Ten would be damned if they would let an outsider know they didn't know.

"Just a demon-stration, your honor," Vergetta offered, a broad grin breaking out over her face.

"A demonstration?" Domari echoed.

"Of course! We're demons, right? So...never mind," she averted the subject hastily, when the judge showed no signs of getting the joke.

The others glanced at her, but she gave them a hasty wave as if to say, *Leave the talking to me, girls. We can use this.*

"Look, your little prison might hold Scammies, and it ought to hold scam-*mers*, if you understand what I'm saying, but I'd like to point out that you couldn't keep a Klahd wizard behind bars for even one night, and believe me when I tell you darlink, that after another night or so those walls aren't going to hold *us* any longer. And look at the evidence: we can come and go as we please. So why don't you just let us leave? I promise you from the bottom of my heart, that when we go you will never see any of us again. Ever."

The judge looked genuinely tempted. Vergetta could tell that she was beginning to get through to him. She hoped so; it had been an exhausting time, staying up all night bashing at the walls. She wasn't as young as she used to be. It was one thing for young Charilor, who went out partying for a week, then could come home fresh as a daisy and beat up a neighboring army, but for the older folks it was tougher. She hoped the judge's resolve wasn't as durable.

Domari cleared his throat. "It's...just not that simple, madam. There's the matter of the psychological harm that you may have caused to the population. When you have an expert of the magnitude of Zol Icty himself condemning your device, it becomes quite a serious situation. So many of our fine people have required virtual deprogramming to return to their normal lives..."

"Psychobabble!" Oshleen protested.

"Psycho-what?"

The slender Pervect rose to her feet, giving a raised eyebrow to Vergetta. The elder female handed off the talking stick without protest. Oshleen had obviously come up with a good wrinkle on her own.

"It's nonsense. It's clear that he has no faith at all in your citizenry. In their mental resilience. I mean, look at the wonderful device—you admitted that you tried it and enjoyed it yourself. How could we, as honest merchants, have believed you could not tell the difference between fantasy and reality? You're smarter than that," she added, in her most persuasive voice. Oshleen undulated forward, as far as her chains would let her. "He's the one you ought to arrest."

"I...I can't do that." But Oshleen had gotten him so confused that he didn't know what to think. "What surety will you give to remain away from Scamaroni forever? Besides refunding the money to our honest citizens for the goggles."

"Refunding the money...?" All of them gasped at once.

The judge looked at them impassively. "Unless you wish to remain in our slowly deteriorating jail for the duration of your potential sentences. And after the last few days, I am inclined to hand out maximum sentences. I will allow you to confer."

He smacked his gavel on the desk, and retired from the courtroom.

The Pervects put their heads together. "We can't do that," Loorna hissed to the others. "It'll eat up all of our remaining resources."

"Which would you rather have, our resources or our liberty?" Charilor countered, then stopped herself with a grimace. "What am I saying? Never mind...but we weren't the ones who were running around town last night! We *can't* come and go as we please. They just think we can."

"We can recoup our losses in some other dimension," Monishone argued. "We'll take the intact pairs elsewhere."

"There aren't that many intact pairs," Paldine retorted. "There's no chance of getting our investment out, not when Zol Icty himself has condemned the goggles. The word will spread faster than a dance craze. We're stuck. There are very few dimensions where a toy like that will pass the marketing research test."

Vergetta set her face grimly. "We have no choice. Someone has left us with only one option, and if I ever get my hands on that someone, I have a use for all those broken sets of goggles, bubbies, and I don't mean making a mosaic."

Paldine sighed. "I'll handle the negotiations."

It took longer than a day for Zol to finish his encounter session. Bunny, Tananda and I sat at his feet throughout the process. By the time his audience finally cleared the meadow beside the river I had a new respect for my hired expert.

He managed to prove to me that you can sell a million books by convincing people that there was something wrong with them, and that they can only solve the problem by reading the book. When Zol spoke in that calming manner of his, he made it sound as though the problem was minor, and they could fix it themselves by following the guidelines that he laid out. He put the most positive possible spin on their struggle, promising them that even if they didn't see quick results that they were still on the right path. No wonder he was famous throughout all the dimensions. There wasn't a thinking being alive who deep down didn't feel fundamentally flawed. Zol tapped into that feeling, but he persuaded them that it was okay.

On the other hand, he was genuinely good at picking up the traits that a race largely shared. He told the Scammies that they were too gullible for their own good, falling for the most convincing story or the newest toy. But then he sold them copies of his latest book.

What bothered me was that he didn't see anything remotely hypocritical about that. I honestly think he did believe in his own advice, and a practical way always to have it on hand was to own the book. I wondered what he would say was wrong with Kobolds.

The final book was at long last signed. We were left in a meadow of trampled grass. Zol drained his teacup and set it daintily on the saucer.

"Thank you," he told to the proprietor of the café. "It was good of you to lend us your establishment for such an extended session. I hope we didn't inconvenience you too greatly."

The restauranteur, looking exhausted but still dazzled, pumped his hand. "It's been an honor, sir. An honor! Zol Icty, in my café!"

He shook hands with all of us. I noticed that his staff of three were sprawled in chairs against the wall. No pastries or sandwiches remained under the glass domes, and the huge containers of the local lemonade, tea, coffee and milkshakes had long ago been emptied. They hadn't lost a thing by having a famous author descend upon them for an impromptu shrink-fest.

Zol paid his own tea bill, over the protest of the café owner, and blipped us all back to Wuh.

The *bamf* of our return brought Gleep running from the stables, where he must have been taking a nap.

"Gleep!" he cried joyfully.

I managed to fend him off before he knocked me over. Zol petted him and produced a few bags of Kobold snacks out of his satchel for him. Gleep settled down on the floor to crunch up the shiny packets.

I looked around. Montgomery's inn seemed to be completely vacant. Not one of the tables underneath the ferns was occupied. The lights behind the bar had been extinguished. I glanced out into the street. It was devoid of Wuhses.

"Hello?" I called.

Tananda frowned. "Is something wrong?"

"Where is everyone?" Bunny said.

Gleep's pointed ears perked up. In a moment, I heard the noise that his more sensitive hearing had detected: the sound of footsteps rushing towards us. Down the stairs came Montgomery, the innkeeper. He rushed towards us with arms extended.

"I am overjoyed to see you!" he exclaimed, embracing us all one at a time. "Welcome back, Master Zol," he greeted the author shyly. "We are very glad that you are safe."

"You are very kind," Zol beamed. "It was a productive trip, I must say. So many minds cleared! And how have things been here?"

"Exciting, if I may use so bold a term," Montgomery hesitated, glancing at us for permission.

"Okay by me. Where's Wensley?" I asked.

"Oh, we didn't know when you were coming back, good Masters and Mistresses, or they would have waited for you."

"Waited for us for what?" I inquired curiously.

Montgomery's fat cheeks shone with emotion. "The revolution, Master Skeeve!"

"The *what?*"

"Wensley was so very impressed, sir, as were we all, at the way you went to save people in a dimension that you didn't even know, and how you went back again at the risk of your own safety to save Master Zol—just like that!—when you saw that he was in trouble. Well, I have to say that we were ashamed. Wensley called a mass secret meeting, sir, and spoke as how we ought to take more of a hand in our own defense. He was very strong on the subject of non-cooperation. Now that only two Perverts are still in the castle he thought that it was time we take action, sir! And so many people agreed with him! I agreed with him, but he pointed out that I had to wait for you..."

"Action?" I interrupted him. "What kind of action?"

Montgomery drew himself up proudly. "Wensley says behooves us to make an attempt to wrest the leadership of our people out of their claws, er, hands."

"He's been fomenting a revolution?" Zol asked.

"Well...yes."

"Good for you!" Zol exclaimed.

"WAIT A MOMENT!" I shouted. "Just exactly what kind of action does Wensley have in mind?"

"Why, they're going to go in there, and throw out those two Perverts," Montgomery explained, as if surprised that I didn't understand. "Should be easy as pie, now that there's only two of them."

My tongue went dry, and I realized that my mouth was hanging open. "Where are they?" I demanded.

Montgomery peered at the timepiece on the mantel. "Oh, I suppose they'd be up at the castle about now."

"No! They'll be killed!" Bunny gasped.

"But there's only two of them, against thousands of us," Montgomery replied, hurt.

"That's like saying there's only two tornadoes," I retorted. "We've got to go stop them."

We gathered up Gleep and raced toward the castle, leaving our puzzled host behind us. As soon as we were out of the door I took to the air. Flying is controlled levitation, pushing against solid objects with my mind to move me along. I lifted Bunny and carried her along with me. Zol and Tananda took to the air under their own power. Gleep dashed ahead. We had no time to waste.

"Perhaps we should have taken Wensley with us to Scamaroni," Zol mused, as we flew. "We could have advised him on the sensibility of confronting Pervects directly."

"I wanted to take him," I pointed out with some asperity. "but you persuaded me not to."

"Heavens, you are right," Zol replied, surprised. "This is all my fault. Wuhses are such followers normally. I underestimated him. He adapted to a positive example much more strongly than I thought he would. And he was behaving in such a threatened fashion that I feared it would do him more harm to be thrust into a new situation. I did not take into account the effect new stimuli might have on him when he was left behind in a venue he considered to be safe. You are a catalyst, Master Skeeve. You're making a leader out of him. He has gathered followers of his own."

"And now he's leading them into a bloodbath," I growled.

"But the threat *is* limited," Zol pointed out, as Gleep rebounded off the corner of a candy shop to turn into the main street.

My mind more on what I might find ahead than what I was doing, I narrowly missed the edge of the same building.

"It is possible for a group of that size to overpower a pair of Pervects. It is not as though they were at their full strength." Zol insisted.

"But they don't know what they're doing," Tananda reminded him, grimly. 'I don't think even Wensley has a real plan."

"Then we must persuade them to retreat and reconsider their actions!"

"We have to get them to get out of there before they get hurt," I declared.

We rounded the last corner until we could at last see the castle. As Montgomery had predicted, thousands of Wuhses were marching through the unguarded gate. Some carried flaming torches. They were all shouting.

"Baaa-aaad Pervects! Baaa-aaad Pervects! Go home! Go home! Go home!"

A green face with bat-wing ears appeared in the window of the Pervect Ten's headquarters. A shower of rocks came flying up from the crowd and spattered against the castle wall. The face withdrew hastily. I thought I saw Wuhses in the room behind her.

Suddenly, I felt as though someone had yanked my stomach and dragged it down through my toes. I fell heavily to the ground. Bunny dropped on top of me.

"Skeeve!" she squealed.

"I didn't do it," I protested. "The magik is gone!"

A great disturbance was brewing in the energy lines above and beneath me, draining them of power. I had felt this sensation before, but I didn't want to believe that it could possibly be what it was: the Pervect Ten pooling their strength, drawing on an incredibly deep well of magik.

There was a huge flash of light. When it cleared, the thousands of Wuhses marching and chanting in the courtyard had vanished without a trace. The street was silent.

I groaned, overwhelmed with grief at the tragic and unnecessary loss of life.

"They're back."

# Chapter 19

*"You say you want a revolution?"*
N. Lenin

"That's it!" Vergetta howled, dropping the hands of the two Pervects on either side of her. "I can't stand it any longer! I did not need this on top of just getting out of jail. *Everyone's* grounded. No exceptions!"

"What the hell brought that on?" Niki wondered, taking a quick glance out of the window. The spell had worked. The street was empty of life.

"You're the ones who let the place go to hell while we were gone," Paldine accused her. "Why don't you tell *us.*"

Niki gawked at her. "*We* let it go to hell? Did it really take all eight of you to find out that you'd laid an egg in that other dimension? A few of you could have stayed here and helped keep order. But *no-o-ooo.* You left two of us—*two of us*—having to play hall monitor for an entire country, and *now* look what we had to do!"

"Those intruders must have been watching us," Tenobia grunted. "Look how they knew to come in with us to avoid being toasted by the barrier spell. They've been planning this for a while."

Loorna kicked a pile of papers that had been cast to the floor by the invaders. "This place is a mess! It doesn't look like they have dusted in here in days."

"Well, sure," Niki snarled defensively, "I could have been cleaning up in here, if I didn't have to oversee the distribution of merchandise in the morning, monitor factory operations all day, and still have time to work on special projects. That's why we have all those janitors!"

"Did it ever occur to you you're complaining about the color of the dragon's nail polish just before the paw comes down and smashes your worthless carcass into a grease stain? Those janitors just facilitated an attempted palace coup," Tenobia reminded them.

"That's right, girls," Nedira soothed, trying to make peace. "We have bigger problems than dusty bookshelves."

"This is totally lame," Caitlin snorted, sitting down at her computer and tapping in the data off the sheet Oshleen handed her. "I mean, you didn't make a single gold piece on the whole Scamaroni enterprise. You lost all of our investment!"

"Give your elders more respect, dear," Nedira corrected her. "We were up against unfair opposition."

"Yes, the Klahdish wizard," Vergetta grumbled. "The one who really escaped."

"Did anyone get his name?" Tenobia asked. Oshleen reached down into her cleavage and pulled out a sheaf of papers.

"I always knew you stuffed. What's that?"

"The court docket," the accountant replied, with a haughty stare. "They wouldn't let Paldine see it. We'll send it back when we're through with it."

"I can't read this merde," Loorna sneered. "It's in Scammie."

"Ugh," Oshleen groaned. "I knew we should have bribed the bailiff. He could have read it to us."

Caitlin waved an imperious hand. "Give it to me. I'll run it through the translator." The smallest Pervect spread the papers out in front of her screen and typed in a command. The computer started humming. In a moment a huge rectangle projected itself upon the wall. "There."

"Smee, Smee," Niki mused, running down the names that appeared in the document during the target dates. "There's a Glee here, a Skeeve, and a Paneer."

"Cheesy," smirked Tenobia.

"Save the cheap jokes. So, which one is our wizard?"

"We heard of a Skeeve when we were on Deva," Vergetta offered. "But we heard he's retired. What would he be doing on Scamaroni?"

"No idea," Loorna rejoined. "What the hell, we're out of there now. We'll just have to pick up where we left off, pay our suppliers and start over." Niki snorted. "What?"

"You have no idea what's been going on since you left," the scientist growled.

"I notice that this place is a mess," Charilor taunted.

"Eat a bomb. We can't pay our suppliers. While you were out the stupid sheep have been in and out of this place every damned day, sneaking out money and goods. They've been on a buying spree that you would not believe."

"Oh, now what have they brought back this time?" Nedira groaned.

"You name it," Caitlin innumerated, having her computer flash more pictures up on the wall. "One day a clothing fad: genuine fur socks. Poorly tanned, I might add. They'll start stinking any time now, maybe even before the novelty wears off. Then, the very next day everybody had to have shutterbug viewers. And today Niki's been confiscating flight candy. If there was anything more annoying than Wuhses, flying Wuhses is it."

Vergetta nodded. "And they've been ripping us off to pay for them."

"All but today," Niki replied. "I finally took what was left of the treasury and stuffed it in the safe."

Paldine sneered. "You should have done that the first time."

"No, I should not have done that the first time," Niki disagreed. "You know what goes in that safe never goes away. You can always get it back again by reaching in to where you put it. Whoever invented it was a Pollyanna who believed everybody in the universe was honest. If the Wuhses knew that this chunk of change could be resurrected every single time it was spent they'd be committing grand larceny all over the dimensions, and I won't be responsible for that."

Vergetta sighed. "I can't disagree with you. So, now what? We're further in the hole than we were before. We don't want debt collectors showing up looking for payment we can't give them. Like it or not we are responsible for setting these fools straight, finding another source of cash, and stopping up the holes once and for all."

"Now will you believe me when I say we need to get that D-hopper away from them?" Loorna asked.

The elder held up her hands in mock surrender. "All right, all right! You were right and I was wrong. Get it."

Loorna grinned. "That will be my pleasure."

"Anyone have any ideas for our next business venture?" Vergetta asked the room.

"Oh, come on!" Paldine protested. "We just got out of jail! Who can innovate under those circumstances?"

"Honey, we've got to hit the ground running," the elder female urged. "We've had setbacks, sure, but I don't want to be stuck here forever."

"Besides," Niki smirked, "*I* wasn't in jail. I *have* been working. What do you think of this?"

With a flourish she reached under the big table and produced a palm-wide cylinder with a plunger on top.

"Signature chop?" Monishone asked.

"Half right," Niki grinned, hitting the knob on the top. Businesslike little blades dropped out of a concealed midsection. "It chops. It purees. It mixes. Put it down on top of raw food and it makes a meal out of it. Automatic safety doors so idiots can't stick their fingers in the blades or the heating element."

"Technology?" Monishone snorted.

"Don't knock it. I think it'd sell in more places than your stupid toy. It doesn't use electricity, it doesn't need magikal energy to run. All power is provided by piezoelectric contacts. It's very simple technology. Even a moderately smart monkey can operate it."

"So the Wuhses will have no trouble making them?" Charilor said, pointedly.

"The one thing I can't fault these sheep on is manual dexterity," Niki assured them. "We've got the capacity for mass production. I've already had our concealed shop stop making the glasses. Crom knows what we'll do with six thousand un-sold units. We can't break them down *en mass*. The magik re-leased would probably blow up the castle. We were lucky there were no accidents on Scamaroni."

"We'll find something to do with them," Vergetta assured them. "If we have to let them go at a loss to the Deveels, well, that's life."

"In the meantime, we need to make it a priority to find that damned D-hopper!" Loorna ordered.

"All in favor?" Vergetta asked, putting up her hand. "Ten in favor. None opposed. The motion carries. Go get 'em, ladies!"

"What about the Wuhses?" Nedira inquired, concerned.

Vergetta waved a hand. "They're fine. Every single one of them got blipped back to his or her home. About now they're discovering that they can't get out the door, the win-dow, or even up the chimney. They can all sit in tonight and think of their sins. Tomorrow morning the magik seal will release, and the Wuhses will be free to go to work as usual. The minute they're back home again, wham!" She smacked her palms together. "They don't go home, they find them-selves there anyhow. A few nights of early curfew might re-mind them that they've got responsibilities, too, so they should act like adults and stop getting in our way. As for their bellwether," she raised a clear glass globe off the table and shook it, causing the small object inside to go tumbling through the liquid that filled the interior, "he's going to spend his time-out with us for a while."

Sadly, Zol, Tananda, Bunny and I returned to the inn. Gleep's drooping ears and scales pretty much defined the mood of all of us. We were in complete and utter shock. I was numb. I kept tripping over paving stones, never even feeling the bruises on my legs and shins.

"I never thought they'd react so brutally to a challenge," Zol repeated for the sixth time. "It's...genocide. Wiping out a crowd of protesters so callously, well, it just goes to prove that I know very little about Pervects. I can see why other races do refer to them once in a while as Perverts."

"I'm almost ready to call them that myself," I agreed, hardly able to believe what I had seen. "Poor Wensley!"

"Maybe he got the D-hopper back," Bunny suggested. "Maybe he just blipped out of here." But she didn't sound as though she believed it.

"Who's going to explain to Montgomery what just happened?" Tananda asked.

I straightened up. "It's my job. Wensley hired me to come in and help him. I'll have to inform his fellow committee heads." I sighed. "I should have listened to Aahz. He told me that I was out of my league on this mission. He was right. I wish he was here."

"You did the best you could," Bunny assured me, coming up to take my arm. "Wensley did this on his own. You didn't tell him to, and you weren't here when he made his plans. Look at it this way: what would Uncle Bruce do if one of his lieutenants went off and got himself killed because he was underprepared?"

"I suppose he'd still pay for the funeral," I offered glumly.

"I doubt it," Bunny retorted crisply, though her large eyes were full of tears. "But I'm sorry for Wensley."

"It was a hero's passing," Zol intoned solemnly.

Montgomery was cleaning glasses behind the bar when we entered. "Evening, Masters and Mistresses," he greeted us blithely. "I wouldn't presume to tell you your business, but may I suggest a nice glass of wine, or something stronger? If I looked like one of you, I'd tell myself that I needed it."

"We do," I agreed, sliding into the booth that we had more or less come to regard as our own. "Master Montgomery, I don't really know where to start. We have some bad news for you. The revolution..."

"...Went all wrong," the innkeeper finished for me. "I know it. Ragstone, my potboy, told me all about it."

I peered at him, wondering if I had heard him incorrectly. "It went worse than 'all wrong,'" I stated. "It was a total failure. There were no survivors. Where was Ragstone watching from?"

"Oh, he was in the thick of things," Montgomery declared.

"He was on the drawbridge?" I asked.

"He was up the stairs on the way to the Pervects' big room," Montgomery replied, looking around at all of our puzzled faces. "He said they never had a chance. One minute he was about to break down a door with my best barrel-rolling stave, and the next minute there's a big flash of light and he's back here."

"Here?" I echoed.

"Aye, in his room. Which he shares with Coolea, my stable lad. Both of 'em as puzzled as a crossword. You've never seen such faces," the innkeeper chuckled.

"They're alive?" I demanded. "But we thought the Pervects had killed them all."

"I bet the boys wondered if they was dead," Montgomery grinned. "Finding themselves at home looking at the ceiling. We're all surprised, too. I thought like you did, that they might put down armed resistance with force, but maybe the Pervects are more merciful on us poor misguided souls than we would've been on them."

Zol's eyes danced. "This is more material for my study," he asserted eagerly, pulling out his notebook and tapping in several lines. "What a fascinating turn of events."

"And your employees weren't harmed at all," I pressed Montgomery.

"Well, except none of 'em can go out and about. I was right surprised to see you come in. I thought it didn't work. We've all tried to go out, but it's as if there's no door there."

"That," Tananda announced, once we had all gotten over the shock, "is one powerful group of magicians. Two couldn't have done such a mass working by themselves. Not even ten of them could have. What we saw them do the other day to combine their power has to be unique. I feel outgunned and outclassed."

"And yet they temper their actions with mercy," Zol muttered, writing furiously. "Intriguing."

I thought for a moment. "It doesn't sound like mercy so much as a warning. They don't want to destroy their workforce. They'd have to train thousands of new Wuhses to do the work."

"But what about our revolution?" Montgomery said.

Zol gave a rueful smile. "And with such a demonstration of power, will you refuse to do your work tomorrow?"

"No!" the innkeeper exclaimed, his slitted pupils wide. "No, I'll get up early! I'll work late. Providing we can all get out of here in the morning, that is."

"What about Wensley?" I asked.

"Oh, he don't live here, Master Skeeve. You ought to try his house. And on the way past, if you'd be so kind to drop in at Carredelest's delicatessen? He lives above his shop. There's not a bite to eat on the premises, and I can't get out of here to pick up my order."

"Sure," I agreed, absently. "Where does Wensley live?"

# Chapter 20

*"There's something funny going on here."*
                                    G. Carlin

"I'm sorry," responded a petite female Wuhs with dark curls, through the window of a pleasant blue house several blocks from the inn. "My mate is not here."

"That's strange," I murmered, almost to myself. "Everyone else was returned to their homes."

"He could be with his parents," Kassery suggested apologetically. "They are not well. He is there as often as he is here. I applaud his eagerness to be a dutiful son."

"Hmm." I nodded slowly. "That might explain it. Could you tell us how to get to their home?"

"They don't live in Pareley," Kassery offered. "I could send them a note...if I could leave here, but at present I am finding it difficult...very difficult. Is it possible that I might be allowed an explanation of my temporary indisposition? Not that I am upset about it, of course," she added hastily.

As quickly as I could I told her what had happened. "No, no, no," the female shook her head disbelievingly. "This is not my Wensley. It couldn't be."

Following Kassery's instructions, we traveled out a few days' journey into the countryside to a small village in Rennet, in the midst of a great forest just beyond the borders of Pareley. Gouda and Edam, Wensley's mother and father, the local apothecary and schoolmaster, were as puzzled as we were.

"He hasn't been here in some weeks," Gouda explained, serving us tea in a scrupulously clean kitchen. She was a plump little woman, with soft, very deft hands. "He said he's involved in a project for the common good. I might make a guess, though you can tell me if I'm wrong, and I probably am, that you are involved in that project?"

"I think we are the project," I explained. "It's just that we've lost track of him." I glanced at the others, and they nodded. No sense in worrying them, when they could do nothing.

"I thought as much. It's clever of him to bring demons to enrich our local Wuhs culture, when all the others he knows are bringing back inanimate souvenirs. Why, they can't talk, can they?"

I knew plenty of knickknacks that could talk, and more, but I didn't believe then was the time to bring that fact up. "He definitely had...has a purpose for us," I said, hastily correcting myself. I had to stop talking; my concern for the missing Wensley was making my tongue trip over itself, and it really didn't need the help. "We're trying to live up to his expectations."

Gouda smiled. "He's such an intelligent boy, so curious, though I probably shouldn't brag about him to you...but would you care to see some pictures of him as a child?"

"He's still not here," Wensley's wife informed us, when we called upon her on our return to the capital. She regarded us with wide-eyed fear and hope, the latter of which I hoped we could justify by discovering his whereabouts and restoring him to his family.

"He'd surely be returned nightly, if he was still around," Montgomery told us, as he escorted us upstairs to our rooms. "We're all still having to have our secret meetings in the day-time. Once the sun sets, bang! It's cutting something fierce into my trade. But on the other hand, my lunch business is going very well," he added, talking loudly to the air.

"Are you being spied upon?" I inquired.

"Never be too careful," the innkeeper replied. "The Pervects seem to be here, there and everywhere these days."

We joined one of the secret lunchtime meetings, held with great ceremony in the back room of a tavern owned by a Wuhs named Crozier not far from the central factory. The situation had clearly worsened. Everyone was going a little stir crazy at having been under house arrest for a week. The Pervects had succeeded in intimidating them into compliance with every whim, no matter how trivial. Not that the Wuhses need much intimidating, mind you.

"We're all going to work," Gubbeen admitted to us over a mug of beer, "but we're not enjoying it. That's putting things strongly, I know, but it isn't only my opinion. I wouldn't say such a thing myself, not unless I was assured of wide support from my friends and co-workers, that is."

"The Pervects have to go," I declared, causing most of my listeners to dive underneath the table, and emerge only when it became apparent that the ceiling wasn't going to fall in on them. "But the problem is that there's no easy vulnerability that we can exploit to get them to leave. We still have to find where they're weak, and push on it."

"But they are not weak!" Ardrahan, the female "committeefriend" exclaimed, and confided to the ceiling, "They are all powerful and strong!"

"More Wuhses than ever are being taken in for extended personal conversations," Gubbeen whispered. The Wuhses who worked as janitors nodded their heads vigorously, but were afraid to say anything aloud. They had been sitting and listening to us with their mouths clamped tightly shut except to eat.

"Where are they being held?"

"In the, er, basement apartments," Ardrahan stammered, with a glance at the silent cleaning staff for corroboration.

"Is Wensley down there, too?"

"He is not...there, good Master Magician," said one of the janitors, a female with silver scattered through her black curls. "The only ones that we are, er, hosting, are those whom our visitors wish to speak to under conditions where they...aren't interrupted."

"I know about the interrogation chambers," I burst in, making them dive underneath the table again at my direct phrasing. "Is there anywhere else in the building where he could be?"

"We are fairly certain that we ought to be able to state with some degree of certainty…" one of them began.

"YES OR NO?"

"Uh, er, no." They looked taken aback that I forced them to provide a one word statement. I tried to remember that Wuhses were generally nice people, and that the frustration I was feeling was my own.

"And he's not in anyone else's home? Then he must be in a public building. Like, one of the factories, for example."

"I don't see how any of the missing Wuhses could possibly be concealed in the factories, Master Skeeve," Gubbeen protested. "Our workers clean every facility every day. The Perverts see to that." Here he gave me a hard look.

"It's not my fault they managed to come back," I retorted. "I know how disappointed you are but I did my best to make sure they stayed out of your dimension. They're tough. You knew that. I have a lot of respect for Pervects' abilities, both magikal and otherwise. They're fantastic negotiators. If I hadn't been thinking wishfully I might have guessed that they would have gotten themselves out sooner or later. I'm sorry it was sooner."

Gubbeen grumbled to himself, but he didn't say anything. I intimidated him, too, and I'm one of the least terrifying people I've ever run into, but Wuhses terrify easily.

"All right," I offered in a soothing voice, "you're probably right. How could anyone live in a factory? I'm only trying to look in all the corners, hoping to find my friend while we try to figure out what the Pervects are up to now."

I had to admit that it was a setback to have the eight turn up again so soon. Zol was at a loss to explain their reappearance.

"I don't understand it, Master Skeeve," he had stated apologetically. "I gave my testimony to the judge. In my opinion the perversion of minds is one of the greatest crimes in existence. They should have remained in custody for at least thirty days. Per victim."

But it hadn't happened. We were still dealing with ten Pervects instead of two. If I hadn't given Wensley my word, I would have been back at my studies. No, that's not true: I was worried about his disappearance, and while it had only offended me at first that the Pervects had gone from contract employees to de facto rulers of their country, now that I had seen them in action I was incensed at their callous disregard for the Wuhses.

"So we have to go back to the drawing board and formulate a new plan. Does anyone have any ideas?" I asked.

"N-n-nno," the assembly bleated.

I didn't think so. I felt sorry for them. I just wished that they wouldn't keep looking at me for leadership. But I guess it went with the territory. If Wuhses were capable of making strong decisions, they wouldn't be in this mess.

Being under the yoke of the Pervects, even by proxy, made it hard for me to think. I was going back daily to Klah to check on Buttercup. The war unicorn did fine on his own, grazing in the fields behind the inn and putting himself in his stall at night, but I could tell he was getting lonely. I brought Gleep back with me so the two of them could play while I thought. I was eager to resume my normal life, but I had a job to finish.

"All right," I sighed. "May I take a look in the factories?"

Gubbeen lowered his eyes. "I regret, Master Skeeve, that only authorized personnel may be admitted during business hours. For safety reasons, you understand."

"Really?" I asked, looking from one Wuhs to another in mock surprise. "What happened to the legendary Wuhs hospitality? All I want is a tour."

"Oh!" Gubbeen's mouth dropped open. "I apologize, Master Skeeve. How terrible of me to misunderstand you! I am so ashamed you had to ask. We would be so pleased...No one has ever wanted a tour before. Of course!"

Parrano, a lanky male with a full head of thick, pale curls, bustled ahead of us importantly. "This is so rare, to have visitors," he told us eagerly. "Normally only our directors come here. They are most particular. We have strict standards of quality."

As in every place the Pervect Ten had held sway, the building was ridiculously clean. The structure itself, a plain square of stone blocks, had none of the charm of the Wuhs town. Built by the Pervects not long after they had arrived, it had been plunked down in what had been a park, convenient walking distance from several residential areas. A few pleasant lawns with formal flower beds and clusters of bushes were maintained at the perimeter, but as one got closer to the structure itself, the ground was covered by flagstones polished to a gleam. I noticed, and Tananda could not have failed to observe, that every approach could be covered by a single person standing opposite any corner at a distance of less than a hundred yards. The factory was more easily secured in an emergency than the castle.

A couple of Wuhses in boiler suits followed us from the door, sweeping and polishing the floor where we had walked. I could have been offended, but I didn't want to attract any attention from the Pervects, and I did not want to get my hosts in trouble. All I wanted was for us to investigate and see if we could guess what the Ten was up to next.

The wooden door that Parrano led us through seemed unusually heavy for its size. I sent a pinging thread of power into it, and discovered it was a sandwich of metal concealed in between planks of wood. I followed Tananda's eyes to the ceiling overhead as we entered the showroom. A pair of disembodied eyeballs bobbed in the corners, one turned toward the door through which we had just come, and the other aimed at a smaller door at the rear of the room. There were frames on the walls with swags of curtains, but the windows in them were fake. It did look as though they were hiding something, but what?

Bunny attached herself to Parrano, asking questions. As I've mentioned before, the former Mob moll had a gift for keeping the attention of every male in the room upon her, even ones who were not strictly of her species. In this case,

Wuhs physiognomy was similar to Klahdish, so I noticed that
when he didn't concentrate, Parrano was addressing his answers to her cleavage, which was very much on show in the
low-cut, nearly transparent blouse she was wearing.

It might sound strange to say I was immune to it; I wasn't,
but I could admire her wiles for what they were: window dress-
ing; and admire the intelligent person underneath all the more.
I also had her analyzing how the factory ran: its efficiency, its
potential output, the ratio of cost versus profit. I was curious
as to why the Pervects were even interested in such a low-end
industry. Bunny understood the fundamentals of business better
than any of our crew except maybe Aahz, and she had managed to surprise even him over the years with her insights.
Parrano was proving to be an encyclopedia on the subject of
his precious factory.

That left Tananda, Zol and me free to examine our sur-
roundings. I hoped that the person on the other end of the
security spy-eyes was also male. If it was one of the Ten we
were in trouble, but I was hoping they had more on their minds
than the day-to-day operation of a concern that had been running smoothly for years without outside interference.

"You say this is one of fifteen facilities in Pareley?" Bunny
cooed, running her finger along the top of a display case. She
rubbed her thumb against her fingertip, managing to make the
little gesture look sexy.

"Yes," Parrano stated proudly, "but ours is the oldest. We
have been providing quality wares to Wuh for two years, but
with skills running in an unbroken curve—I mean line!—back
over three hundred years."

Six Wuhses were in the room with us, but their eyes
were on their work. Three pairs, a male and a female in
each, were engaged in different kinds of needlework. One
pair was embroidering flowers on little squares of cloth.
One pair was knitting sweaters: he a powder-blue cardigan
for an infant, she a yellow V-neck substantial enough for a
very large adult. The last two were crocheting doilies. I

cringed at the sight of the last; I used to have a great aunt who crocheted endlessly. Whenever she came to stay with us she brought us a bale of lacy white things that had to be put out on display along with all the other ones she'd give us over the years (that my mother carefully picked up and put away when my aunt left), that could not be touched, and could not under any circumstances get dirty. The craftspeople, knowing that they were on display to offworlders for once, were wielding their tools carefully. I could tell they were proud of their work, but they kept glancing up at us through their eyelashes, seeking approval.

"These are our most average needlefolk," Parrano explained.

"They're really good," I responded without thinking.

The factory manager's mouth opened in shock. "It's very kind of you to be so extravagant in your praise," he began. "You know, the art is taught to all Wuhses equally."

I glanced at Zol, who was giving me one of those "use your compassion" expressions. "I'm sure everyone's equally good," I corrected myself.

He relaxed, and the seamstresses went back to their work. I kept looking around. So far, I had spotted nothing suspicious or even out of place for a firm that made simple fabric handcrafts. Why was there so much security equipment here?

Niki rolled the dolly out from underneath the stamping machine and stood up. She wiped oil off her hands with a rag and threw a nod to one of the Wuhses who ran the press. Obediently, the Wuhs ran to the switch on the wall and threw it. The pistons started slowly, then increased their tempo until they were threshing deafeningly up and down. Niki put the rag in the pocket of her coveralls and watched the process with a critical eye. The steel in this dimension was brittle and inferior, but they had to rely upon it until they could afford to bring in good ore from Dwarrow. Not that these pathetic rats deserved it. They treated her like a prison guard, jumping in fear every time she opened her mouth. Could she help it if most dimensions suffered from inadequate dentition?

Come to think of it, Wuhses didn't really need decent teeth: most of what they ate you could suck through a straw. Natural predators had been bored out of existence long ago.

Niki wasn't far away from a demise from ennui herself. She longed to get back to her own string of manufacturing plants on Perv. They could probably use an overhaul. If she had been coming up with innovations to make machines run faster and better on a miserable backwater like Wuh, then they had to be light-years ahead at home.

"All right, all of you," she barked. "Back to work."

She pointed at their work stations where the conveyor belt passed, bringing parts of the food choppers to them to assemble. One by one they started jumping over the bar at the back of their seats. "Cut that out, dammit! You'll make me fall asleep! Walk around like civilized creatures. What would your mothers say?"

"Madam!" Curdy, her squeaky-voiced office assistant came running. The plump little lambkin had soft white hair and big round eyes like a stuffed toy. Niki turned to her, bored.

"What's your problem?"

"Strangers in the factory."

"What?" she barked. Curdy gestured and started running back toward the office. Strangers? They had had a security breach in the castle, for all that Monishone had denied there was anything wrong with a room-sized spell going for a walk on its own. It must be the same intruders. Who else would want to get a look at a warehouse full of doilies? "This section is on lockdown! Don't let anyone in here but me! Got that?"

# Chapter 21

*"Espionage and information gathering
is a time honored method to prepare for a conflict."*
N. Hale

"Levitate, Master Skeeve," Zol whispered urgently. "I have never seen you so agitated."

I took his advice. The tray of refreshments in my hand, full of precious china set on delicate crocheted circles alongside crisp napkins that were obviously produce of this facility, immediately stopped rattling. The thread of magik literally lifted it out of my hands and moved it easily it from the serving area of the cafeteria toward a table with available seats.

"Sorry," I offered sheepishly. "For a moment I was brought back to my childhood. My aunts and grandmothers always had things like this. They made me carry it, to show what a good little boy I was, then yelled at me when I broke something."

"There is no harm in giving you a standard to which they wish you to live up," Zol lectured, sternly, "but it is never fair to exceed the physical abilities of the person one is teaching."

"They meant well," I defended them faintly, but to be honest I was thinking not just of my female relatives, but of my friend, mentor, teacher and partner Aahz.

He always pushed me to the levels that he knew I could reach, even though at the time I was certain he must be wrong. He had tried to dissuade me from undertaking this mission, and I had ignored his advice. Had he known that I was overstretching myself? I hoped not. I found myself both missing his company and dreading our next meeting at the same time.

After some urging Parrano had taken us on a tour through the shop floor section of the factory. My first view of a thousand Wuhses embroidering was nearly enough to make me turn tail and run back to Klah. It was the most spectacularly boring enterprise I had ever seen. The hands holding the needles rose and fell, rose and fell in a spiky tidal motion. You could literally hear a pin drop as occasionally one of the sewers dropped a fastener on the ground.

This was the main support of the Wuhs economy? If I hadn't already known that the Pervects had another concern going somewhere, I would have thought they were insane relying upon what Aahz called "tchotchkes" and "schmattes" to provide a livelihood for thousands of families, not to mention turning a profit for the Ten.

Row after row of workers, stitching by hand or running a length of cloth through a pixie-powered machine, turned out pile after pile of white, cream, pink and yellow tea towels. I didn't think there was that much tea served anywhere in all the dimensions.

We looked in every door and under every single thing in all of the rooms we visited, but there was no sign of Wensley. Many of the people knew him, but no one had seen him since the day of the riot. Everyone was convinced he was dead. I didn't want to believe it.

Some of the goods the Wuhses made were for sale in the cafeteria. Bunny and Tananda went eagerly to look over the offerings while Zol and I got some refreshments. We sat down at a table full of Wuhses, and I tried to draw them into conversation.

"So what do you do?" I asked for the forty-third time, no longer caring if I got an answer.

"I tat lace table runners," twinkled a little white-haired granny, her hands going together and moving as if she was holding a shuttle and spool. I always noticed that when you asked someone how they did something, they would tell you verbally *and* describe it through body language. She bit off an invisible knot, then her horizontal-slitted eyes peered at me sharply. "You look like you could use some decent table linens, visitor. Look for my name on the tags, and you'll be sure of the most basic quality."

"Thanks," I smiled, trying to sound appreciative, though lace table runners would be as useful to me as water-soluble handkerchiefs.

"How about you?" I inquired of a blunt-faced male with a pot belly. He took in a breath suddenly, as though my question had called his mind back from far away.

"What?"

"What do you do here?" I inquired.

"I embroider tea towels," the Wuhs intoned dully. "I sew daisies and jonquils. I like yellow."

His hands started to go through the inevitable display of his art. I watched curiously, as instead of the motions of drawing a needle up and down, he seemed to be stacking various items on top of one another, stretching overhead and dragging down a pencil-like device to touch the items then letting it go. Next, both hands reached to his left and came back holding an invisible cylinder which he set down over the parts already before him, screwing it down and finally hitting an unseen plunger a couple of times with the palm of his hand.

"What kind of tea towel is that?" I asked Zol.

"I like purple," uttered the Wuhs next to him, mechanically. "I do very fine lilacs and lavender sprays." But the motions he went through were the same as the blunt-faced male.

"Do you know, Master Skeeve," Zol replied, after a few moments study, "it's no kind I've ever seen before."

"I sew roses," a third Wuhs began.

"I make leaf motifs."

"We missed something," I muttered to Zol. "We have to go back in there and find out what is going on."

Tananda leaned over my shoulder at that moment. She had an armful of linens, and pretended to display one for me.

"The spy-eyes are all turning this way, handsome. Should we do something about them?" I started to turn to look, but she gripped my shoulder with iron fingers. "Don't look this way. Not with your own face on."

I felt icy fingers running down my back. Hastily, I reached out with my mind for the nearest energy line. Fortunately, there was a strong one running through the building, a possible reason the Pervects had chosen to build on this site. There was no time to warn Bunny. I saw the look of puzzlement on the face of the Wuhs serving her at the kiosk as she changed from a Klahd to a Wuhs in the middle of the transaction. Not an everyday occurrence for either one of them, but my assistant handled it with aplomb.

She put her hands to her cheeks and felt them. "Oh, my! My illusion spell wore off! I've got to go now."

She hurried to our table and handed me her purchases. "Shall we go now?" she urged pointedly.

Zol and I were already standing. The Wuhses who were still "assembling" tea towels that weren't tea towels paid no attention, but the keen-eyed old female watched us with interest. We started edging toward the door.

When my hand touched the knob, a klaxon began to blare out. "Intruder alert! Intruder alert! No one is to leave the building. Repeat: no one is to leave the building."

I heard a rumbling noise, and felt a drain on the energy line below my feet. One of the Pervects must be in the factory.

"How do we get out of here?" Bunny asked.

"Not easily," Tananda asserted. "This place seals up tighter than a drum."

I glanced around. "Just start walking toward the exit."

As I said that, sheets of metal slid down and sealed off the doors and windows of the cafeteria. I reached for the D-hopper. "Where shall we meet? If there's any possibility they can zero in on where we've gone I don't want them following me home. K—I mean, my dimension can't handle it."

"Kobol," Zol suggested promptly. "Meet you there."

The little gray man vanished. The Wuhses broke into shrieks and cries of alarm. They immediately stampeded toward the metal-covered door and started pounding on it.

"So much for an unobtrusive departure," I mourned, and started to dial the D-hopper. At that moment the wall behind the sales kiosk opened up, and a stocky Pervect female in a coverall stamped through. She made straight for us.

"You!" she shouted, pointing at us. "Come here! I want to talk to you!"

Without hesitation, I grabbed Tananda's and Bunny's hands and yanked them into the mob of bleating, milling Wuhses. Where was that line of power? I summoned up as much energy as I could and stored it inside me.

I felt a touch of power on the back of my neck like a clamp attached to a derrick. The Pervect was trying to pull me towards her! Knowing how much her species hated fire, I flung a ball of crackling heat over my shoulder at her. She ducked, swearing, as a hundred tea cozies shaped like sunflowers burst into flames. Her spell let go.

As soon as I was free I burrowed deeply into the crowd. I noted as many of the faces as I could then, in my mind, I erased the Wuhs features we had just assumed, and exchanged them for new ones. The Pervect could not easily identify us now. She would have to grab everyone, and by then, I intended to be long gone.

"Skeeve!" Tananda hissed, looking about her for me.

When I put a disguise spell on others, they see themselves with their new faces, but I still see them as they really are. I set the D-hopper for Kobol, threw one arm around Bunny, and grabbed Tananda's wrist with my other hand. As the Wuhses whimpered in terror about the angry Pervect and the burning display, I pushed the button.

Niki grabbed a can hanging from a string on the wall and shouted into it.

"We've had a security breach! Spies! Two Klahds, a Trollop and an I don't know what it was! I think we've found our magician."

In a moment a voice crackled in her ear. "Did you catch them?"

"No, they boogied out of here. Someone or something must have tipped them off." She glared around the room at the Wuhses, now all plastered against the far wall in terror. "I'm going to find out who."

"We're already working on it," Caitlin replied. "Over and out."

"Who were they?" Loorna roared at the Wuhs.

After they had hung up with Niki, the Ten had opened the snow globe prison on their table and restored the Wuhs inside it to full size. The rabblerouser who had actually invaded the castle and led a thousand of his countrymen into the Pervect Ten's very own headquarters didn't look like such a hero now. His vest and trousers were torn, his pale hair and face dirty, and his white shirt showed the effects of having been lived in for a week straight.

Vergetta's keen nose wrinkled at the smell he emitted. She snaked up a cluster of power and threw it at him. There. Dry-cleaned, no charge. Loorna tossed her a grouchy look, but Vergetta ignored it. Why should they all suffer for the length of time it took to wring information out of the Wuhs?

"W-w-who, dear lady?" he panted. "I d-d-don't know who you're talking about."

Vergetta, in her seat next to Caitlin's computer, groaned. That was all they had managed to get out of him: evasions and bad grammar. Apart from his name, of course, which was Wensley. "That's whom, bubalah. I don't know about *whom*."

"Shut up," Loorna snarled at her senior. She turned back to the prisoner. "Answer the question!" She grabbed the chattering male by his shirt front and shook him. "Where do they come from? What do they want?"

"They've got some kind of chutzpah, walking right into our place without a by-your-leave," Vergetta declared. "Must be pretty confident, or pretty dumb. I'll take votes either way."

"So?" Loorna demanded, as designated interrogator, "Who are they? Industrial spies? What's your connection with them?"

"What makes you think this sorry little sheep has anything to do with transdimensional travelers?" Oshleen asked, in a bored voice, filing her nails with a twelve-inch rasp. "Plenty of people know we're here. When we started having to seek out venture capital to try and recoup our losses we had to let them know where we were. Niki's intruders could be industrial spies who are taking advantage of the fact that we are having some unrest to rip us off."

"It could be bill collectors," Tenobia grumbled. "I told you these stupid Wuhses would spend us out of house and home."

"They usually send a notice before showing up," Oshleen reminded her, "and I've been keeping them placated with small payments. It has to be that wizard."

"It's a coincidence! It's snoops from some other concern on Perv."

"The timing's suspicious," Loorna retorted, dropping her prisoner to confront Oshleen. "I've been around a long time, and I don't believe in coincidences."

"What were they looking for?" Paldine asked. "I've kept my research hush-hush. The dimensions where we're planning to sell this gadget haven't got enough magik to blow their noses, let alone shake Niki on her own ground. There's a high-powered wizard out there."

"It's probably this Great Skeeve," Charilor interjected. "He's the one who got us locked up on Scamaroni. Well?" she turned to the Wuhs, who cowered in the corner.

"It's bill collectors," Tenobia insisted. "Who knows what the Wuhses bought in the last week? With the treasury empty there's no money for the Wuhses to steal to pay for their purchases. They're looking for saleable assets or collateral."

Loorna lost her patience. She jumped at Wensley and held him high in the air by his collar.

"Talk!" she shrieked. "Where is that damned D-hopper?"

"I don't care if you torment me, foul green viragoes," Wensley choked out, drawing up his narrow chest as far as he could over his little round belly. "I will not betray my friends."

"Oh, now it sounds like he read a book," Charilor sneered.

Caitlin laughed. "What would you know about reading books, you rave queen?"

"Girls!" Nedira snapped. "He's confessing, and you won't even let him speak."

"I am not confessing," the Wuhs protested, then clamped his plump lips shut. The Pervects looked at each other in disbelief.

"A Wuhs with a backbone," Vergetta hooted. "I never believed such a thing existed."

"Threaten to tear his legs off," Caitlin suggested.

"Talk, or I'll tear your legs off!" Loorna shouted.

"Now shake him until his teeth rattle."

Loorna shook her fist, and the Wuhs's limbs flailed like those of a rag doll.

"Wait a minute!" she demanded, looking at the youngest Pervect. "Who's conducting this interrogation? You or me?"

"Oh, you can, if you really want to," Caitlin yawned, leaning back in her chair. "I figured as long as you were going by the book I could just coach you. It saves time."

"Why isn't anyone taking this seriously?" Paldine asked. "Our future is at stake here."

"I am. You're pretty brave for a sheep," Loorna hissed right in Wensley's face, "keeping your mouth shut. Got some Dutch courage from somewhere? I don't smell any alcohol on you."

"I need no alcohol. I know I don't have to tell you anything!"

Loorna grinned. "Well, I don't know if you've ever taken a look downstairs in the dungeons of this sweet little palace of yours. You keep talking about how your ancestors were always so peaceful, cooperative and nice, but I'm here to tell you that there is some pretty nasty torture equipment down there that even Pervects would never have thought of using on another living being. I am just on the edge of taking you down there and using some of it on you. Or," she leaned close enough so that the Wuhs could see the gold flecks in her bright yellow eyes, "we'll make you eat some of our food. Talk!"

# Chapter 22

*"What does this have to do with
assembling the Death Star?"*
G.M. Tarkin

"Whew!" I whistled, as we emerged in the tidy gardens of
Kobol. Zol stood up from the marble bench where he had
been waiting for us. "Do you think that Pervect got a good
look at us?"

"I think we must assume," Zol replied, "that she did see
us as we were, undisguised. And if she did not, there were
plenty of witnesses to our tour. I think you must assume that
she will have a full description of us very soon. The Wuhses
are more adept at self-preservation than they are at maintaining discreet silence."

"You mean they'll save their own skins," Tananda
translated.

"More than that: the odd behavior that we all witnessed
among a segment of the workers indicates to me that they
are engaged upon an enterprise of which even they are un-
aware. You saw the look of stupefaction on the faces of
those males. They all believe that they make handcrafts,
but it is clear from the involuntary re-creation of the re-
petitive motions they went through that it could be nothing
of the sort. Since Wuhses cannot keep a secret they must
not know it."

"The situation is worse than I thought—worse than
Wensley thought," I stated grimly. "Not only are the Pervects
in total control of the country, they're bending the minds of
the inhabitants. It's inhumane."

"What do you suppose it is that they're making?" Bunny
asked. "It seemed when that fellah pounded on the top that it
looked like something mechanical."

"Some kind of armaments?" Tananda guessed. "But it's nothing I've seen anywhere, in or out of the Assassins Guild."

"It does rather look like a weapon of some kind," Zol suggested. "How curious. There must be a spell on some part of the process to fool the conscious mind into believing that they are still performing their usual functions."

"That would be why we never found out who was making those glasses," I mused, thoughtfully. "Nobody would remember doing it. Do they plan to take over *another* dimension?"

"Or to sell to one," Zol suggested. "These are enterprising women, and you will have observed that they did not need arms to take over Wuh or Scamaroni. In one they are already successful, and in the other they would have been, if not for your intervention."

"Next time I'm going to make sure they're captured and stay under lock and key," I asserted, pounding my fist into my palm. "*All* of them. We have to get back into the castle to figure out where they're going and head them off."

"Oh, we don't need to do that," Zol informed me. "Now that my notebook has been in contact with their computer, we can access their drive remotely." To my puzzled expression he explained, "we can see what they see in their magik mirror."

"I thought you couldn't get through their encoding," Bunny queried.

"We don't need to. My countrymen back on Kobol broke their basic program code. What they are working on at any given moment is not going to be stored under lock and key. We can spy upon their plans as they make them. I merely need to be in the same dimension, preferably upon the same energy line."

"You can't do it from here?" I asked. "On Perv they could communicate with the banks on Deva through their computers."

"That was with the cooperation of the Devan computers. The Pervect Ten will surely not want us reading their plans. We need to be close for my subterfuge to work. Our only fear then will be discovery."

"I'll keep us hidden," I vowed, grimly. "I won't fail again. I owe it to Wensley's memory." A thought occurred to me just then. "You know, I hate to say this, but it's just as well that he isn't around any more. If we had plotted this out in front of him he would have blabbed to the Ten about us."

"We're having to do this because of you, honey," Vergetta confided to the snow globe on the table as Niki dragged in the first invitee.

All their threats of torture, all their shouting and shaking had done nothing to dent the resolve of the Wuhs leader, Wensley. Vergetta had to admit to herself that she was pretty impressed with the little guy. It took a strong person to defy a Pervect, let alone the whole *minyan* of them. Big, brave Trolls had broken down in tears when faced with the Ten in full fury. Even a bowl of purple Pervish gumbo had not been enough to make him open his mouth. A miniature picture of defiance, he sat crosslegged and arms folded on the bottom of the paperweight.

"Let's see how long you hold out when you see us take some of your friends apart."

The little face turned away from her. Vergetta grinned.

"First things first," Tenobia demanded, when the fat Wuhs with black curls had been flung into the "hot seat," a chair in the middle of the room.

They had drawn straws to see who got to be "Lady High Executioner," and she had won. In celebration she had put on a silver bustier and a tight black skirt that she usually saved for wild parties at home on Perv. The ensemble looked suitably dangerous and very impressive, the virtual caricature of a dominatrix torturer. The Wuhs's eyes nearly started out of his head at the sight of her. She smacked her palms down on the arms of the chair and leaned into his face.

"Where's the D-hopper?"

"I d-d-don't know what you mean, madam..." Gubbeen babbled. "It's not my department to keep track...we are the friends of public health...the D-hopper is more of a safety issue...."

Charilor came back upstairs, grunting under the weight of a vast, lumpy bag. She threw it on the stone floor in front of the Wuhs. It clanked and banged like a suit of armor in a garbage disposal. Their guest nearly jumped out of his seat at the noise.

"I don't have it!" Gubbeen exclaimed, his eye on the sack, though none of them moved towards it. "I haven't had it for ages. It's been my turn...I mean, I would have safeguarded it on your behalf, but I really don't know, dear ladies, Ardrahan had it last time I saw it...please don't hurt me!"

"I don't know why we didn't do this six months ago," Loorna grimmaced.

She kicked open the folds of the bag and extracted a metal implement with a rotating wheel and several long, sharp strands of metal. She pointed it at Gubbeen and rotated the little handle that made the tines clash violently against one another. The Wuhs recoiled into his chair, trying to meld with the wooden staveback.

Vergetta recognized the device as a whisk they used to aerate hot drinks. She hadn't seen it for months. It had probably gotten dumped into the hold-all drawer in the kitchen, or shoved into a box in a storage closet. She smiled. Obviously the Wuhs, who had never seen one, was making up his own uses for it in his head, and none of them made him comfortable.

They played with him a while longer, going up the threat scale from kitchen implements to sports equipment, and through to genuine torture devices, but the Wuhs continued to shriek out that he had given them all the information that he had about the missing D-hopper. They had no choice but to believe him. He was so overwrought that Vergetta called a halt to the questioning. Nedira escorted him down to one of the padded cells in the basement to calm down a little bit before they would let him go.

Vergetta waved her arms, bringing Wensley out again.

"We were interrupted, darlink. Your friend wasn't much help. Would you like to cooperate a little?"

"Never," the Wuhs declared. "We will be rid of you and your foul enterprises soon. The Great Skeeve will see to that!"

"What's this?" Vergetta demanded, leaning close to make sure she had heard him correctly. "What about the Great Skeeve?"

"He. He will defeat you." Wensley made a gesture that included every Pervect present. "All of you!"

"You?" Oshleen asked, narrowing her eyes. "You hired the Klahd wizard?"

"You got us thrown in jail? Fined? You got our merchandise confiscated!" Paldine gritted out crime after crime. She started toward the pale Wuhs with her claws out.

"That's it," Vergetta exclaimed, getting in between them. "*You* stop," she told the marketing specialist, then turned to point at Wensley. "*You* get a permanent time-out while I figure out what we are going to do with you."

She waved her hand, and the Wuhs was restored to his spherical prison.

"But you heard what he said!" Paldine exclaimed, trying to get around her elder.

"Yes, and what good will it do to tear him to pieces? It won't solve our problem. But now we have at least some of the answers. We've been looking for the cause of our troubles all over the dimensions, and it was right here under our noses. I bet the Great Skeeve got Zol Icty involved, got him to condemn us for a favor."

"If it really was Zol Icty," Oshleen cautioned. "Skeeve's supposed to be such a great wizard it was probably one of his illusions."

"Here's the next one," Niki grunted, hauling in another Wuhs.

"We'll finish with you later," Paldine promised Wensley, gold veins standing out in her yellow eyes. "Count on it."

"Cashel's your name, right?" Tenobia asked, planting a silver spike heeled boot on the Wuhs's knee and sticking her fists into her hips. "I've seen you in the castle a lot lately. But you don't work here, do you? Where do you work?"

"Factory number nine," Niki supplied.

"Right. So what are you doing down in the treasury all the time? You wouldn't be the one who's always extracting money, even though you know that we've got rules about requesting hard currency."

"M...money, dear ladies?" Cashel gulped, his eyes darting warily to all the various pieces of hardware that Tenobia was idly fondling. "I wouldn't break rules, not at least ones I understood to be absolute strictures against ...certain behaviors..."

"Just what did you think that money was for?"

The Wuhs looked up hopefully. He must have thought he knew the answer to this one. "...Er, buying things?"

"What things?"

"...Uh...things for you?"

"No, you fool!" Tenobia roared, throwing up her hands in exasperation. "Supplies. Staples. Building materials. Food. Equipment. A consulting contract that your leaders signed willingly two years ago! Things for *you*! Your spending habits are driving us crazy!"

Cashel looked from one Pervect to another in deep confusion. "Then...I don't understand, ladies, why you're upset. We're buying things for us. I mean," he added, recoiling at the furious expression on Loorna's face, "whoever's taking the money. It's certainly not *me*. I'm in favor of public support, really."

Vergetta shook her head. They were getting nowhere. Naturally the ones they interviewed were *never* the ones who had brought in new merchandise or stolen the money. It was always somebody else.

"Who has the D-hopper?" Tenobia interrupted before the Wuhs could start another string of evasions and lies. "Who had it the last time you saw it? Answer now!"

"Coolea," Cashel sobbed, dropping his face into his hands. "Yesterday. He ought to be back by now. I hope. He really wouldn't listen to the instructions, he was so eager to see other dimensions..."

Nedira threw a nod to Vergetta, picked one of their invisibility cloaks off a hook on the wall and vanished out of the chamber. It was the closest they'd come to current information, and they wanted to check up on it before it changed hands again.

Cashel was led out, still pleading his innocence but bleating earnestly that he would never again take anything that didn't belong to him. Vergetta popped Wensley out of his spherical prison.

"Honestly, darlink," she told him, "would it be so bad if anyone told us the truth? You have anything else you want to say?"

Wensley pressed his lips together and shook his head.

"Wait a minute," Caitlin spoke up, "Nedira's coming back."

The motherly Pervect was among them a second later. Vergetta had to pop Wensley back into his prison so as not to distract the stable boy, who wore an awestruck expression when he realized he was in the presence of the full force of the Pervect Ten. Shaking her head ruefully, Nedira held up a bag.

"Banana-skin shoes. The Deveel who sold them to him is probably still laughing."

"'Slippers,'" Vergetta groaned. "That's such an old one, honey, it plain amazes me that you fell for it. But you're just a kid. What'd you pay for them? A silver piece? They're not worth more than a copper or two, and usually they come with a free banana inside each one."

"Four gold pieces a pair," the boy managed to get out.

"Aaagggh!" Tenobia shrieked, waving her fists. Coolea fled behind the chair for shelter. She pounded on the table. "Every junk seller in all the dimensions must be looking out for you morons, to unload the most useless trash they've got!" She gestured angrily at the others. "I feel like locking him up and throwing away the key."

"No," Oshleen smirked, grinning widely enough to make the Wuhs sway with fear, "send him back and make him ask for a refund."

"The Deveels?" the boy gasped. "No! No! Oh, please, good dames, spare me! Not a refund!"

"Good idea," Nedira agreed with her allies. She grasped Coolea by the shoulder. The two of them disappeared.

"Slippers!" Tenobia pointed a finger at the glass sphere on the table. "You people make me so furious I could eat you, except your lily livers would give me indigestion! After all we've done for you!"

The little figure in the snow globe on the table looked thoughtful.

"All right," Vergetta grunted. "Let's try and get some business done."

# Chapter 23

*"It's so good, it practically sells itself!"*
from the promotional material for the Edsel

A shaggy-coated herdbeast bleated in my ear. We were sitting among them in the shadow of the king's statue in the park at the other end of town from the castle, on the energy line that supplied power to the Pervect's computer. I had disguised the four of us as beasts to blend in.

Unfortunately, that was earning us some unwanted attention, Tananda especially. Whenever I used an illusion spell to make us look like the denizens of a dimension, she always insisted on being made a *beautiful* whatever-it-was. In this case, that meant she was the prettiest ewe in town, and every ram in the field was doing his best to get her attention.

Bunny was less enamored of sitting in the middle of a smelly feed lot, and didn't care what kind of a herdbeast she looked like. Normally she would be neck and neck with Tananda, insisting on the current standard of beauty, but at the moment she was watching Zol avidly as he linked his little notebook to the Pervect's magik mirror. I noticed that Bytina, having touched Zol's computer, now had exactly the same pictures appearing in her little looking glass. It seemed that infinite links could be made very easily.

"The ironic thing," Zol began, as his long fingers flew over the button board, "is that the easiest way into a system is through its security gates. The least safe mode for a computer is when it is operating."

"Stands to reason," I replied. Though I knew nothing about computers, I knew something about systems. "When you're in the midst of a mission, the last thing you have time to do is watch your own back."

That was why I had had partners. At the moment I was in the "back-watching" position, and Zol was gathering the information we needed.

Zol gave me a luminous smile of approval. "Precisely, Master Skeeve! I never ceased to be amazed by your capacity for comprehension."

I smiled back, a little uneasily. Not that I didn't enjoy basking in the little gray man's fulsome praise, but after having to pry compliments out of my former associates with a crowbar I mistrusted someone who threw off accolades whenever...he felt I'd earned one. He seemed just a little too easy to please. He didn't seem to notice my discomfort.

"Now, by looking at the active components, the open books on the desktop, so to speak, we can see what they have been doing today. Hmm...they have a weather-prediction program...that one they are using hasn't got the latest updates. The prognostication section has a flaw. It foretells firestorms when it means light rain. It's given rise to panic in some dimensions, as you might guess. Yes, see here?" he pointed at the center of the mirror. "'Partly sunny, with widespread devastation toward evening.' There's a partial letter home...and the operator has played over five hundred games of solitaire, with a 7:1 win-lose ratio."

"Whew!" I whistled. "I'd have liked to hire her as a dealer for the casino our partnership once owned. She must have very fast fingers."

"Oh, they aren't physical cards, Master Skeeve; they're magikal projections. You can play hundreds of different card games on a magik mirror like this. Unfortunately, in everything but solitaire, your virtual opponents tend to cheat."

"Just like real players," I nodded.

"But among all of this detritus they are working on plans," Zol said, his huge dark eyes reflecting the light coming from the small square mirror. "We are in the enviable position of being able to monitor their every move. See this? Men, machinery, logistics, principles of generalship...They *must* be out for empire-building. This is bigger than I ever dreamed possible. Marvelous!"

"Marvelous?" I echoed.

Zol beamed at me. "Yes, seeing how the minds of Pervects work. Released from the ease of their own dimension's comforts, they set their sights on spreading their influence across the multiverse. What an opportunity to observe! Untrammeled ambition! How the two halves of their nature intersect! They seek to Per*vert* the course of the future in these places, to Per*vect* their vision."

"Well, it won't do," I snapped. "This isn't an experiment, it's all these people's lives. Their *real* lives. It cost our friend Wensley his life, in case you have forgotten."

I'd forgotten how straightforward you Klahds are," Zol offered sincerely. "Please accept my apologies. I became too enthusiastic a scholar, and forgot to be a loving, caring being. I am so sorry." The big dark eyes turned sad.

"He's not upset, Zol," Bunny hurried to assure the author. "Are you, Skeevie?"

I winced. She knew how much I hated to be called Skeevie, so she must be trying to make a point. "But what do we do?"

"You must use that Klahdish sensibility," Zol told me. "Confront them. Head them off and prevent them from achieving their latest objective."

I peered over his shoulder. "Can we tell where they're going this time?"

"Yes, indeed," Zol replied, enlarging a map so I could easily read the name in the center. "Ronko."

"It slices. It dices. It cooks. It even cleans itself if you dunk it in water," Paldine expounded to a roomful of potential distributors.

Ronko ought to be ideal dimension, she had argued to her companions; they loved gadgets of all kinds, putting even Perv in the shade when it came to techie-toys. She leaned over the Formica podium with one of Niki's inventions in her hand.

The development of the dimension was at about the era of early sit-coms, perfect for a gadget like hers.

"It has only *one moving part*. You push it down. When it pops up, you push it again. When your food looks the way you want it to, you stop. It's so easy an animal can use it." She didn't add, "like you." She might have thought it, but she would never say it.

"That's not in the sales brochure," complained one of the Ronkonese in the front row.

She knew he was going to be trouble from the beginning. His tanned face was wrinkled and lined as if he had spent too many an afternoon out with his pocket fisherman, obviously a veteran of thousands of intense sales pitches.

"Well, you can confide that to a buyer when you're trying to sell him one," Paldine countered, getting exasperated. "Exclusive information they can only get from you!"

"Is it safe?" asked a Ronkonese female, raising a pencil in the front row next to Paldine's "problem child."

"Of course it's safe. You think I could have gotten an import license from your government if it hadn't passed a dozen tests first?"

Paldine turned the business end down onto her palm and pounded the plunger up and down a few times. Then she displayed her unmarked hand to the audience.

"If it's not food, it won't cut. In other words, don't try to use it to shred those confidential documents, folks; it won't work." An appreciative chuckle ran through the room.

She went through flip charts showing sales projections, giving them every wrinkle she had worked out to attract the attention of the average and below-average buyer. They might be scared witless of her looks, and they were wise to pay heed to that discomfort, but no one listening could deny that she knew what she was talking about.

If her master's program in marketing at the Perv Academy of Design hadn't been enough to teach her her business, a full century at Bushwah Tomkins and Azer had certainly cemented her reputation as an innovative sales thinker. She had won the coveted Euphem Ism Queen title twelve years running. Since the Pervect Ten usually undertook accounting and refinancing contracts she hardly ever got to stretch her advertising muscles, and she was enjoying it.

The first two posters on her flip pad were okay, and she knew it, but the third one was the big bombshell, the sell-all ad. When she revealed it the room burst into applause. She built on it by going from there to newspaper ads, sponsorships at halftime shows, sandwich boards, and direct mail. A pleased murmur ran through the room, as she showed them the potential profit per type of ad purchased. Paldine built upon the growing enthusiasm.

"But nothing works like word of mouth. Stress convenience! Stress price!" she urged them.

"Are you trying to tell us how to do our job?" the pain in the butt in the front row asked, raising his voice so all of his fellow pitchmen and women could hear him.

Paldine had had enough. She bared all her fangs and walked right up to him. When she was an inch from his face she whispered, "No." The Ronkonese recoiled, then looked puzzled. "I'm telling you how to sell our item," Paldine roared. The force of her voice pushed the troublemaker back into his chair, his fluffy hair plastered backwards on his head. "If you don't think I'm an expert on a product that *we* invented, that *we* put all the features into, step right up here and explain it to me."

For a moment the sales force looked as nervous as Wuhses. Paldine was satisfied. She had gotten her point across and without bloodshed. It didn't hurt that some Pervects in the past had paved the way for her by proving that they were not demons to be trifled with. In fact, the point had been proved so well that most of the Ronkonese were crowded against the back wall trying to edge warily toward the door.

"All right," she rallied them. "Then get out there and make us some money!"

# Chapter 24

*"Interesting place. Wonder what they sell here?"*
M. Polo

It was a good thing that we had such an experienced dimensional traveler as Zol with us. Even Tananda had never visited Ronko. The route from Wuh had taken us through three intermediate hops, each into dimensions less than friendly to Klahd metabolism. I would never have tried such a transit on my own.

Gleep had perked up every time we materialized in a new place, but seemed to understand that no matter how interesting the smells were coming from that primeval swamp or those volcanoes, it was more important to stay close to us while Zol calculated the next jump. In the meanwhile, I kept wards around us, sealing in a bubble of air that we could breathe.

The second hop left us teetering on a boulder perched on a mountaintop that threatened to topple over and plummet us into an avalanche of bright blue snow. Even Gleep looked nervous as we all wobbled with our arms out, trying to keep our uneasy perch from overbalancing.

At the conclusion of the third hop we found ourselves on level ground. Well, at least it wasn't moving. The city around me, for it was a city, swooped upwards on both sides of the street on which we were standing. I had been in cities before, including the filthy and dreary burg on Perv that Aahz hailed from, but I had never seen one like this before.

Instead of plain boxes, the buildings on either side were made in fanciful shapes. To our left was a turreted castle covered with bright yellow tiles. Next to it, a squat fortress made of green stone seemed to beckon us toward its portcullis with concentric arcs of lights that blinked in sequence from the outside inward, over and over again. Across the street stood a vast rough wooden box, fifty feet on a side, with what was the mother of all bird's nests on it, each straw as thick in diameter as my body. That was just a relative sample of the structures we could see from where we stood. And the signs! Hundreds of them were plastered on all flat surfaces, from the sides of big vehicles to entire walls of soaring buildings. Brilliant orange, pink and blue ribbons of light were shaped into letters and pictures. We couldn't read any of them, but the illustrations above and around them made their meaning clear. They were advertisements.

I enjoyed looking at them. Everyone in them looked cheerful, healthy and prosperous. I couldn't help being interested in what they were so cheerful about. The street was full of traffic, both foot and vehicle. I pressed my back against a handy lamppost so I could see the giant posters without getting in anyone's way. The denizens of Ronko were similar in shape to Klahds, though they were slightly smaller in stature, like Zol. All of them were talking on small devices or playing with square toys that beeped or bobbing their heads from side to side as they walked.

"It doesn't look like the Pervects have started their strike yet," I observed. "Maybe we've gotten here first and can head them off."

"I'm afraid you are incorrect, Master Skeeve," Zol replied. "We are too late."

He pointed. My eyes followed the line of his finger.

On the side of the biggest building we had yet seen was a gigantic representation of a Pervect female wearing a military uniform. Serpentine yellow eyes caught passing glances and held them, daring one to look away. The Pervect in the picture held an object which I didn't need to have anyone tell me was what the Wuhses in the factory were assembling. It was a cylinder about the length of my forearm, with a plunger at one end and wicked-looking blades protruding from the round casing at the other.

"It's a weapon," Tananda mused critically. "It must be nasty, if it has to have a safety casing like that around the business end."

"I wonder what the poster says?" I asked.

Bunny held up Bytina. "She translated it for me. Look."
Bunny held the PDA under our noses. There, on the little screen,
was a miniature representation of the huge advertisement. Instead of the square script of the Ronkonese, curly letters in
Klahdish spelled out an order.

"We want YOU to join the growing army of happy
Pervomatic users!"

"It's a recruiting poster," I growled.

Zol's dark eyes went wide. "How could we have missed
the clues?" he demanded, shaking his head at his own naiveté.
"It was there on their desktop: they were looking for a force.
But for what purpose?"

I smacked my fist into my hand. "To take over other dimensions. They supply the weapons here on Ronko, then use
the Ronkonese as a strike force somewhere else. It's brilliant."

"What are four of us going to do?" Tananda asked.

"Gleep!" protested my pet.

"Sorry, Gleep," Tananda replied, scratching him around the
jowls. "Five of us...And if your suggestion is join up, I may
love you like a brother, but the answer this time is a flat no."

Having seen how complications can set in even in such
a straightforward enterprise as trying to disrupt an army
from within (for further information on the last time my
companions got involved in an operation like that I draw
your attention to the fine book *M.Y.T.H. Inc. in Action*), I
shook my head.

"We're going to shut them down," I informed them.

"How?" asked Bunny.

"I don't know yet," I admitted. "I'll figure it out on the
way there. Bunny, can Bytina lead us to this recruiting office?"

"You bet," she answered, pleased to show off her pet's
prowess.

"No, wait, Master Skeeve," Zol halted us. "If you will
allow a little advice? It is not enough to attack a single outlet, as you saw before. You need to reach as many people as

possible." He pointed to a shop window where people were gathered to look at screens similar to computers but somehow not as sophisticated.

"Black and white," Zol explained, "not as advanced as in some dimensions, but all-pervasive here on Ronko. I seem to recall having been interviewed some years ago at a media outlet, though I cannot recall precisely where it is." He turned to Bunny.

She touched the tiny keyboard, and an arrow filled the round mirror. Bunny held the small device level, and gestured over her head. "This way."

I glanced into the screens as I passed. The images in them didn't look black and white to me, but a spooky gray blue and chalky white that made the beings pictured look otherworldly. But I was the demon here. Maybe that looked good to the denizens of Ronko.

The "television station" was a building off to itself at the edge of a big park square. It had been built like one of its own screens, a huge box with a glass front. Inside Ronkonese hurried around three-walled rooms with lights, boxes on wheels and hand-sized padded sticks, which they pushed in front of one another's faces.

I told my story to the receptionist. She gestured us to a seat, and we waited. The lobby had a wall of screens, each showing a different activity. On one, a male gestured with both palms at a map. It had a smiley sun face and a frowny rain cloud facing one another over a dashed line that separated rough halves of the geographical area pictured. In another, a cheerful looking female in a frilly apron held up a cylindrical bottle and a sponge. I guessed she was promoting some kind of cleaning product.

In a while, an eager little Ronkonese female came out to meet us. She was dressed a lot like Bunny often did, in a trim skirt suit with a ruffle at the neck.

"I'm Velda Skarrarov," she introduced herself, shaking hands with all of us and ending with a pat on Gleep's head.

The fact that we all looked very different from natives of Ronko, or that we had a dragon with us, seemed not to faze her at all. "I'm very interested in your story. Will you come to my studio with me, please?"

We followed her through the chaotic hallways. Velda talked to us over her shoulder as she negotiated her way, striding past busy men in headsets pushing big pieces of equipment. "I'm an investigative reporter," she confided. "They all think I'm insane, a girl trying to make it as a rough and-tumble journalist, but I know they're wrong."

"They are," Zol replied, keeping up with her effortlessly. "Why, in a few years it will be the norm to see females in your position. Be strong, be intelligent, and when the time comes, be generous to your detractors. They can't see what you do."

"Why, thank you," Velda smiled. "I really appreciate your confidence. Of course I know who you are. I'd like to interview you after I speak to your friend."

"With pleasure," Zol assured her.

I didn't like the television station, and I could tell Gleep felt as uncomfortable as I did. A shrill whine permeated every room all of the time. There was no escape from the sound. It made Gleep flatten his ears sideways. I wished mine were as mobile.

"It's the monitors," Velda informed us. "They don't like to work, and they want us to know they're unhappy. They don't like to suffer alone."

"Misery loves company," Zol intoned. Velda regarded him with the same sheeplike expression Bunny did. I could tell she was falling under his spell.

"Can we get back to the reason we're here?" I insisted, with some heat.

"Oh, yes!" Velda exclaimed, gesturing us into an office, once again with only three solid walls. The fourth was a section of the vast window that made up the front of the building. She showed my friends a line of chairs against a wall, and pointed me at a seat in front of a row of hot lights. "Please sit there."

The room was very plain except for a panel behind us that looked like the cityscape we had admired on the way there. Opposite it on the far wall were several big monitor screens, with different scenes on each one.

Two big boxes were wheeled in that looked like siege cannon except that the gun end had a glass lens in it. Each contraption moved on a platform with three or four Ronkonese to steer it. A woman appeared wielding a powder puff and an eyeliner pencil. She applied both to Velda and then to me. Tananda and Bunny, safely out of the way, giggled at my discomfiture.

"Ready?" Velda asked me, as she settled herself in the seat opposite mine in front of the lights. "Tell me your story."

I told her the entire tale, beginning with the arrival of Wensley in my study, going on through his description of the Pervects' domination of the Wuhses, our surveillance of them in their lair, their attempt to take over Scamaroni, and our discovery of the new plot we had discovered against the Ronkonese.

"Those things that we saw in the poster," I explained. "We think they're weapons. I believe that the Pervects intend to use your people as soldiers, assembling an army that will be under their absolute command."

"But Ronkonese are very independent thinkers," Velda countered. "We wouldn't make a good army to attack anyone else."

"But you wouldn't know you were doing it," I pointed out. "I told you they've also invented these mind-bending spectacles. If you were wearing those you might march on an unsuspecting enemy thinking you were doing no more than, say, cutting up food."

Velda nodded sagely. "I thought those Pervomatics sounded too good to be true," she said. "I thought they were just food choppers, like the ads say."

But I wasn't listening. My attention had been drawn to a Ronkonese female on one of the blue-white screens.

"Today on the Happy Homemaker," the cheerful female chirped, "we're pleased to introduce you to the greatest new labor-saving device of the age, the Pervomatic. Just put all your ingredients here on the worktable," she narrated, piling hunks of meat and vegetables together, "place the Pervomatic over them, pound on the plunger, and before you know it, you have a hot and tasty Pervect patty, every time! Your family will love them!"

"Food chopper," I repeated faintly.

"Yes," Velda said. "That's what they've been selling them as. But if, as you say, they have the potential to be weapons, then that's a big story! Tell me more. It'll be all over the evening news! You've made my reputation, Mr. Skeeve!"

"I'm sorry," I blurted, getting to my feet, as the whole reality of my error slapped me in the face. "There's been a terrible mistake. Never mind. Um. I'm sorry. It's actually a really neat item. You ought to buy it. Uh, goodbye. Please don't run this story."

Velda looked shocked. "But I have to," she insisted. "It's news. It's big news."

"No. I...you can't. It's wrong. I was wrong!"

"I must speak for my young friend," Zol interjected, stepping in between me and the glass-eyed cannon. "This interview is at an end."

Velda glared at him. "But we haven't gotten into all the details yet!"

I didn't wait to hear any more. I had to get a breath of fresh air. I rushed out of the studio and into the street. I had to get away. I looked around me wildly, hoping I could remember how to steer the D-hopper to get me home.

But a firm hand closed around my upper arm, and a familiar shape looped around my legs.

"Gleep!" chirped the latter.

"Hold on there, handsome," insisted Tananda, the proprietor of the aforementioned hand. "Where do you think you're going?"

"Anywhere," I replied desperately. "Away. Out of here!"

"All right, then," Tananda agreed, with a glance at Bunny and Zol.

The landscape around us vanished.

# Chapter 25

*"If you don't want egg on your face, don't make omelets."*
B. Crocker

"I feel really stupid," I exclaimed, as we arrived back on Wuh. I didn't want to endanger any of the locals, so we landed behind the statue in the park instead of at Montgomery's inn.

"I saw what you saw on that screen," Zol informed me gently. "It would appear that we have erred in our judgment. I did try to talk Velda out of running the story, but I doubt I have dissuaded her. Ronkonese believe strongly in word-of-mouth communications."

"I ought to go back there and try and straighten it out," I declared, wishing not as much that I could get away from my friends as that I wanted to get away from myself. "I have been a complete idiot. I'm supposed to be a hotshot, experienced magician, but I have made every single rookie mistake that Aahz was always pounding me over the head for. I made all those assumptions about the Pervects' plans, but I never looked at one of those things up close. A food processor!"

I clutched my head. A gigantic ache was hammering in between my eyes like a troll with a mattock. It wanted out if it killed me, and I almost wished that it could.

"Don't," Zol replied softly. "It's a mistake anyone could have made."

I groaned again. Not anyone. Just the Great Skeeve. Just a guy who had had too much success too soon in the last few years, knocked his own supports out from underneath his own feet and tried to jump right back in the first time someone asked him for help without using any of the experience that he had supposedly gained. I made a decision there and then. I turned to the little gray man and put out my hand.

"Zol, I want to thank you for all of your help. It's been a privilege meeting you. I know you were going to stick around, but after today there's going to be nothing left to see."

Zol's thin black eyebrow went up his gray forehead. "Why the farewell?"

"Because I'm going to resign," I informed him. "I've made a total mess of this whole mission. Those things we thought were weapons were labor-saving gadgets. The Pervects were just trying to sell them. The same probably went for those spectacles. All I've done is make a fool of myself and of all of you. I'm going to find Gubbeen. He seems to be the ranking Wuhs around here. I'll tell him I'm sorry, but I can't do what he wants. It may be too late, but I'm going to take Aahz's advice. This mission was too much for me. I'm willing to admit it."

"Oh, Skeeve, that's not true," Bunny cooed, winding herself into my arm. "You can't quit now."

"I'd better," I told them, "because I've made nothing but bad decisions all the way through this."

"Things might not have gone the way you thought they would, Tiger," Tananda purred, burrowing close on my other side, "but you made the right moves. It's not your fault if the plans didn't work out the way you expected them to. You're not finished yet. I've never known you to be a quitter." Her soft lips were next to my ear, and her voice dropped so only I could hear it. "I know why you wanted to take this mission. You wanted to learn on your own, to be able to fail on your own. Okay, but that doesn't mean that you stop after you fail. Right? You try again. Humiliation's not fatal, even if it feels as though it ought to be."

I turned crimson with shame. She was right. I would never have even contemplated backing out of a contract when I was the president of M.Y.T.H. Inc., or leaving a friend in the lurch even before that. Not that I had had too many friends until the day Aahz exploded into my life.

Gleep, not to be left out, plumped down at my feet, making the ground shake, and wound his long neck around all of us. He gave me a big slurp on the face which, with both arms full and my legs immobilized, I was powerless to avoid.

"Those choppers and the spectacles were made by unwitting slave labor," Zol reminded me. "A situation which is still ongoing. And the Wuhses are not yet freed of the Pervects' rule."

"But one of my friends was killed," I reminded them sadly. "I'm afraid to put anyone else in harm's way."

"Isn't that our choice?" Tananda replied, shaking her head with a little smile on her face. "I've been around the dimensions for a while, and I'm not taking a risk without both eyes wide open."

"I may not have been as far around…" Bunny began, then shot an apologetic glance at Tananda, "no offense—we Klahds don't live as long as you Trollops."

"None taken," Tananda waved, without ire.

"…But I know that you're right, and they're wrong. It's as simple as that."

"Elegantly put, Miss Bunny," Zol applauded.

"You're right," I acknowledged, giving her a warm hug, then letting her go. "You're all right. I felt sorry for myself—really sorry for myself—but I won't let that stop me again."

"Oh, look, there he is!"

I turned at the sound of a female voice. Kassery stood on the edge of the park jumping up and down and waving her hand vigorously at us.

"Master Sk—aagh!" the petite, darkhaired Wuhs cried.

Suddenly she choked, grabbing at her throat. She dropped to her knees, her face turning purple. I glanced around in horror. Tananda was throttling a handful of air. I threw a ward in front of Tanda's hands, cutting off the flow of magik to her target, then I ran to help Kassery to her feet. She was gasping for breath. I carried her to the steps of the statue and laid her down.

"Why did you do that?" I asked Tananda.

"Sorry," Tananda snapped out, sounding not at all apologetic. "Thinking on my feet. It was the only way I could think to shut her up before she finished shouting out your name. We're trying to be incognito here. You know damned well that the Pervect Ten will be out for your scalp pretty soon."

My fault again. I should have brought us in with disguises in place. Hastily I remedied the omission, transforming us all into Wuhses. "I apologize, Kassery. Are you hurt?"

"No, I am all right." Wensley's mate stood up and clutched my hands. She seemed more than all right. Her eyes were glowing, almost full of hope.

"What is it?" I asked.

"I have just heard a rumor at Montgomery's," the little female whispered. "Wensley is alive! Gubbeen saw him in the castle."

At first I felt nothing at all, then as her words sunk in joy welled up inside me until I could no longer contain it.

"Whhheeeeeee-HAH!" I cheered, grabbing Kassery around the waist. I kicked off against the ground and flew high into the air, higher than the treetops. He hadn't been killed after all!

The world around me turned white. I realized that in my enthusiasm I had zoomed all the way up into the clouds. I stopped, and looked down. Four tiny specks on the ground in the center of the green sward were looking up at me. Talk about stupid overreaction, when I had just chided Tananda for the same thing. Kassery was clinging to me with all her strength.

"I'm so sorry," I stammered, throwing the illusion of birds on us so that our descent would be more unobtrusive than our ascent. "I bet you're afraid of heights. I didn't mean to scare you."

But the little female's eyes were shining. "I'm not, but thank you for being concerned. It is true what they say, that you care for those you serve, with all the affection a father shows his children. You are as kind and as powerful as your reputation paints you." She gave me a shy kiss on the cheek.

I was glad the illusion covered my face. It felt like it was on fire with embarrassment.

"Believe me, I'm not," I insisted. "I'm just an ordinary Klahd. Ask anyone."

"It's a good thing Aahz didn't see that," Tananda teased me, when we landed. "He'd have been all over your rear end for playing rocket ship."

"What's a..."

She gestured upward. "That was a pretty good imitation. So what was that I heard before you two decided to recreate 'Fly Me to the Moon'?"

Since it was daylight I had no idea in which direction the moon lay, but we pulled Kassery around the corner of the statue so she could tell us her news.

"What do you mean, sales are down to zero?" Paldine asked in disbelief.

"Sorry, ma'am," the Ronkonese representative rattled out, not really wanting to look her directly in the eye. "A bulletin from the Bureau of Consumer Affairs rescinded your safety certificate this morning."

"*And* reissued it this afternoon! I've just spent four hours arguing the matter with the board, and they agree with their original license. Our item is *fine*."

The rep spread out his hands apologetically. "Yes, but if there was even a *question* of a hazard issue the public gets absolutely crazy. The recall has made the talk shows, newspaper headlines, even getting talked up in 'man on the street' interviews. The reinstatement will get a mention in small print in the 'Corrections' page of the newspaper tomorrow morning. No one will notice it. I'm sorry."

"But why?" Paldine pleaded. "Everyone was for it! You all like it."

"I love it," the rep said frankly. "I'm keeping mine. It's cool. But this Skeeve guy got a lot of press when he denounced it on television this morning..."

"Skeeve!"

"Yeah. Do you know him? A Klahd."

Paldine drew her face into a grim set. "A soon-to-be-*dead* Klahd. What did he say?"

"Read it for yourself." He tossed a newspaper across the desk to Paldine. She read the front page story which was embellished with a picture of a really young Klahd male with blond hair. That was the way the Deveels in the Bazaar described Skeeve the Magnificent. This article described him only as Our Confidential Source. Dammit. How could he have found them? Why was he doing this? The Ronkonese rep looked at her questioningly.

"I'll be back," she informed him. No sense in killing the messenger, no matter how tempting the prospect was. "Don't box up the merchandise yet. We may still be able to move it. Once this Skeeve is history."

"I spent hours looking for him, but the reporter who did the original and, it seems, only interview, said he blipped out of there without finishing answering all her questions. She asked if I wanted to offer her an exclusive tell-all. It was all I could do not to reach down her throat and pull her gizzards out."

"Never mind," Vergetta soothed her. "We'll find another place to unload the Pervomatics. Meanwhile, I think we've found our leak."

She gestured to the "hot seat," where a tall, pale-haired Wuhs sat with Tenobia's knee across his thighs.

"An old lady told us that you took a couple of Klahds through the factory," the "torturer" hissed. "Confess!"

"But madam," Parrano protested. "Tours are not against the rules."

"They saw our special project!"

"W-w-what special project?"

With a questioning tilt to her head, Charilor held up an eggbeater.

"Never mind the small stuff," Tenobia growled. "Bring me the gumbo!"

This Wuhs had already heard the stories from Gubeen and Coolea; he was babbling out his entire life story and apologizing for every misdeed, minor, major and imagined, that he had ever committed. Sweat poured down his silly face as he tried to scramble away from the purple goo in the bowl. "I'm sorry! I'll never do it again! I swear to you, ladies, I swear!"

"All right, all right, all right!" Vergetta exclaimed, pushing Tenobia away from her victim. "I believe you."

That declaration was little consolation to the Wuhs, who had passed out cold at the sight of the pseudopods of bubbling stew pulsing out of the bowl at him. Niki slung him over her shoulder and trudged downstairs to put him into a cell to recover his wits. Charilor picked up the gumbo and a spoon.

"No sense in wasting good food," she commented.

"But if that gibbering fool didn't show them the Pervomatics," Oshleen pointed out, "then this Skeeve saw through the concealment wards. Damn, but this Klahd must be packing some fierce firepower. His reputation must be true."

"As strong as ours?" Nedira asked.

"Well, it would have to be," Vergetta agreed.

"I'll pit my wards against anyone's magik!" Monishone protested.

"Then how did he figure out where we were going? What we were making? The Pervomatic hasn't been anywhere but the factory and Ronko!"

"He wouldn't have to have seen them at the factory," Caitlin spoke up. They all turned to the littlest Pervect. She pounded her hands down on her keyboard. "He hacked us. I've got a power signature on my computer that came in not too long before the trouble started on Ronko."

"He's got a computer?"

"Why not? He's got a credit card. I found his credit history on line between Deva, Klah and Perv."

"How'd he get into your system?"

Caitlin avoided the eyes her elders, ashamed to be caught off guard. "My bad. I didn't think I'd have to put locks on the back door to this thing, not since this is the only computer in the entire dimension, but it seems I was wrong."

"Wow," Charilor scoffed. "She actually admits she was wrong about something."

"I think all these Wuhses have been lying to us," Loorna growled. She threw a hand at the glass prison on the table. "That one claims that they hired him to get rid of us. I think they brought the Great Skeeve here to bankrupt us so that they can keep us here *forever*."

"I want to go home!" Oshleen wailed.

"Right," declared Vergetta, putting her hands down decisively on the table. "This means war. He can't be in too many places at once, no matter how tough he is. We'll have several fronts. If he shuts one down, then we'll have the others. He can't cover every dimension. We'll diversify, get into places before he knows that we're there. And we'll shut *him* down. We are the Pervect Ten. The second he comes back here, he's history."

Oshleen raised a slender eyebrow. "What makes you think he's coming back?"

Vergetta picked up the snow globe and shook it. "We've got his friend."

# Chapter 26

*"What do you say to a little revolt?"*
F. Castro

"In a paperweight?" I repeated, not for the first time.

"In a crystal sphere," Kassery said, huddled with us behind the statue. "I couldn't say if it was used to hold down paper or not. Many of those invited by the Pervects to...to go and converse with them...claim that they have seen him."

Trust a Wuhs not to be able to make a straightforward statement about anything. "Are you sure it's him, not an illusion?" I said.

"Well, I would hesitate to doubt such upright members of the community," Kassery waffled, "but I have also heard Coolea say something similar. He claimed that he saw my mate standing before our tormentors, then was whisked away."

"I believe that would confirm that it is he," Zol suggested. "If the Pervect Ten meant to frighten their interviewees with the thought that they, too, could become a permanent guest they would leave him on display. Pervects are not subtle people."

"That's true," I agreed. "All right, that's it. I've been feeling guilty because I believed I had driven Wensley to a suicide attack. That had me stuck for a while, but I'm not stuck any longer. We're going to get him out."

"How?" Tananda asked, reasonably.

"The only way to do it is to beat the Pervect Ten into submission," I insisted. "We strip away their strength and put them at our mercy."

The looks on my friends' faces ranged from astonishment to open pity. Even Gleep wore a puzzled expression.

"Ten Pervects at *our* mercy?" Bunny asked.

"Are you sure you are feeling all right?" Kassery inquired, with tender solicitousness.

"I'm fine," I informed her. "I'm better than I have been for ages. I'm not crazy. I know how we can do this," *I think.* "We can't beat them if we go at them head to head, but we're not going to; we're going to hit them where they live—literally."

Tananda watched me carefully. "It sounds like you want to commit organized suicide. Mind letting us in on your plan?"

"It's not organized suicide, or suicide of any kind." I looked her squarely in the eyes. "A good general never wants to go into battle. I learned that from Big Julie. But when you have to, you go in to win, one way or another. Where you can't win openly and honestly, you win any way you can, because the enemy is going to do the same thing. Right? And you know me. I don't want any of us to get hurt, not even the Pervects, if I can help it. To do that I need your help. All of you."

Tananda's moss-green eyebrows climbed her forehead. "I'm not sure I like the way this is going. Excuse me for being skeptical, but I signed on to watch your back, and I will. I'll do anything you need me to, but I'm not even a little sure what you want to do is possible."

"Trust me," I pleaded. "You might like what I'm going to suggest. At least I'm hoping you might. At least, I'm hoping you won't throw me through a wall for suggesting the first step I want you to take. I need you to go back to Scamaroni and look up your friend Scootie."

A half-grin appeared on her face, and her shoulders shifted unconsciously as she considered it, not unfavorably, I thought. "And ask him what?"

I whispered in her ear. She let out a long giggle, took my face between her palms and gave me a big kiss right on the lips.

"See you later, handsome," she waved. There was a loud *bamf* as she vanished into thin air.

"What can I do?" Bunny asked eagerly.

"Nothing right away, but I'll need you and Bytina to help with negotiations with the Ten."

"Why Bytina?" Bunny asked, with wide eyes.

"Access," I grinned. "With what I have in mind we may not be able to speak with them directly. Bytina may be the only way we can communicate with them. I'm going to trap them inside their own fire spell."

"How?"

I waggled my eyebrows. "Tanda's gone to get the means. I hope."

"How may I help, Master Skeeve?" Zol inquired.

"Insights," I replied, though I didn't tell him how I planned to use the opposite of whatever he said. "Tell me how the Ten are likely to respond when we throw our one-two-three punches at them."

"Ah!" Zol exclaimed. "A three-pronged attack. Very clever. I see that Mistress Tananda is one step. The fire spell is another step. But what is the third?"

"For that I'll need about thirty packets of Kobold snacks," I grinned.

Zol's big dark eyes crinkled with merriment. He glanced at Gleep, who looked innocently from one of us to the other.

"This is why you are such a successful magician," Zol said me, as he picked up his notebook for a quick trip back to Kobol. "Innovation. Would you care to join me, Miss Bunny?"

"I'd love to," my assistant replied. The two of them vanished. One more item off my mental checklist.

"Can I help?" Kassery inquired shyly.

"I need to meet with as many Wuhses as possible," I said. "Tonight or tomorrow, in Montgomery's inn."

"A secret meeting? Can I tell them what it's about?"

"It's simple," I responded. "Everyone has a stake in getting the Pervect Ten to leave. It's time that some of you Wuhses step up and help out. I promise that no one will get hurt. They might get yelled at, but they face that any day."

Kassery nodded. "I will begin to organize it. They will be there." She rose from her crouch on the stone steps.

"Oh," I added, "and can you look after Gleep for me for a little while? I have to run back to Deva to pick up a few things."

Gleep looked disappointed, but Kassery regarded my dragon warmly. "It would be my pleasure," she responded, hooking her hand through his collar. My pet followed her with reproachful looks over his shoulder, but I knew better than to take a dragon shopping with me at the joke shop in the Bazaar.

We reunited at Montgomery's that evening. Kassery, Gleep and I waited at the table in the corner that had come to be our headquarters. As Bunny and Zol appeared, I was careful to throw a disguise spell over them. After the debacle on Ronko, I was certain that the Pervect Ten were very angry with me. I figured the safest possible place to be was right underneath their noses, but I saw no reason to advertise the fact, either.

Bunny's eyes were bright with excitement. "Oh, Skeeve, I had such a good time! Kobolds certainly know how to throw a party. They updated Bytina's communications program, and I think I got messages from everyone in the dimension!"

"Mission accomplished," Zol informed me, patting his satchel. "Is there any other way in which I might aid you?"

"There is one thing," I began.

Just then, Tananda reappeared. Her clothing was a little disheveled, but she had a smile on her face, and she was humming happily. I reached out to extend my disguise spell to her, but I was unable to cover up her olive-skinned beauty with the semblance of a sheep-woman. I smiled smugly. Mission accomplished.

"If you wouldn't mind," I queried Zol, "I would appreciate your help with a research project."

Tananda ambled over to me and placed a small object on the table. I noticed that as we leaned in to look at it, our faces changed from Wuhs to our respective races.

"But what is it?" Bunny asked.

"It's a stone," I informed her. "At least, I think it's a stone."

"That I can see," my assistant replied, with some asperity. "I may be able to play the dumb moll but you know I'm not."

"Sorry," the Trollop apologized, grinning. "Skeeve didn't know what he was going to get. It's a piece of stone from the Volute courthouse wall."

"This will do it?" I asked, nervously.

"Mmm-hmm," she hummed, running a sensuous finger along the décolletage of her tightly laced tunic as if remembering a pleasant sensation. "He swears it. *Precisely* what he said is 'It makes more of itself.' That was the best he could explain it, and believe me, I asked him several times. He was not inclined to mislead me at the moment. He's just not a magician." She raised her eyebrows meaningfully, and I did not want to ask her under which circumstances Scootie was sworn to honesty. I could guess.

"What is it?" Bunny insisted.

"It contains a portion of the enchantment that created the anti-magik field inside the jail on Scamaroni," I explained.

"But what's the use in that?"

"What's the biggest advantage the Pervect Ten have over us?" I asked her.

"That they can mop up the floor with us?"

"That's only if they can reach us," I pointed out.

"But so can any Pervect," Bunny asserted reasonably. "Between their magik and their strength, they can pound any Klahd or any Trollop into jelly."

"No," I corrected her, "what makes the Ten unbeatable is their ability to combine their magikal talent into ten times ten, to command forces that make my talent look like a drop of water in an ocean. If I can figure out how to duplicate this spell, we can knock out their power."

"Which still leaves them able to mop up the floor with us," Tananda pointed out. "They don't need their magik to tear us to pieces."

"Not if they can't reach us," I replied. "You see, if they can't use their talent, they can't dimension hop."

"Out of what?"

"Remember their fire protection spell? The one we took for a walk the first day we came to Wuh?"

Tananda made a noise. "Will I ever forget it? I like being around hot stuff, but that goes outside the definition."

"That's the one. We get them inside it, but we turn it inside out so they're trapped. If they can't use magik, they're not going anywhere. Then we have negotiating power."

"And how are we going to get them to wait politely in their chamber while we steal their powers and lock them inside their own security spell?"

I agreed with them. "For that, we're going to rely upon Wuhs power."

Since the Wuhses were still under house arrest during all non-business hours the only time they were able to attend a secret meeting was just after dawn and before they had to report for work in their shops and factories. Thirty or forty Wuhses crowded nervously into Montgomery's main room.

"We do not wish to be late, Master Skeeve," Gubbeen reminded me, watching through the window as the sun climbed with distressing rapidity up the eastern edge of the sky.

"Then I won't waste your time," I said. "I'm ready to fulfill the deal we made, but to succeed I am going to need your help."

"Us! W...w...well, you're the one Wensley hired," Ardrahan protested.

I raised an eyebrow. "How badly do you want these Pervects out of here?"

"Er," Gubbeen thought about the question for a moment, "a lot?" The others nodded their heads vigorously. That seemed to be the general consensus. They were willing to agree upon that concept.

"Enough to risk your life?" I inquired, pushing a little harder.

"Uh," Cashel gulped, "well, now that you mention it, not *really*. It hasn't been so bad with them here now, you know...new things to do, new industry getting started..."

I interrupted him. "Do you want to end up in a bottle like Wensley?"

"No!" the Wuhs protested. He began to back out, but there wasn't room in the crowded inn. "I mean, if it's not necessary, but they have their own opinions on how they want to deal with us, you know. Everybody has his or her own style, and who am I to condemn that, right?"

"Well, here's the good news," I told them. "I need your help, and it won't be fatal *or* painful at all. How about that?" The Wuhses looked surprised. I had begun with the worst possible scenario, and dropped the level of threat until it was under their threshold of panic. I did my best to keep from smiling as they discussed the matter between themselves, but I wasn't going to wait long for their answer. "Well?"

"I believe," Gubbeen began, "that the risk assessment is favorable to our continued comfort. All in favor of assisting Master Skeeve...?"

"Yah. Ya-a-aaah. Yaaaah," the others bleated in agreement.

"Opposed."

They all looked at one another. That was the biggest reason I had not approached each Wuhs privately. In public, they had to hang together, or face peer pressure to accede. I was right.

"Sheep," Tananda muttered.

I rubbed my hands together. "Good. Now, here's what I want you to do. One week from today..."

I now had to undertake the most intense course of study in my life, more difficult even than when I was trying to learn Dragon Poker in a week. Montgomery lent me a small, unused root cellar as my study, since we didn't want an inkling of what I was doing to circulate. The Wuhses were terrified of the Pervects, but they loved to talk among themselves. A secret which they crossed their hearts and hoped to die before telling was open knowledge before the next round of drinks was on the table. I watched it happen over and over again. Therefore, Gubbeen and the others were on a need-to-know basis only, as far as the specific details of our upcoming attack were concerned.

It was easy for me to say I could break down the components of the anti-magik spell and figure out how it worked, but since it did dampen any magikal probe that I threw at it, it made it harder to figure out what made it tick. Zol offered me his assistance.

"We can employ statistical analysis and field emissions to discover what sets it off," the Kobold stated, setting up his computer at the far end of the table. We discovered that inside a certain range the stone prevented either his notebook or Bytina from operating in this dimension. Bunny kept her little PDA at a protective distance from the sample.

"What puzzles me is what our source told Tananda," Zol reminded me. "'It makes more of itself.' What can that mean?"

"I don't know." I peered at the rock more closely. I had had plenty of time to study the walls during my incarceration, but I had not seen the bricks reproducing. "Maybe we have to give it something to reproduce with."

We tried soaking the stone in water, wine, oil, and several less savory fluids. We fed it sugar, plant food, even people food, but it continued to sit there. I went back to Klah for the grimoires Garkin had left me. Everything in his books was oriented toward channeling power, not getting rid of it.

"Maybe it's like yeast," I suggested. We broke it up into little pieces. We mixed it with dirt, then gravel, then chunks of rock. We heated it in fire, cooled it in ice, added practically every ingredient I could think of. I surrounded it in a field of magikal energy, then let it dissipate. Nothing happened until we mixed the wall parts with sand. The chunks of rock started making a hissing noise. A lather began to gather on top. I reached out a finger to touch it, but Zol yanked my hand back.

"Don't touch it!" he cautioned me. The sizzling noise got louder. "I believe it's working!"

"But why sand?" I asked, watching as the foam covered the mass and enveloped it in a seething, heaving, glowing lump. Heat blasted outward from it, singeing our eyebrows. We retreated to the far end of the cellar. "Why would that work when rock like the original piece wouldn't?"

"Because of its relative translucency," Zol explained. "I believe that what you have just witnessed is a textbook example of near-clear fizzin'."

I was too fascinated by the process to ask for a clarification. It was working.

It took a few days to produce a couple of buckets full of the anti magik material. Tananda provided security on the cellar, making sure that no one came down to see what we were doing, although my yell of "Yee-hah!" probably raised a few eyebrows. I emerged from our laboratory, frizzled hair and all.

"Are we ready?" Bunny asked.

"We are," I announced, triumphantly. "The coup will proceed on schedule."

# Chapter 27

*"But that trick never works!"*
R. J. Squirrel

Niki shouldered into her coverall and gulped down the rest of her coffee.

"Almost whistle time," she told the others, who were in various stages of trying to wake up.

Oshleen peered up from her ledger full of red ink with gold lines showing in the yellows of her eyes. Vergetta threw aside her copy of the Perv News, their sole link with civilization in the dreary Wuhs backwater.

"The new line is running like a top. No trouble from the Wuhses. They went right from Pervomatics to personal reminder pixies. The hypno chamber is really good. Even I almost forget what we're doing when I leave there."

"Should patent it," Caitlin stated, tapping away at her keyboard. "Look at the potential applications for secret installations. There might be government contracts in a device like that."

"Oh, great, that's all we'd need," Charilor groaned. "The government already forgets half the stuff it's doing. Do you really want to add deliberate black holes to that?"

"I guess not," the little Pervect shrugged, not looking up from her screen. "Should patent it anyhow. Won't keep the Deveels from copying it, but at least we'll have a legal reason for ripping their lungs out if we catch them."

"I can't believe that there's been no heroic attempt to rescue you, little guy," Vergetta told the paperweight in the middle of the table. "Nobody throwing themselves on the ramparts, no one scaling the walls, nobody battering down the door. Looks like all your friends are a bunch of Wuhses, eh?" She laughed heartily at her own joke. The Wuhs didn't join in.

"There was a retraction in the *Ronko Gazette* from the Great Skeeve," Paldine announced. "I saw it when I went to pick up our stock. What I can't figure out is why."

Vergetta looked dubious. "Why which one? Why he got in our way, or why he apologized?"

"The apology is the weird part."

"Looks to me like he backed out of his contract with Shorty over there," Tenobia declared, aiming a manicured thumb at the Wuhs on the table. "Nothing's happened for a week. He probably went back to his batcave with a big fat zero. Probably just figured out he's as likely to get paid as we are."

The can hanging from the wall jangled. Niki frowned at it, then went over to pick it up. She listened, the scowl growing deeper.

"Something's wrong at Factory #9," she told the others as she let the cylinder drop. "The Wuhses are refusing to sign in." The can clattered again. She snatched it up and shouted into it. "I'm coming! What??" She threw it down. "Factory #2. They're protesting for better parking spaces."

"I'll go," Tenobia volunteered. "I'll give them *parking spaces!*"

"Don't all of them walk to work?" Nedira inquired.

"It's probably a notion one of them picked up on another dimension," Tenobia snarled. "Ironic, isn't it? They found something for free that's still a pain in the rump!" She vanished.

The can jangled again. And again. The Pervects grabbed for it, another rushing off to handle each fresh situation.

"Hold on!" Vergetta shouted, as Charilor was about to blip out to handle a riot at Factory #3 about microwave popcorn privileges. "This is too fishy. Someone's trying to get us all going in a dozen directions at once."

"Skeeve," Oshleen sniffed. "He's back! But where?"

A shout from Caitlin made the remaining four turn around.

"We got him," the smallest Pervect announced smugly. "He's trying to read our computer again!"

Her hands danced over the keyboard. Vergetta smiled her admiration as a ball of blue lightning built up in the air around

Caitlin's head. As the little Pervect hit ENTER, the surge dove back into the computer and down the line. She crossed her arms. "That'll fix him."

I jumped to catch Zol as a jagged ball of power leaped out of his notebook, knocking him flat. We were in a room of the castle on the same floor as the Pervects' headquarters waiting until the room was empty. Gleep sat in a corner happily crunching up more Kobold treats than I had ever let him have before.

"What happened?" I demanded.

Bunny lifted the little gray man's head. His eyes fluttered open.

"Coley," he gasped. "Where's Coley?"

I lifted the notebook and handed it to him. The screen had been blown outward, and all the lights were dark.

"No!" he cried. "Oh, Coley!"

He cradled the little computer, patting its case and rocking it. Tears ran down his face. The computer was ruined. Zol muttered nonsense to himself.

I was shocked. It was the most emotion I had ever seen from the impassionate little Kobold.

"They're joined for life," Bunny reminded me.

"Zol, we've got to move soon," I whispered. "How many are left?"

The Kobold whimpered at me, his big dark eyes open and anguished.

"He's in no shape to help us," Tananda whispered back. "A Kobold and his computer are one of the great love stories in all the dimensions."

I made a quick decision. I pulled the D-hopper out of my boot and handed it to Bunny.

"Take him back to Kobol. See if they can do anything for Coley. We can handle the first part, at least."

Bunny nodded. "I'll be back as soon as I can." She kissed me. My heart sang. "Good luck!"

I grinned. "No warrior ever got a better sendoff to battle."

She blushed prettily and pushed the button.

"That leaves three of us," Tananda reminded me.

After their cowardly attack on Zol I was more determined than ever to drive the Pervects out. "That will be plenty."

We hefted our weaponry and sneaked into the anteroom. Gleep's stomach rumbled audibly behind me.

"Shh!" I hissed.

Gleep looked at me apologetically. "Gleep sorry."

The Pervects weren't listening for small noises. They were shouting at one another. A clanging noise added to the clamor. I crawled close enough to the door to listen.

"More riots!" the eldest one yelled. "What is it, every single Wuhs in Pareley decides this is the day to protest our rules? They're insane."

The jangling came again.

"Hello! Factory #8. Fix it yourselves, you miserable sheep! One of you go. Hurry."

I heard a *bamf* of displaced air as a Pervect vanished.

Mentally I complimented Kassery and Bunny. They had been riding herd on the designated protest teams all week long. Bunny in particular had been incredibly good about getting them to promise to cooperate at the designated moment. With her background in handling Mob men, the Wuhses didn't have a chance to waffle or back out. It looked like all her convincing had paid off.

"Let them riot!" shouted the elegant one in the jumpsuit. "Who cares if the Wuhses riot? There's a magician gunning for us. Concentrate on him! Find him!"

"That power surge ought to have knocked him out," the little one at the computer snapped. "He's flat on his back. He ought to be easy to find. Follow the power line. Take a tracer from my CPU."

If they had a means of locating computers by magik I was glad Bunny and Zol were no longer in the dimension. I peered through the crack in the door. Four left. Weren't they ever going to leave?

"Gleep?" my pet asked quietly. He wore a collar filled with anti-magik dust. I hoped that would protect him from the fire spell. If he felt any heat at all he had orders to back off and lure the Pervects to him. It would have the same effect of clearing the room that I had in mind.

I glanced in through the doorway. The old one, the very young one, the elegant one and the tough one in the miniskirt were still in there. Time was running away! How could I get in and lay my anti-magik floor if they didn't leave? Time to take action!

I gestured over my head. Gleep gave me a happy grin, nudged open the door with his nose, and trotted playfully into the middle of the Pervects' chamber.

"Well, look at that, a little pet dragon," the elder Pervect said, bending over to beckon Gleep to her. "Come here, little dragon-cutie-pie. What are you doing here?"

"Dragons aren't native to this dimension," the little one warned her. "It's some kind of trick...!" But it was too late.

POOT!

*"Aaaaugggh!"*

The inevitable happened. The effects of processed carbohydrates hitting dragon digestive juices manifested itself strongly in the enclosed room. The air didn't actually turn green, but it smelled as though it should have. Gleep stood in the middle of the stone floor, looking very pleased with himself. Then he stuck out his long, forked tongue and blew a raspberry at the four Pervects. Flicking his tail playfully, he galloped out of the room. The Pervects let out a cry of fury, and went running out after him, past us and into the hallway. I checked the status of the spell to make sure the little flames were pointing inward now, hoisted my buckets and charged in.

"Hurry," Tananda urged me. "Phew!"

The gaggingly awful smell Gleep had left behind drove me to my knees, but I used a form of the "pushing" spell I knew to clear out the air.

"Look!" I cried joyfully, pointing to a clear glass globe on the table. "There he is!" A small figure was jumping up and down inside it. Wensley.

There was no time to free him now. I stuffed the sphere into my pouch. Tananda and I emptied our buckets into the center of the room and used brooms to push it over the surface of the floor in a big square.

"Do we have to get it everywhere?" she asked.

"Keep it more than an arm's length from the wall. I don't want it to take out the fire spell. I need that. Look! It's soaking right in." The disenchanting sand seemed to dissolve right into the substance of the floor.

"If it replicates itself," Tananda pointed out, "then eventually it will work its way outward and put out the fire."

"I hope we can get this done before that happens," I replied. But I was worried about that, too.

Screaming and the sounds of breaking crockery allowed us to monitor Gleep's progress around the castle. I had instructed him to cause the maximum possible disruption, and it sounded as though he was taking my orders to heart. I hoped that the other Pervects would come running to help. When I was only half-finished covering the floor the sound seemed to grow nearer.

"Not yet, Gleep," I muttered desperately. We couldn't even become invisible. All magik within arm's length of the bespelled floor had been dampened. "We're not ready!"

It must have been a lucky gust of wind or a shift in the old building's foundation, but the door into the hallway swung shut just before Gleep thundered past it with the Pervects in hot pursuit. It was about time something went our way on this assignment.

I surveyed our handiwork. The anti-magik dust had soaked into the floor, leaving only a slight sheen to show where it lay. I tried throwing a fireball into the room, but my spell fizzled almost as soon as it left my hand. I grinned.

"Now, to get them all back in here," I declared.

"First thing we have to do," Tananda insisted, dropping her broom and shouldering a bag full of her own special equipment, "is to get their attention."

Loud clattering in the direction of the kitchen told us where Gleep had led them. I levitated the two of us past all the traps and spells that were supposed to prevent intruders and were now impeding the Pervects from intercepting the dragon who had made their room temporarily uninhabitable. Cursing, they had to dispell their own magikal obstacle course as they ran. Gleep let half the attacks roll off his tough hide, and blew out the other half of the defenses with blasts of flame.

He spotted me as we ducked into the long hallway that led to the butler's pantry, the laundry room and several other side passages. Wheeling almost on his tail, he bowled over his pursuers, and came charging towards us. I readied an illusion spell for the moment he crossed the threshold, transforming him into a mouse. The Pervects hammered past the doorway of the pantry, backpedaled and glanced in.

"Gleep?" squeaked the mouse.

"He must have gone down one of the other passages!" the elegant one shouted.

"We'll split up," the miniskirted one ordered.

"Call for reinforcements," the little one panted.

"I'll get the others back here," the elder one insisted. "You keep looking. I'll bet this Skeeve is here somewhere."

I grinned. They were absolutely right.

They all took off in different directions, but within minutes reassembled in the hall heading for the main stairs. Tananda vanished, heading to a point over the stairway where she had some little surprises ready. I could almost count backwards in my head, then...

*"Eeeeeee!!!"*

A plague of wood spiders came plummeting out of the air onto the heads of the Pervects. These weren't real arachnids, but an animate growth like an active moss Tanda had discovered while "camping out" in another dimension (well, that's what she had called it). The longlegged plants enveloped the Pervects with fibrous threads, wrapping them up like mummies. The females' feet got tangled up, just in time to slip on the spongy marbles scattered on the floor from another package in the Trollop's bag of tricks. Yelling, the four clutched at one another, dancing madly to stay upright. They cannoned into one another, and rolled head over heels down the stairs. Being Pervects I knew the fall wouldn't hurt them, but it *would* make them mad.

I had been counting on Bunny to set off the next wave, which let a gaggle of herdbeasts loose from the reception chamber where they'd been penned up since before dawn. I reached out with my mind, lifted the latch, and flung open the door. Baaing in panic, the herd thundered out, heading for the main door and freedom. Before the Pervects could tear all the wood webbing off, they were in the middle of a mini-stampede.

Into the midst of this mess, another Pervect appeared, the efficient one in the coveralls.

"Vergetta, what's going oooo-nnn-nnn-nnn!"

The marbles claimed another victim. She catapulted down the stairs and landed on her fellows, who were just picking themselves up off the floor. They all fell down again. Another, the plump motherly one, blipped into the middle of the disarray.

"What is going on here?" she cried. "Who-oo-oooa!" And down.

Six. It was time to let myself be seen. Wearing the disguise that Aahz and I had worked up for my "audition" as court magician of Possiltum, I stalked out onto the landing and raised my arms. The main door slammed shut behind the last of the herdbeasts. The open windows banged closed, and the torches on the walls dimmed and flickered.

"There!" the elegant one shouted. "There he is!"

Bolts of fire and lightning flew at me, from not one, but two directions. I spun on my heel. The slim female in the long robe had reappeared on the landing. I glanced up. Tananda was gone. I threw up my hands, spreading out a ward. Her lightning bolt bounced off, and I "disappeared"

in a cloud of smoke, courtesy of a bag of flash powder. The Pervect magician doubled over coughing. Before it cleared I was flying through the hall overhead, aiming toward my next vantage point. The object was to lure the Pervects, all ten of them, back into their chamber all at the same time. I had seven.

Gleep wasn't idle. I bounded up toward the ceiling in time to avoid being run over by my pet, who was being chased by two Pervects dressed in exactly opposite styles. One had on the most conservative two-piece suit I had ever seen, and the other was in a spiked leather bustier and stockings. It takes all kinds, I mused. Nine.

All we were missing was the grouchy one. I had presumed I was going to catch a few fish upstairs in the main headquarters as they popped back from the Wuhs riots, then found they couldn't pop out again. I hoped fervently that she was there. It was time to lure the rest of them back into the trap we had set.

Sailing towards the second floor anteroom I lit off a series of rainbow blasts of light designed to bring the Pervects running my way. Without Bunny I was going to have trouble with the next part of my illusion, but I was willing to improvise. I alit on the mantel of the fireplace, where I'd gotten stuck the first day. Now it was a perch to keep me from being trampled by the Pervects.

"Sst! Skeeve!"

I glanced down and saw the gleam of a familiar head of red hair. Bunny! A thin gray hand waved.

"Ready, Master Skeeve!" Zol whispered.

I beamed. My force was back up to full strength. It was showtime.

From two different directions the Pervects converged upon the hallway, one group pursuing Gleep, one following my beacons. At my signal, Bunny turned Bytina toward me.

I spread out my arms and in my most impressive voice I boomed out, "Greetings!"

My magician image, vastly expanded, appeared on the wall of the headquarters. Yes, there was the tenth Pervect waving her arms, evidently trying to figure out why her transportation spell wasn't working.

"He's in our workroom!" the eldest shrieked furiously. Together, the remaining nine of the Pervect Ten went charging into the chamber with Gleep right alongside them. I saw him take a deep breath.

I crossed my fingers. The timing was very tricky. The second the last Pervect crossed the threshold, Gleep breathed out a long tongue of flame. It struck the big tub of flash powder Tanda and I had left on the Pervects' table. A vast cloud of smoke filled the room, accompanied by coughing and hacking. Gleep came lolloping out of the midst of it as if he hadn't a care in the world. He was largely immune to anything having to do with smoke and fire. I watched carefully as he exited. The little flames marked his passage, and turned their points inward. The Pervect Ten were trapped.

When the smoke cleared, I was sitting crosslegged on the air facing the door, my disguise dispelled.

"Greetings," I announced. "I am the Great Skeeve."

# Chapter 28

*"When you have the upper hand, use it."*
M. Jordan

Coughing, the Pervect Ten turned to face me. I had to admit I felt a little sorry for them. I'd made the mistake of being at ground zero more than once when using flash powder, and the effect was lung-searing. I preferred to be well away by the time it deployed. Gleep came trotting over to me, expecting a pat on the head for a job well done. He got it.

"Who the hell is the tot?" the eldest demanded, waving her arms to clear the air.

"Watch who you're calling a tot!" Caitlin grumbled. "Yeah, who are you?"

"Greetings, ladies," I repeated, spreading my hands and floating higher in the air on a wisp of thought. "I am Skeeve the Magnificent."

"You?" the angry one declared. "You're going to be Skeeve the Grease Spot when I get through with you!"

I threw a finger toward Bunny, who turned Bytina to face me. My face, magnified about sixty times, appeared on the wall of the chamber, and my voice echoed out of the computer on Caitlin's desk.

"Halt!" I shouted. The very volume caused them to stop in their tracks.

"I serve the Wuhses, and they have empowered me to deal with you. So deal you shall!"

"I'll tear him apart," the heavy-browed one snarled.

"Me first," snarled the one in the leather skirt. They all started moving towards me, claws out.

"Don't!" I shouted, as they made towards me. "Look at the walls around you. My dragon reset the wards so the flames are facing you. I know that Pervects are vulnerable to fire. Do not try to cross the threshold."

"That's our spell!" the robed one protested.

"Formation, ladies!" the eldest one ordered. "Let's wipe this snotty little brat out of existence."

They all joined hands and closed their eyes. I braced myself. I had watched them send a crowd of a thousand Wuhses each back to their individual homes with a single spell. They were the most powerful magikal force I had ever encountered. If they could break through my preparations I was finished. I waited...waited...waited...then....

Each of them opened one eye and peered at the others.

"Someone is not concentrating!" the eldest chided them.

"Yes, we are," the elegant one complained. "Something's wrong!"

The leather-skirted Pervect pointed at me. "He...he's dispelling our magik! All of it!"

"How could he?" the one in the bustier said. "He's a Klahd."

"A Klahd who knows one more trick than you," I replied, loftily. "That's all that it takes, really. While you were bumbling around in my obfuscation spell..."

"You mean choking on your flash powder, sonny," the elder interrupted me. "We may be impressed by your tenacity, but we've seen the sleight-of-hand tricks before."

"Fine," I shrugged. "I don't mind if you see the mechanism of my trap *now that you're inside it*. The anti-magik shell comes from the jail on Scamaroni. You can't blip out of there, because neither spells nor magik items work inside it."

They gawked at me. The skirt-suited one recovered her wits first. "It *was* your voice we heard that night. You were there!"

"Uh-huh," I acknowledged, pleased that they were finally starting to catch on.

"What do you want?"

"I want you to cease your unfair control over the Wuhses. They are tired of living under your yoke and having you rob them blind and make them work for you as slaves to make you rich. They want you to pack up and leave, and stop draining their treasury. Otherwise, you can stay here. We'll even shove food through the barriers for you, but won't take them down unless you meet certain conditions."

The one in the coverall gawked openly at me. "Making *us* rich? You've got the wrong slaves here, pal. We can't even collect our fee!"

It was my turn to goggle. "What fee?"

The elegant one groaned, as if I was too stupid to live. "These fools hired us to work for them. They brought us in as financial managers. Our assignment was to straighten out the kingdom's cash flow problems. These moronic Wuhses have been undercutting our efforts at every turn. Did they tell you that? Did they tell you that we've managed to get them out of debt and keep them out of debt, but only by scaring them into submission? That we were able to stay on top of their out of control spending up until the last three weeks, when *someone* has gotten in our way every time we were going to get ahead."

"We've been here over two years," the littlest one moaned. "If they'd just cooperated we would have finished with our contract and been on our way in six months. That's what it was supposed to take."

"Don't talk to him," their magician complained. "He's just here to cheat us and throw us out."

"No, I'm not," I goggled, honestly appalled. "Tell me about it."

"Not under these circumstances," the eldest one told me firmly. "We don't deal under siege."

I lowered myself to the ground and headed toward the door.

"No, Master Skeeve," Zol called to me. "Don't go to their level. Maintain your advantage."

But I was through listening to his advice. What the Pervect Ten said made sense. I had observed from the beginning that the Wuhses dealt in a sidelong and cowardly fashion, except Wensley.

Wensley! I reached into my pocket and drew out the globe. The little figure in it jumped up and down. "Stop! Stop! Stop!"

"How do I release him?" I asked, holding up the sphere.

"Just release the wards," the robed Pervect gestured.

With my mind I opened a little door in the side of the glass ball. Suddenly, Wensley was beside me. I steadied him as he staggered, then he rushed toward the Pervects. I ran after him through the blinding flash of light.

"Hey, stop!" I shouted.

But I was too late. Wensley threw himself on his knees in front of the eldest Pervect.

"Dear lady," he pleaded, "I most humbly apologize."

"What is this?" I demanded. "Wensley, what are you doing?"

He looked up at me. "I had no idea how hard we were making it for them. We are not used to having anyone give us direct orders. Let us say that...we didn't take it well."

"I'll say, sonny!" the elder declared. "You've driven us clean out of our minds with all of your nickling and...you say you're sorry?"

"I am, truly," the Wuhs vowed. "I'll do anything I can to help make it right."

"Well, for a start, you can tell your hired gun here to stop interfering in our business ventures!" the skirt-suited one insisted. She walked over and whacked me on the chest with the back of her hand. "We're doing all this for your benefit. You people have been making it almost impossible for us to live up to the terms of our agreement. We're businesswomen. We have a reputation across thirty different dimensions of being the Pervects to come to when you need something done right in the minimum possible time, and you're doing a hell of a job of undoing years of hard work in a matter of weeks."

"I'm really sorry about the misunderstanding," I informed them, rubbing the sore place with my fingertips. "I didn't realize until I saw one used that those Pervomatics really were food choppers. But if it's so straightforward, why were you concealing from the Wuhses what they were working on? It looked pretty suspicious."

"Because these sheep, in case you haven't noticed, have all the morals of jackdaws," the eldest sighed, sinking down into a chair. "They'll take anything and rationalize that it's okay as long as no one else knows they're taking it. But why didn't *you* come to us in the first place and just ask us what we're doing, instead of putting us out of business in two dimensions?"

I heard a contrite little noise behind me, but I ignored it. I had been wrong enough times on my own in my life that I didn't have to ruin a second reputation to make my explanation.

"I got some advice I didn't understand properly," I shrugged. "It's all my fault."

"Don't let him take the blame, dear Pervects," Zol put in from behind me. "He came to me, and I inadvertently gave him a wrong steer. Please forgive us all."

I glanced over my shoulder. The little gray man stood in the doorway flanked by Bunny and Tananda.

The skirt-suited one pointed a finger. "Aren't you Zol Icty?"

The Kobold bowed. "I have that honor."

She smiled, showing four inch long teeth, an expression which was repeated on the faces of all of the Pervect Ten. "We have *all* your books."

"I'm sorry about your workroom," I told them, as the female in the business suit broke out a keg of wine to toast the new spirit of cooperation. "I think the alteration may be permanent. You can't do magik in here any more."

"As long as the computer runs, who cares?" the little one declared. "I'm Caitlin, by the way. I've been checking the archives on you around the dimensions. You've got a pretty hot reputation, for a Klahd."

"Thanks, I think," I replied.

Tananda shifted impatiently. "Hey, handsome, are you going to let us in, or do we have to stand here and watch you drink in front of us?"

I had to transit through the brilliant flash of light twice, once to open the fire spell outward, and once to accompany the rest of my companions into the room.

"Tananda's one of my former partners," I introduced my associates. "Bunny's my administrative assistant."

The tallest Pervect eyed Bunny curiously. "Aren't you a beauty queen?"

"I was on one occasion," Bunny explained. "I'm really an accountant."

"You are?" Oshleen continued in astonishment.

I remembered her now. (For those of you who missed our previous encounter please see that fine volume *Myth-Told Tales*, available from your finer stockists.)

"So am I. What do you think about secured investment in growth industry?"

"Depends on the track record of the companies involved," my assistant replied, instantly falling into the secret language of finance. "Are we talking seasonal or year-round value?"

I instantly lost track of the thread of conversation. Money management was not my long suit.

Vergetta, the eldest, waved an admonitory finger at Gleep, who regarded her with utter innocence.

"He's not going to...you know...again, is he?"

"Oh, no," I assured her, mentally crossing my fingers. I exchanged glances with Gleep. I think I saw understanding in those round blue eyes that now was not the time to upset the delicate balance.

"Good. *You* I remember," she turned to Tananda. "You and a couple of big lugs were the ones who ruined our plan in the Bazaar."

"You bet we did," Tananda declared, holding her ground, "extortion's not welcome there."

Vergetta sighed. "It wasn't supposed to go that far. We were just offering services. You think it's easy, after spending a day arguing with creditors, to go and clean a dozen offices and shops? You think I *like* scrubbing toilets?"

"But, five gold coins a week?"

"Pervects always charge top coin for their services," Zol explained. "They believe they're worth it. You should have paid it."

"Too much," Tananda disagreed, shaking her head. "We did the right thing putting you out of business there."

Vergetta patted me on the arm. "You're right not to follow this little guy's advice, Sonny. But it was very clever, what you did to us. You could be a Pervect. You, too, Honey." She held out her wine glass to me for a refill.

"I'm in your debt," Wensley told her, leaping to get the carafe off the table and fill it for her. He hadn't left her side since he had been freed from the snow globe. "I'd like to help undo the mess I made."

Vergetta didn't hesitate. She frowned at him. "From what we've been able to find out about your hired gun here, this guy is Mr. Connected. We need to dump all the merchandise the two of you made impossible to sell."

"Me?" Wensley squeaked. "Why?"

"Because you hired him, Bubby. If he's got any advice to pass along, you have to ask for it."

Wensley turned beseeching eyes to me. "Will you, Master Skeeve?"

I felt guilty about my part in the enterprise, too, so I thought hard for a moment. "Why not the Bazaar?" I suggested.

"Why not?" Vergetta echoed. "Because your little Trollop friend there got us banned for life."

"And I'd have done it for longer, too," Tananda growled, her cat's eyes glowing. "You should have seen the black eye she gave me! And poor Chumley was sore for a week! Nobody beats up on my big brother but me!"

"Only two of you have been banned," I reminded them, thoughtfully. "Besides, you don't need to have a shop in the Bazaar to have your goods sold there. I know the Merchants' Association. If I put your exclusive contract out to bid they'll be undercutting one another in no time. The Deveels will love Pervomatics and...and..."

"Storyteller goggles," Monishone, the robed one, put in shyly. "My invention."

"That name's got to get changed," Paldine, the business-suited female, interjected briskly. "I'll come with you to handle the negotiations. When? We want to get some black ink back in the ledgers."

"As soon as we're done here," I assured her.

"We could have used that Bub Tube," Oshleen was saying passionately to Bunny. "We needed it. I hoped to use it to instill a little responsibility into these Wuhses. What do you do when everyone seems to agree, and when they don't they just sneak off and do what they want? Pervects are much more straightforward. We just tell someone what we want, and if they don't do it, we tear their heads off."

"Don't play dumb with me," Tenobia was telling a wide-eyed Gleep, who was gnawing on a table leg. "I was a dragon-tamer when I used to work for the circus. You guys are much more intelligent than you let anyone know."

Eavesdropping with interest, Zol took out his little note-book and began to tap away on his button board. It looked as though Coley had been restored to his original condition. He even had a new red metal band around his middle.

"Say," Caitlin perked up, noticing the device in his hands. "Isn't that an InfoDump Mark 16?"

"Yes, it is," Zol beamed. "His name is Coley." With pride, he put it into the littlest Pervect's hands and began to explain all its features. In turn, she showed him her computer. We were all getting along so well, we had forgotten about the object of our presence there.

Oshleen and Paldine put their heads together over a spread-sheet. The two of them compared notes with several of the others, all of whom seemed pleased. They brought the proposed figures to Vergetta.

"Very nice," she nodded. "What with our projected earnings we'll be able to buy out our contracts and go home in no time. Even the Wuhses will prosper, since they're doing the

manufacture. I've been dying to throw out the line of tea towels for a year."

"We could be home in time for the spring fashion line,"
Oshleen sighed.

"But what about us?" Wensley asked.

# Chapter 29

*"It's been real!"*
W. Disney

"What about you?" Vergetta echoed. "You Wuhses will be on your own. It's why you brought in the big tough magician and his friends, isn't it?"

"Well," Wensley began, "you ten have been essentially in charge of everything for the last two years. If you pull out and go home, then...we will collapse. We'll go back to the way we were before. Sink into debt." His slitted eyes were wide with fear.

"Then you need a new government," I suggested. "One with backbone."

"Led by whom?" Wensley asked. "Who could possibly step in and tell people how to do what you've been doing?"

I looked straight at him. "You."

His voice rose up into an even more strangled squeak. "Me?" The Ten look him up and down.

"Why not you?" Tenobia said. "As Wuhses go you've been pretty assertive. You have shown some leadership potential."

"Oh, no," Wensley protested, abashed. "What an unkind thing to say."

"Not where I come from," I stated firmly. "In fact, calling something 'average' is almost an insult. You could be in charge of Wuh's rebirth."

"Oh, I *couldn't.*"

"Oh, yes, you could," Zol insisted. "Why, with the example of the Pervects before you, you could create a government that all Wuhses would be proud of."

"But they hurt people's feelings, and they step on toes," Wensley complained. "Someone will have to say 'no.'" He looked alarmed. "I don't know if I can do that."

"Sure you could," I informed him.

"My friend," Zol began encouragingly. "You need to reach inside yourself for the resource you showed in going to find Master Skeeve..."

The Wuhs looked even more alarmed. I stiff-armed him out of the way. "Wait a minute, Zol. This kind of therapy really should be left to a specialist in assertiveness." Zol looked puzzled but Vergetta grinned.

"One side, Honey. Allow me." She took the Wuhs's face between her hands. "Kiddo, starting tomorrow, we're going to reopen both of the old product lines. You guys are going to have to leave behind your old handcrafts, which weren't selling anyhow, and start making anything that our inventors here come up with."

"Well, of course," Wensley agreed, as amiably as anyone could with his cheeks flattened by Perv claws.

"And in the meantime, you are going to take lessons from us. We're gonna teach you how to think like a Pervect, walk like a Pervect, talk like a Pervect, and above all...eat like a Pervect. Think about it! What could add more fire to the belly than a real, honest Pervish meal? Once you can muscle a bowl of Potage St. Auugh down your throat, handling a bunch of Wuhses who want to spend your money on a complete set of last year's Superbowl tickets should be a piece of cake. What do you think? I can go and rustle up some stew right now."

"You're too kind," Wensley gasped at the very thought of Pervish food. "Really, it's very considerate of you to think of my nutritional needs, but I'm sure there must be another way to instill the virtues..."

"Doesn't put the lead in your pencil the same way, Sonny. Should I go get some for you? You can eat it right here. I insist. You'll love it."

Wensley seemed to be going through the most incredible internal discomfort. He wriggled and squirmed, but Vergetta had a firm hold on him. Gradually his protest worked its way up to his mouth. A nasal hum emerged.

"..Nnn..."

"What?"

"...Nnn...nnn..."

"I can't hear you!" Vergetta bellowed, leaning close. "What did you say?"

"Nnn...nnn...nno...No!" Wensley shouted. His eyes flew wide at his own boldness. "I did it! I said no!"

Vergetta wore a smug smile. "Once. You said no once. But you'll get used to it."

"Excellent!" Zol exclaimed. "There, do you see? And every time you need to say no in the future, you can picture this lady's most impressive persuasion."

"Congratulations," Charilor cheers, slapping him soundly on the back. "You're president."

"Oh, I can't be. That will take consultation with all of the other committees. They may have views they wish to offer..."

"Nobody will disagree with you," Niki interrupted. "If there's anything I've ever learned about you Wuhses, it's that if you tell them something's got to be, they just accept it. Face it. You're in charge now."

Wensley looked astonished, but pleased. "I...I don't know how we can ever thank all of you."

"Oh, you've got our bill, darling," Vergetta reminded him. "You'll pay it. Put it on the debit side of the clean new slate you're starting today."

"And you can buy my books for everyone to read," the little gray man added. "That way you will have a written guideline to mental self sufficiency. I'll be delighted to offer you a bulk rate."

Wensley called a mass secret meeting to announce the outcome of the morning's action. Most of the Wuhses came out of curiosity, to find out who had torn whom apart. They were all thankful to see Wensley alive and well. He and Kassery wouldn't let go of one another, kissing and whispering together. Bunny sighed.

"It's so romantic," she kept saying. I don't know why that made me feel uncomfortable, but it did.

When we had all the committee leaders safely stuffed into Montgomery's inn and sealed the doors closed, I thanked them all for coming.

"We've reached a new understanding with the Pervect Ten," I explained. "You all know my friends. I'd like to introduce our guests. I think you know them?"

Into the midst of the Wuhses a loud *bamf* heralded the arrival of the Pervects. There was a general stampede for the doors. If we hadn't barred them magically I would have lost my entire audience in five seconds.

"You have nothing to worry about!" I shouted over the panicked bleating. "From today onward you will be led by a Wuhs. The Pervects will go back to being consultants, answerable to him, as they were supposed to be from the beginning."

"But who?" Gubbeen asked curiously, once we had coaxed him back to the table. "Who is this Wuhs who will lead us?"

"Wensley," I announced, putting my arm around the hero of the day. "He'll be a great leader. He was ready to sacrifice himself for your greater good, and he's ready to serve you in a less life-threatening capacity."

"But," began Ardrahan, puffing herself up indignantly. "The style with which we are most comfortable is for everyone to have an equal voice in all decisions."

"Not any more," I informed them. "That didn't work. That's how you got in trouble in the first place. Wensley's ready to take all your input and be fair in his judgment, but the final decision has to rest with him. He's in charge now."

As Niki had predicted, the committeefriends conferred and complained, but in the end they agreed with everything we told them to do. The Pervects were relieved. Wensley and Kassery were elated and awed but ready to try. The disenfranchised spokesWuhses were doing their best to influence the new leaders to see their points of view. And I was ready to go home.

"Well, that's that," I stated, shaking hands with Zol Icty. "So, are you going back to Kobol now?"

"No, indeed," the little gray man informed me happily. "I am going to stay here to observe the Pervect Ten assist our young friend there in finally putting Pareley back on the financial map, and then I will go back to Perv with them. I want to study them very closely for the new book I am researching: *I'm Okay, You're Pervect.* When it's finished I'll send you all copies."

"I'll look forward to it," I thanked him. "I'm going back to my studies. I've still got a lot to learn."

"You're on your way," Zol assured me. "I was very impressed with both your application and your wisdom."

"I'm sorry," Wensley said, turning to me with some embarrassment. "But we can't pay you yet. Wuh is on the financial mend, and your fee will just send us back again into negative territory. I'm sorry."

"How about an in-kind fee instead?" I said.

Wensley looked uncomfortable, but nodded. "We owe you so much. What do you have in mind?"

"It's something you already have," I explained. "I'd like to have your D-hopper."

"But you don't need one," the Wuhs said, looking puzzled. "You can already travel the dimensions."

"I know," I acknowledged, "but I do need it. What about it?"

He looked at the others, who were clearly urging him not to give up their precious D-hopper, but he nodded. "It's caused enough trouble here," he decided at last. "I think that once we learn responsibility there will be plenty of time to learn how to travel between the dimensions."

"Thank you," I asserted, tucking the device into my belt pouch. Bunny and Tananda gave me odd looks, knowing I had one just like it in my boot. "Good riddance to it," Loorna insisted, producing the device. She slapped it into my palm.

Paldine came up to join me. "Come on, Skeeve the Magnificent. We've got some Deveels to dazzle."

Oshleen came over to envelop me in a massive, bonecrushing hug. "Any time you need some quality financial work done, honey, you've got a freebie coming."

"I've got a top accountant, thanks," I replied. Bunny, who had not even noticed she had tensed, relaxed and smiled brilliantly at me.

"Well, any time you need someone's hindquarters chewed off, we'd be glad to help out," Charilor offered, showing her teeth.

"Gee, where were you a couple of weeks ago?" I asked, innocently. "I was looking for an organized force to throw out a bunch of Pervects who had taken over another dimension."

To give them credit, the Pervect Ten laughed.

"You've got chutzpah, bubby," Vergetta chuckled, crushing my hand in a tight grip. "Don't be a stranger. Okay, ladies, back to the castle. We've got glasses to enchant." She glanced at Wensley. "Come with us, Sonny. You might learn something."

Tananda, Bunny and I slipped out of the hastily-convened auction going on between members of the Devan Marketing Association. Once I had introduced Paldine and had her display the wares she had to offer, the bidding began at the top of everyone's voice. I had finally gotten a chance to try the Storyteller Goggles (soon to be renamed), and I was sorry my misplaced enthusiasm had deprived the Scammies of them. They were terrific, and the Deveels knew it, too. The Pervomatic also sold itself in a matter of seconds.

I had volunteered to stay, but once I had persuaded Hayner and the others that these Per*vects* were friends of mine and that any discourtesy to them counted as if it was being done to me, none of them paid much attention to us. I was glad to escape because, as I have said before, one of the few things about the Bazaar that I *don't* miss is the noise.

Paldine leaned across to shake hands with me before I left. "I don't know who the Pervect is who befriended you before," she whispered, "but he's lucky. I hope he knows that." I felt a wrench somewhere around my midsection. "I'm the lucky one. He's been a good friend to me."

Out in the street, where the voices of Deveel merchants and customers weren't bouncing off the walls of a tent, I relaxed.

"Care to join us for a milkshake before we go?" I asked Tananda.

"I have to get to Trollia," Tananda informed us, shouldering her small bag. "If Chumley's not in the hospital with a hernia he'll need me to referee between him and Mums. I've already left them long enough."

"I'd better get back to my studies," I agreed, taking my D-hopper out of the side of my boot. "I've left them long enough, too."

"You know, you don't need that thing any more," Tananda nodded. "You know enough places in the dimensions that if you practiced you could use a travel spell instead to hop between them."

"The D-hopper's not foolproof," I replied, "but it works almost all the time, which is more than I could promise right now, considering how tired I am. I don't want to take a chance and get lost, and I sure don't want to be responsible for getting Bunny lost."

"All right. Take care of yourself, handsome."

She kissed me warmly. I regretted again that she'd come to be a big sister to me. I could no more imagine us having a relationship than I could with Bunny. I respected them, but I felt both of them outclassed me.

Tananda winked at Bunny. I grinned, sensing some sisterly communication between them that I couldn't translate, but I'd learned from long experience not to obsess over.

I handed over a bag containing 500 gold pieces and gave it to Tananda. "Here's your share of our fee. Zol didn't want to be paid. I've made good to Bunny, too."

"You don't have to do this," Tananda protested.

"Yes, I do. Please." To my relief she accepted it. "And please take this, too."

I handed her the other D-hopper. She looked a question at me. I took a deep breath and plunged in.

"If you see Aahz I want you to give it to him. Tell him...tell him if this would make it more convenient to visit once in a while I'd like him to have it."

"'Don't be a stranger,' huh?" Tananda translated.

I dug a toe in the dirt. "Uh, yeah. I mean, if he wants to. I'm the one who pushed away from everyone else. Maybe I'm getting over the funk I was in. It's up to him. I just want him to know...he's welcome. I miss him. Studying's a lonely occupation."

"Keep it up. I think you're going to be one hell of a good magician."

She kissed me thoroughly. An affectionate farewell from a Trollop can make you feel like you've been embraced by a tornado.

"The same to you: don't be a stranger," Tananda waved as she sauntered off down the aisle between tents.

"I don't want to be," I murmered quietly. "It'll just take time." I turned to Bunny. "I hope all this hasn't ruined your feelings about Zol Icty. He's quite a guy."

Bunny smiled. "Let's just say my understanding has matured a little. I still like him a lot, and I love his books, but I'm going to reshelve them in the fiction section of my collection."

I grinned. "Shall we go?"

"Yes, indeed. I hope that Gleep and Buttercup haven't trashed the inn since this morning."

Tananda unlocked the door and let herself into the dim anteroom. I waited until she turned around before I sat up. She stiffened for a moment, then relaxed.

She came over to me, reached into her belt pouch, and came out with a D-hopper.

"This is for you, Aahz," she smiled.

I accepted it with a wary look. "What's he using?"

"The same one he had before. This one was his fee for helping out the Wuhses—his whole fee. He just handed it to me and told me to give it to you."

"What for?" I growled.

Tanda tipped her head to one side. "I think you're smart enough to figure that one out. He misses you."

My eyebrows went up. "He's something else," I declared. "How'd he do?"

"He did fine," Tananda assured me. "He did really well. He's a good man. You know that. You saw him. I got you there in time so you could watch the fireworks."

"Yeah," I muttered, thinking back with pleasure to the sight of ten Pervish females running after that darned dragon and getting penned up in their own spell. "He did okay."

"He did more than okay, and you know it, Aahz." Tananda chided me.

"He didn't see me, did he?"

"No."

"Good," I sighed, putting my feet up on the ottoman and leaning back with my hands behind my head. "Just because I'm not his teacher any more doesn't mean he's not still my student."

"Well, I'd better get home to Mums," Tananda smiled. "I left my suitcase half-packed in my room. I hope Chumley's still in one piece. Wait until I tell him Skeeve made friends with the women who beat us up a couple of months ago. Hey, take care of yourself, Aahz."

She gave me a big hug and a kiss, and headed off toward her room. I poured myself some wine and settled back to contemplate the ceiling some more. A D-hopper. The kid sure knew how to send a message. I wondered if and when I would ever take him up on it.

A knock on the door disturbed my reverie. I cracked the door, but kept my shoulder against the inner edge. You could never be too careful, even in the Bazaar.

Standing outside was a thin, blue-faced individual with thinning white hair. I had never seen his species before, but I knew a bill-collector when he saw one.

"I'm looking for The Great Skeeve," the visitor announced.

"He ain't here."

"This is his last known address?"

"I don't answer questions like that, especially from people I don't know," I growled, showing all of my teeth. The little guy gulped, but soldiered on.

"Well, he owes us over three hundred thousand gold pieces, and if he doesn't pay up," he concluded with a feral grin and a thumb jerked over his shoulder toward a couple of really big bruisers that I hadn't noticed before, "our collection agents will be happy to take the matter up with him personally."

# Robert Lynn Asprin

Robert (Lynn) Asprin was born in 1946. While he has written some stand alone novels such as *Cold Cash War, Tambu, The Bug Wars* and also the Duncan and Mallory Illustrated stories, Bob is best known for his series: The *Myth Adventures of Aahz and Skeeve*; the *Phule's Company* novels; and, more recently, the *Time Scout* novels written with Linda Evans. He also edited the groundbreaking *Thieves' World* anthologies with Lynn Abbey. His most recent collaboration is *License Invoked* written with Jody Lynn Nye. It is set in the French Quarter, New Orleans where he currently lives.

# Jody Lynn Nye

Jody Lynn Nye lists her main career activity as "spoiling cats." She has published 25 books, such as *Advanced Mythology*, fourth and most recent in her *Mythology* fantasy series (no relation), three SF novels, four novels in collaboration with Anne McCaffrey, including *The Ship Who Won*; edited a humorous anthology about mothers, *Don't Forget Your Spacesuit, Dear!; The Dragonlover's Guide to Pern; The Visual Guide to Xanth;* and written over seventy short stories. She lives northwest of Chicago with two cats and her husband, author and packager, Bill Fawcett.

*To read the continuing Myth Adventures of Skeeve, Aahz, Gleep, Tanda and the others, look for*

# Myth-taken Identity

by Robert Asprin and Jody Lynn Nye

**coming
September 2004!**

COMING IN **2005** FROM MEISHA MERLIN

AND

# ROBERT LYNN ASPRIN

A new omnibus featuring three early,
stand-alone novels:

# THE BUG WARS
# COLD CASH WAR
# TAMBU

This collection will also include
**Cold Cash Warrior**
a role-playing novel by Robert
Asprin and Bill Fawcett

**Watch our website for further
updates!**

# The Mythology of
## Jody Lynn Nye

*Applied Mythology*

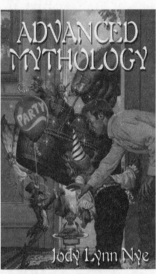

*Advanced Mythology*

"Whimsy is a delicate and dangerous kind of writing to attempt. To make it work takes a special kind of writer, one skilled at splicing the real world together with the new and unreal one seamlessly enough not to leave any telltale roughness around the interface. Some writers, surprisingly good ones, never get it right. But Jody Lynn Nye has mastered this difficult art, and succeeds in making it look easy. These books are a graceful and enjoyable romp."
—Diane Duane

Coming in September 2004: The first novel in a brand new series—military SF with a twist!

## _THE WOLFE PACK

# Come check out our web site for details on these Meisha Merlin authors!

Daniel Abraham

Robert Asprin

Robin Wayne Bailey

Edo van Belkom

Janet Berliner

Storm Constantine

John F. Conn

Diane Duane

Sylvia Engdahl

Phyllis Eisenstein

Rain Graves

Jim Grimsley

George Guthridge

Keith Hartman

Beth Hilgartner

P. C. Hodgell

Tanya Huff

Janet Kagan

Caitlin R. Kiernan

Lee Killough

Jacqueline Lichtenberg

Jean Lorrah
George R. R. Martin
Lee Martindale
Jack McDevitt
Mark McLaughlin
Sharon Lee & Steve Miller
James A. Moore
John Morressy
Adam Niswander
Andre Norton
Jody Lynn Nye
Selina Rosen
Pamela Sargent
Michael Scott
William Mark Simmons
S. P. Somtow
Allen Steele
Mark Tiedemann
Laura J. Underwood
Freda Warrington
David Niall Wilson

# www.MeishaMerlin.com